A WREATH OF DEAD MOTHS

Recent Titles by Gwen Moffat

CUE THE BATTERED WIFE
THE LOST GIRLS
THE OUTSIDE EDGE
PIT BULL
RAGE
VERONICA'S SISTERS

A WREATH OF
DEAD MOTHS

Gwen Moffat

This first world edition published in Great Britain 1998 by
SEVERN HOUSE PUBLISHERS LTD of
9–15 High Street, Sutton, Surrey SM1 1DF.
This first world edition published in the U.S.A. 1998 by
SEVERN HOUSE PUBLISHERS INC of
595 Madison Avenue, New York, N.Y. 10022.

British Library Cataloguing in Publication Data

Moffat, Gwen
     A wreath of dead moths
     1.   Aircraft accidents – Scotland – History – Fiction
     2.   Suspense fiction
     I. Title
     823.9'14 [F]

     ISBN 0-7278-2219-5

Typeset by Palimpsest Book Production Ltd,
Polmont, Stirlingshire, Scotland.
Printed and bound in Great Britain by
MPG Books Ltd, Bodmin, Cornwall.

For Christopher

Scotland

Introduction

He woke without feeling; only images drifted through his mind, like pictures on a movie screen. He recognised them vaguely but he didn't relate to them, didn't even wonder whether this was a dream or reality.

He *had* been dreaming: of the cabin in Crazy Woman Canyon, and him on a hunting trip, after a moose. Outside the coyotes were singing, although it could have been the wind – which was how he knew it was winter; there was never a wind like that at Cow Camp in summertime. When he woke, or thought he woke, he saw that he wasn't in the familiar cabin. He didn't recognise this place so he waited for something to happen. That is, his mind waited; he didn't realise that there was nothing he could do consciously except wait.

He was in some kind of building but the light was poor, and it wasn't the warm yellow glow of a lamp but the cold light of snow. He was tired, pleasantly so; it was too much trouble even to move his eyes. Directly in his line of vision was a wall, and the opening that was admitting the light. There was some kind of framework to the construction but it was made of metal, not wood: spars, not the logs of a cabin. These were contorted and gashed, not orderly as metal should be. He'd seen severed metal like that before. There was a cold smoky smell and a stink of shit.

It was the sounds that brought him to full consciousness. Something was flapping like a big tarp and there was the howling: not coyotes but wind through the torn spars and now, as he identified the opening for a gash in the wall of

3

the construction, the whole scene seemed suddenly bathed in sunshine. His eyes moved then and he blinked, flooded with relief. For a moment there he'd thought he was dead. Now he saw that he was in a long room, a Quonset hut, could it be, and the others were there, all sitting – well, sitting or lying – no one was standing, and no one was moving. This had to be the result of a bomb. They'd taken a direct hit and everyone else was dead. Reluctantly, almost lazily, his mind admitted more feeling. Chuck? Chuck had been sitting a few yards away in the plane. *Plane?* They weren't in a Quonset hut, they were in a B-17, and they were on their way home.

Something moved. "Chuck," he said. "Chuck?" No sound came. He couldn't hear his own voice. Shock, he thought; we've crashed and I'm in shock. A pale face turned to him, a living face. A figure was bending over Chuck who was slumped on the floor, kind of cradled between the legs of a guy who didn't have a face, only a wound like meat where the face should be. There wasn't much blood on Chuck and what there was could have come from the man above him. The survivor smiled. Chuck's tunic was undone, the rescuer was feeling for his heart.

"He's Okay?" the survivor asked, finding his voice this time. "Who are—" But the effort was too much for him. The lovely lassitude returned and his voice died away but he kept his eyes open, smiling weakly at the rescuer, terrifying him.

One

"It crashed in the forties," Bill Hoggart said. "It was a Flying Fortress carrying American servicemen back to the States. It was winter and the cloud was down. The search went on for days. Now there's one for the book! No one survived—"

"I'm not doing plane crashes." Kate Munro looked across the glen to the mountain where a broken wing was lodged in the top of a gully. "There's no human interest," she added. She meant no suspense. She was writing a book on mountain rescues and for that she demanded excitement; she couldn't get involved with a plane crash. There was no sense of urgency: just bodies and the chore of recovering them.

"I was going to say," Bill went on, "no one survived – except there's a story that one of them did, and he kept a diary, but it disappeared – *and* someone was on the hill ahead of the rescuers."

"That's not original. Climbers often imagine someone with them in mist, or close by. It's a trick of the light, or fatigue, or a deer—"

"What about the missing diary?"

She thought about it. "Who were you talking to?"

"The crofters. The Flying Fortress is a local legend."

"So what's their explanation for the diary?"

"People say the team was incompetent. It was RAF Rescue in those days. They should have found the crash sooner and then this guy would have lived. They say his diary vanished because he wrote in it after the crash, that it was seized by the authorities and destroyed."

5

"And who was the man who was supposed to be ahead of the rescuers?"

He shrugged. He hadn't asked the locals about that.

It was the end of a somnolent afternoon and the rocks were giving off heat. In the boulders below the climbers a wren sang a few notes. Bill shielded his camera lens and squinted at the torn wing over a mile away.

"The forties," Kate mused. "Around fifty years ago? There'll be no one left who was alive then – not to have gone up there."

"They need be no more than seventy."

"I wonder why they hit the top. Another few feet and they'd have skimmed the summit and then there'd be nothing between them and the open sea." She sighed. "Poor devils. I hope no one did survive. It would have been lonely up there on a winter's night if you were conscious." She shuddered, then pulled herself together. "But nothing dramatic about it. That's why the locals dream up these stories about missing diaries and ghostly rescuers. A plane full of men crashes on top of a mountain in winter. In a village where nothing ever happens they'd talk about it for decades. And embroider it."

"Nothing ever happens? What are you doing here?"

Their heads turned in unison and they regarded the neighbouring mountain. "Yes," she said, grinning. "They've got Neil Grant."

"And they've embroidered him too: same as the plane crash."

"Oh, come on! Grant *started* civilian rescue in this area. You just can't stand the guy's manner."

"He's an arrogant bastard."

"That's how he comes over on the telly. I mean, the stupid questions rescuers are asked, and never the right ones—"

"He's an overweight, pompous—"

"I don't care what he is now, it's what he's done that's important, and the rescue here on Torboll is going to make a superb climax to the book. A pity it was a corpse, but then the difficulty of recovery makes up for that. Do you realise her rope was frozen so hard to the rock he spent over an hour chipping it clear? Hanging there, twirling under an overhang, his own ropes knotted together: if one of those knots had come apart he'd have fallen a thousand feet. And no communication with the chaps on top because of the blizzard—"

"Save it for the book. But get it right: no way was he hanging under that overhang for an hour – and he had good weather. The snow didn't start until they were on the way down."

"The cloud was low; it had to be pitch-black. Admit it, Bill: he did a sensational job there."

"No more than a lot of men who don't have influential friends in the media. Grant made his name with that rescue and he's been capitalising on it ever since."

"Bollocks! He may be an opportunist, could have used the episode to promote his business, but it's a good hotel in its own right. It would be even if it was run by a wimp."

"Watch him on the box and he tries to give the impression he's landed gentry, like Armidil was the family shooting lodge before they made it into a hotel. You'd never think, to hear him, he'd come off a croft and his dad was a poacher. With a bit of sheep-stealing on the side."

"You *what*? Where on earth did you hear that?"

"It's common knowledge." He was smug. "Talk to Duncan MacRae. He'll tell you."

"Gossip." Her shoulders slumped. She dealt in facts, objectivity was what was needed here; Bill's jealousy stuck out a mile. Wondering what he'd make of it, she asked, "Does he have a private life?"

"Not now, he's too old. He was married once and his wife left him. There could be something between him and his manageress but basically he's a mother's boy. You think I'm kidding? Didn't you know that they'd always lived together?"

"Of course they do – or did when she did the cooking at Armidil."

"She still lives there: in that cottage outside the gates. I'll

7

tell you something: Neil Grant may be the local celebrity but his mother was a bit more than the hotel cook. Hector Stewart goes all soft when he speaks about her."

"God!" He exasperated her, always coming back to trivial relationships when all she wanted was high adventure. "I made a mistake," she said, "asking about his private life."

"If you were more interested in what people are instead of what they do you'd write better books."

"What the hell do you know about writing books?"

"Nothing. I know you though."

Her lips tightened. He was getting uppity. A good photographer, an occasional lover – and she was paying him to illustrate her book, or would be when she had the advance. He might remember that, show some respect. She grabbed her rucksack and started to fasten the straps, glaring at his back. He was wrapping his camera in a sweater: a hard man with not an ounce of spare flesh anywhere, but soft-centred, not exactly clinging but always there, focused on her, totally predictable. No way did he know what she was about.

"Let's get moving," she snapped. "I want to see Grant tonight."

"Evening's his busy time. Besides he'll never talk to you in the back bar; the audience would be too down-market."

"I'll make an appointment." He was impossible. She stooped to pick up the rope. In the bottom of the glen a navy-blue loch was fringed with jade above the shallows, water flashing silver where deer were wading shoreward. She regarded them absently, thinking about the evening, about work and Neil Grant.

Armidil Hotel was a massive Victorian pile of pink sandstone, three storeys high, with towers and pepperpot turrets. Neil Grant was sitting at the window of his turret room checking the details of the Torboll rescue in one of his journals. He was a large man, balding, with a genial mouth below a fleshy nose: an affable-looking fellow but one with careful eyes. Neil didn't miss much. He knew that there was a climber in the area called Kate Munro who was writing a book on mountain rescues, and the grapevine told him that today she'd gone to look at the north face of Ben Torboll, which was why he came to be checking his own report.

He was starting to have doubts about the wisdom of agreeing to an interview. She hadn't sought him out yet but there could be no question of her need to talk to him; he was more than the local expert, he was *the* authority on rescue. He grinned to himself, at himself, then sobered. Everyone said he should write his memoirs. His guests produced autobiographies: lawyers, politicians, media people; he'd had it in mind for a long time. He'd had a fuller life, been more successful than any other rescuer he could think of, but would Kate Munro pre-empt his own book, steal his thunder? Not if Torboll was only one incident in her story surely – indeed it was only one episode in his own life; he'd done innumerable things more dangerous: alone, at night, in bad weather. He winced – some would bear forgetting.

He heard her coming before her Transit appeared: an ancient van rattling down the drive. She drove round the side of the building heading for the stable yard. He gave her a few minutes and went downstairs.

He hadn't seen her properly before, only a figure glimpsed at the wheel of the van. As he entered the public bar, ostensibly to ask how the beer was holding out in the heatwave, he glanced round the tables, nodding, acknowledging that these too were valuable customers. Kate was the only woman present. He caught her eye, saw her hesitate, and then she was approaching the bar: a slim, muscular woman in her thirties, tanned, with short straight hair bleached by the sun, clear eyes, a good jaw, high cheekbones. Nothing intimidating about her.

"So you're Kate Munro." He said it as if he'd been waiting a long time for this moment. "Did you have a good day?"

"Productive." She blinked. Grapevine, she thought – he was

keeping tabs on her. "We were looking at Ben Torboll, taking pictures. Can we talk to you some time?"

"We?"

She glanced over her shoulder as if for support. There was a chunky fellow at her table, clean-shaven but with longish hair. He was studying his beer, aggressive in his detachment.

"Me then," she said. "I'm the writer. Bill Hoggart's doing the illustrations."

"Yes, I heard you were doing a book on rescue."

"Not a definitive book," she said hastily. "And only the more sensational – I mean more technical rescues." She reddened. "That's how you come into it. The time you carried—"

He held up a hand. People were listening, all except Hoggart, now staring out of the window, stiff with hostility. "I can spare an hour tomorrow morning," Neil said pleasantly. "Meanwhile why don't you come round to the other bar after dinner" – he beamed at her – "meet some real climbers. Nine o'clock suit you?"

"Royal command," Bill sneered when she returned to her seat.

She shrugged. "I have to go; it's probably considered an honour for ordinary people to be invited to the residents' bar. I must keep him sweet. You heard him; he's not going to be interviewed in public."

"He would if you had a television crew with you."

"I don't recall the name." Alec Dunbar, the cardiac surgeon, tasted his brandy with appreciation. "Kate Munro? What's she written?"

"Nothing to my knowledge." There was movement in the hall as people came out of the dining room. Neil glanced at his manager behind the bar but Gillean was alert, as ever. A new frock tonight, he noted: pale brown – stone? Unassuming, but that was Gillean: discreet, watchful and totally reliable. A treasure, his mother called her, still harping back to the time when she thought her son would marry Gillean Forbes. Instead he'd married Poppy, the receptionist, who'd cleaned him out and cleared off – with a procurator fiscal of all things. Poppy had hated Gillean. Gillean had no feelings either way, none that she showed—

"Come back," Dunbar said, waving a hand.

"Sorry! You were saying?"

"I asked what she was like. Kate Munro."

"She's – unremarkable. Fit, of course, a little gauche. I've asked her round for a drink."

"I heard a rumour she's interested in your biography."

"Rubbish! I'm just an incident in her book – well, a chapter on Torboll maybe. And that was blown up by the media. In fact, there was no one else capable of going down the cliff. The team was made up of keepers and crofters just in the early days. I was the only climber; it had to be me." Neil grinned. "I had no choice in the matter."

"What about RAF Rescue?" Colonel Linklater had been listening and now he bristled like a terrier in defence of the serviceman. "They were in existence as far back as the forties."

Neil drew a breath. These old fellows had to be humoured – and some of them knew what they were talking about. "They weren't called out to the Torboll accident," he said patiently. "If they had been, I wouldn't have been needed. The RAF had some good chaps in the sixties: trained for snow and ice work."

"They weren't always as good," Dunbar put in meaningly.

Neil's attention wandered, then focused on the hall. "In here, Kate," he called.

She had changed but the blue cotton shirt was hopelessly creased; however, scrubbed and without make-up, she glowed with vitality. Introduced to Dunbar and Linklater she was attentive, almost subdued, on her best behaviour. She said she would drink whisky. "The Macallan," Neil murmured to Gillean.

"Tell us about your book," Linklater commanded, taking the

initiative. "Are you writing it as you go, or collecting all the material first?"

"It's written, all except the last chapter." She gulped the malt, embarrassed now, aware of Neil's eyes on her.

"What else have you written?" Dunbar asked.

"This is my first book. I do short pieces mostly, for magazines and newspapers, a few radio scripts. You wouldn't know my name; I use pseudonyms a lot. Editors say I write too much so I can't write under the same name all the time, something about saturating the market."

"What do you write about?" Neil asked.

"Anything. Climbing, travel, animals, you name it; whatever I'm asked to do."

"Is the book commissioned?" Dunbar asked.

"Oh yes, I couldn't do it otherwise." She sensed surprise; they thought she was just another person who could write a book when she felt like it. She addressed herself to the gaunt one – Dunbar – the one with the warm grey eyes. "The research takes time: all last spring and summer; the writing done during the winter, when I wasn't snow-climbing. I had to know I was going to sell it—" She trailed off, not wanting to mention money, aware that she was being drawn out but not knowing how to take evasive action.

From behind the bar Gillean came to the rescue. "How did you collect the material?"

"From the police and rescue teams, but that only gave me the official reports. I filled the gaps with personal interviews." She put her glass on the counter and Gillean reached for the bottle. "That is," Kate went on, "if the rescue was sensational enough." She smiled at Neil, thinking he looked rather fun, but a bit flushed. He'd have to watch his blood pressure, he was on the single malt too. "After I've done the preliminary work, I go to the site of the accident to find out what really happened. Except on this occasion I saw the site first. Of course I have the official reports on Ben Torboll already."

"What *really* happened?" Neil repeated.

"I don't mean there was a cover-up; I meant, the team reports and police statements – they're just facts: times, weather conditions, injuries. The personal interviews give me the background, like people's feelings, and then there's the atmosphere. I get that from climbing the route."

"With Hoggart," Neil said brightly. "He's her photographer."

"Not always." Kate wondered why he had to bring Bill into it. "Often I'm solo. Bill's along on this trip because I need pictures of Torboll. Torboll's important. But he'll need to come back after the first snow in autumn. It's no good now; the face looks – well, friendly."

"Solo?" Linklater's voice cracked. "You don't mean you climb on your own?"

"A lot of people do nowadays." She was indulgent. He was very old, over seventy perhaps. "I don't do anything hard. After all, most accidents happen to silly buggers, don't they? Inexperienced people. The result of making a mistake."

"Experienced men have accidents," Dunbar pointed out.

"You're right. No one's perfect."

"Accidents are the result of human error," Neil intoned, but they ignored him, fascinated by Kate.

"Suppose you got stuck on a big cliff?" Linklater couldn't accept her casual attitude.

"I'd retreat. Climb down."

"And if you couldn't?" Dunbar pressed, genuinely curious. She wasn't boasting, she was stating facts. This was how she did it. Socially she might be inept, in her own line she exuded confidence.

"I wouldn't attempt a move I couldn't reverse," she told him. Her face changed, lit by a dazzling smile. "How smug! But there's the proof of the pudding: I haven't had an accident yet. I'm very cautious really." Her eyes came to rest on Neil. "You know what I'm on about," she said meaningly and Dunbar was disconcerted, excluded.

Gillean was amused. She wondered if this could be the start

13

of an affair. Neil was obviously on edge, but then it was probably his first contact with a hard woman climber. She was a novelty, and she carried a sexual aura of which she appeared to be unaware. Dunbar was aware – it was there in the softening of the gaunt features, the relaxed body. Perhaps Kate's allure was enhanced by the potency of the whisky that suppressed shyness and allowed the confidence to show. Even the colonel couldn't take his eyes off her and as for Neil, he was beaming like a sixteen-year-old.

Two

"When did you realise that she was dead?" Kate asked, and the abruptness of it threw him. It was next morning and they were sitting in the garden. He had been studying her profile as she stared at Ben Torboll, thinking that she had the intensity of a cat watching long grass. "She'd been there for hours," she went on. "Her rope was frozen to the rock."

"We knew from the chopper pilot that she was hanging. There was no chance she could be alive."

"You went to a hell of a lot of trouble to recover a corpse."

"What else could I do? Cut the rope and let the body drop? The media would have had a field day."

She sighed. She wasn't taking notes. Before them the lawns stretched to the water. A heron was immobile on the margin, poised like a garden ornament. Across the loch the peaks were sage-coloured in the heat haze.

"This isn't going to work," she said.

He stood up, his eyes shining. "Let's go and climb. We'll talk on the hill, or this evening, tomorrow, any time. Who cares? We're wasting a glorious day."

"You said you could only spare an hour."

"That was last night. This is today. Now is the only time that matters."

They climbed all day. The rock was bone-dry, the ledges dusty, but flowers glowed in the shade and the air was sweet with the scent of ferns and crushed thyme. The burns were low and no

15

sound rose from the corries; their cries sounded isolated yet intimate, like the calls of birds.

It was late afternoon when they came out on the summit and collapsed on the dry moss. "Don't suggest another route," he pleaded. "It would be gilding the lily."

"I wasn't going to. I'm bushed."

He turned and stared at her. "You don't look it. Damn it, you're humouring an old man!"

"You don't climb like an old man."

He lay back and watched a vapour trail unfurl itself across the sky. He felt as if he were twenty years old. "What happened to the interview?" he asked. There was no reply. He closed his eyes. They'd been on the next buttress to the one where he'd recovered the woman's body, and they'd never mentioned it. "I've done more interesting rescues," he murmured.

"Tell me about them."

"I can't be bothered. I've kept journals," he added shyly.

"For how long?"

"All my life virtually. All my climbing life. I thought I might make something of them one day."

"Why don't you let me do it?" There was a long silence. At length she resumed. "I could do it better than you." She pursed her lips. "There are things you can't say about yourself that another person can." She sat up, alert now. "I'll finish this book – there's only the one chapter to do – and then I'll write your biography. How's that?"

"Ghost it?" He was still on his back, feeling heavy now, and resentful.

"Ghosting would be in the first person. I said: it needs to be written by someone else."

He sat up stiffly. "I'll consider it. I'd always expected to do it myself."

"No, you didn't. You were uncertain until I said I'd do it. You're being a dog in the manger: all that material and you don't want me to use it."

"I said I'd think about it." He stood up, annoyed, and started to coil the rope. With Hoggart having left for Glasgow to print his photographs, Neil had been looking forward to spending the evening with her: a fitting end to an idyllic day, and now she'd spoiled everything with this suggestion that he was incapable of writing his own story. All the same she could have a point: that bit about her ability to be more objective . . . He might show her the journal containing the Torboll incident, see what she made of it.

They came back to his Range Rover that was parked on the shore of the loch. He rolled down the windows and drove slowly, first on a rough track, then on a narrow road that ran between water and a belt of woodland. They passed a crumbling blackhouse in a glade, its thatched roof sagging into a jungle of nettles. "We farmed there at one time," he told her. "Before we bought the hotel."

"When was that?"

"We bought Armidil in the fifties; a terrible rundown place it was too: an old shooting lodge. The bathrooms had geysers to heat the water. Mother did Bed and Breakfast at first, and any profit went straight into plumbing, mending roofs, wiring, you name it." He smiled. "We worked like navvies. I did some guiding. Dad was gillie and stalker. Mother was chef, housekeeper, chambermaid, everything."

"Did you climb for fun?"

He shrugged. "That came later. At first it was mostly taking the guests on the hill for a fee. That's how I started going abroad: guiding people in the Alps. We were lucky in our timing. There weren't many decent hotels on the west coast in the fifties. Once we got going, the word spread and in no time it seemed everyone who climbed came to Armidil, either to the bar or to stay. My mother saw to the hospitality side of it; I provided the atmosphere." His mind wasn't on the road but that was immaterial, there was no other traffic. "The atmosphere grew," he continued. "Armidil's an institution now. Of course its reputation's had time to evolve."

"It was self-perpetuating."

17

"What? Oh yes, you're right. Once we'd made the move from the croft to the lodge, it was like the start of an avalanche."

"It was a gamble though. You sold the croft."

"No – why do you assume—"

She bit her lip. Money talk. Too intimate. "Why, to buy the hotel," she said weakly.

"No, not at all! The laird virtually paid us to take the lodge off his hands. You should have seen it! Another year or two and he'd have needed to remove the roof to save taxes. It was rotting to bits. We paid peanuts for it."

They reached the village. Cullen was little more than a handful of cottages, a filling station and a store. There were crossroads where the lochside road widened to become the highway to Glasgow, while on the right a minor road ran under the southern slopes of Ben Torboll to another arm of the sea. On the left a few yards of tarmac ended at pretentious gateposts flanking the entrance to the hotel.

Duncan and Linklater were sprawled on a bench outside the front door, overtaken by fatigue in the act of removing their boots. They revived at the suggestion of tea and the party trudged up the stairs to Neil's sitting room where windows were open wide on an expanse of loch and mountains.

Kate thought that a small fortune had been spent on furnishing the room. Bookshelves curved round circular walls, the stereo looked like state of the art, sofa and easy chairs were in rich brown leather. Neil disappeared into his kitchen which abutted on the main building. It was a self-contained apartment, Dunbar told Kate, with the bedroom above this room, also circular. She suppressed a giggle, wondering about the shape of the bed.

They talked about their day. The others had done a modest route on Am Bodach. "Is that wing safe?" Kate asked.

"What wing?" Linklater barked. "Oh, the one in the gully: what's left of the Flying Fortress. We were nowhere near it but, yes, it's safe."

18

Dunbar turned to him. "How do you know? Have you jumped on it?"

"Of course not! I meant: it must be safe, it's been there – how long?"

"Forty-five years," Kate said.

"Is that so? 1949. That's when it came down, Neil?" He had entered with a loaded tray.

"I was just a kid. Kate will know more about it than I do—"

"Not me." She was dismissive. "I'm not doing plane crashes. Bill Hoggart told me about it though. He was talking to the locals."

"Ah yes, that old legend." Linklater nodded. "The missing diary. The man ahead of the rescuers—"

"Presence," Dunbar put in slyly. "No one said it was a man – or did they? *Something* was ahead of them in the cloud: left no tracks. Right, Neil?"

Neil was pouring China tea from a silver pot. He stopped and considered. "I love it. I've not heard that one before: a presence. 'Ghosts' is the usual term, implying it was the spirit of one of the victims."

"The last one to die," Kate murmured, and there was a momentary silence.

It was broken by Dunbar: "Is it still there? Still haunting the gully?"

Neil was indulgent. "There's a white hare, which you're supposed to see only on the night of the full moon. Some folk say that's the ghost."

"Was there a moon on the night of the crash?" Dunbar asked. Neil sketched a shrug. "It's illogical anyway," he went on, "an American serviceman wouldn't come back as a Scottish hare."

"He could," Kate put in. "He might if he had Scottish roots. What was his name?"

Linklater gaped at her. Dunbar blinked. "Of course you don't know who was the last to die," she conceded. "But it would have to be the diarist, wouldn't it?"

They were all staring at her now, bewildered by this sudden turn of an idle fantasy into something which she seemed to be taking seriously. "I'm curious," she protested. "Aren't you, Neil? It happened in your own backyard. Didn't you ever wonder about the victims: what they thought about before they crashed, how long they survived?"

"They all died on impact. There were no survivors."

"I don't know about that." Dunbar, the medical man, was thoughtful. "Fatal injuries certainly, but some may have survived for a few hours. No longer, on a winter's night too."

"But that's the suggestion, isn't it?" Kate pressed. "That not all the injuries were fatal, that at least one man survived and would have lived if the crash had been reached in time?"

Kate didn't eat at Armidil that evening. She declined Neil's invitation and went home with one of his journals to a can of Irish stew. Home was a tent about four miles from Cullen, in a birch wood below Ben Torboll. She glanced at the journal before sleeping but found it surprisingly heavy going and put it aside. Next morning she leafed through it until she found the epic rescue – recovery rather, you didn't rescue dead people.

Once again it wasn't a day for work. There were distractions. A red squirrel arrived to scrape bacon fat from her breakfast plate, curlews were lilting, the sun was hot – and Neil's prose was florid and affected. However, there were the facts, a framework – and there was nothing else to do: Bill was in Glasgow, Neil had gone to Edinburgh to see his accountant. She spent the morning drafting her last chapter, and then she drove to the village to find people who might fill the gaps.

MacRae and Stewart were the crofters whom Bill had talked to in the back bar at Armidil. She found Duncan MacRae on the shore of the loch, his plain modern house hidden from the road by a thick grove of spruce. Between the house and the strand were a few acres of pasture where a small black cow grazed beside a black calf asleep in the buttercups.

Duncan was a brown gnome in limp tweed breeches and

an old-fashioned grey shirt without a collar. His hair was, however, trendily long under a deerstalker that had seen better days. He was polite but distant, even before she mentioned the purpose of her visit; she guessed he was aware of it already. His attitude was partially explained when he – as it were – declared himself. He had been keeper to the laird.

She decided to play it as if she were unconscious of undercurrents: the ignorant researcher looking for material on the antecedents of her subject. They sat on a seat in front of his house and she asked him about the Grants when they were his neighbours. Neil had shown her the blackhouse, she said, and it wasn't far away surely? Was it a family croft, inherited by Neil's father?

Duncan was astonished. "It weren't their place! It were part of the estate, like everything else; they rented it from Sir Ian. Why, they was poor as tinkers when they arrived here; they come in on the back of a lorry. That were before the War. They had nothing – nothing! Just the clothes on their backs, maybe a change in some old bags, and Rory Grant's tools. He called himself a handyman but he could do anything: carpentry, building, plumbing, even wiring. Aye, a jack of all trades were Rory!" He halted, remembering, then added savagely, "And master of all of 'em."

He pulled a tin of tobacco from one pocket, a pipe from another, and lit up, taking his time about it. Kate watched a cormorant land on a skerry and spread its wings to dry. Duncan got his pipe going and went on, still resentful, "The first night they spent in a tin shed on the old quay. Next morning Rory showed up at the lodge, never mind me and the factor: he went straight to the laird and said as how he'd come to mend the fences, drop a few trees, set some slates back on the roof. That one picked out everything as needed doing and never said a word about payment. 'Course he got the jobs, and though I says it myself he were gey clever with his hands – and he got paid – not much, the laird were a close man with his cash, but Rory got took on, and they moved into that old blackhouse this side of the Turkey Burn. And Sir Ian's lady, she give them old bits of furniture as they'd thrown out in the coach house, and clothes, and damty," – his voice rose – "if after all that they didn't get the lodge!" He was furious.

"How could they manage that, if they were so poor?"

"Rory's auntie died and left him everything – but they didna pay much for the lodge, and Sir Ian were glad to be rid of it if truth was told."

"How much?" It was too sharp but he responded, if reluctantly.

"Five, five and a half thousand." His nostrils flared. "And now look at him!" He stared up the loch to where Armidil's pink stone showed above its lawns. "Respectable now, up there with folks that's on television, and members of Parliament, and Americans. He goes to America on his holidays. Why, he's had Prince Charles at the lodge, so he has!"

"He worked for it." She was reproving. "Were you on the Torboll rescue, Mr MacRae?" Putting him in his place.

'Ach no, I was never in the team: playing around with them ropes and pitons, that's not for me."

"I thought local people did go out in the early days."

"Just to search like, not on the cliffs. If someone was missing Sir Ian would have us all out: himself and any of his guests as could handle theirselves on the hill. And the keepers an' others off the estate. And when the RAF started doing rescues, they had a long drive to get here and we might find an injured man before they arrived. And we could always show the way, like yon time the Yankee plane crashed on Am Bodach, not that anyone knew where it had crashed for days, and when we did find the wreck, it were too late. All dead – well, all dead by then: stiff as boards when Hector Stewart and me got there."

Kate was side-tracked. "Why did it take so long to find the wreck? Weren't other planes used in the search, and helicopters?"

"There weren't no choppers in those days, leastways we never saw 'em. Not like now: with yon big yellow machines

22

out every time a hiker twists his ankle, spending the taxpayer's money. They had a plane up looking for the wreck but not at first. Cloud were down."

"I see. So they spotted it when the cloud lifted."

"That's so. We—" He trailed off. He looked puzzled.

"The cloud was down when you reached the wreck?" she prompted.

"It was so. I mind now: the weather were taking up, and there were a wind on top and flurries of snow. The search plane musta spotted the wreck through a break in the cloud. And then the cloud came back."

"Wouldn't the wreck be covered with snow?" He said nothing. "Was it a strong wind?" she pressed.

"Aye, cold as charity it were. 'Twas the third day after the crash they was found." His tone sharpened. "What's your interest in all this? I thought you wanted to know about Neil Grant."

"It's in my book." She was glib. "Did the relatives come over from the States to see where it crashed?"

There was a pause. "I don't know." He went on awkwardly, "It were different then. Wartime. Folk couldn't travel. There was enemy submarines." He stood up. "I got to see to my sheep now." Courtesy was forgotten. She was dismissed.

She drove back to Cullen, drifting to a halt before she reached a row of cottages dozing in the sun. Hector Stewart lived in the first of these; he was the other ancient who had talked to Bill, and one of the few left who remembered the War and the plane crash. But the crash was in 1949, four years after the end of the War; you'd think a man who'd been involved in that search would remember the date. And what was she about anyway, she wasn't interested in plane crashes – but you had to admit that this one was diverting, not the part about the ghost of course, although if one chap had survived, and walked away . . . No, there was no suggestion that anyone had been missing, and the injuries would have kept them in their seats, perhaps able to make slight movements . . . like writing. How did the story about the diary start? Someone had to see it in the first place, even to read it. To steal it? Her eyes sharpened. A large figure was standing in the doorway of the first cottage, looking her way. Duncan said he and Hector Stewart had been first at the crash. She felt a sudden rush, a surge of avid curiosity like adrenalin, and following close on it, a warning. Something was going on here; there could have been someone ahead of the rescuers. He left no tracks but Duncan said there was wind on top and flurries of snow. Blown snow covers tracks. *So what happened to the diary?*

Hector was intrigued. His eyes were faded, greyish, they would have been blue once; he must have been a beguiling character fifty years ago. Even now, well into his seventies, his gaze lingered on her thighs. She was wearing a thin blouse with a scoop neckline and Levis that lengthened her legs. Seated at a careful distance from him on his garden bench she listened politely to his reminiscing about Maisie Grant. She'd explained her interest in the son but Hector's concern was the mother. "She were beautiful," he told her earnestly. "But gey strict. Not church mind, nor even chapel, but brought up right. She'd need to be well behaved; she were in service down in the Lowlands some place. I don't know how she come to take up with that Rory Grant. He were like a foreigner: small and dark, and sly as a sack o' weasels."

A marmalade cat stalked along the garden wall, settled itself on a cushion of sea pinks and regarded Kate with basilisk eyes. On the far side of the road a strip of turf bordered the loch. It was low tide and black timbers projected from the mud. "The old quay were there," he said, following her gaze. "And a tin shack where they slept: him and Maisie – only for a night mind. Then they moved into the blackhouse beyond MacRae's croft." He grinned wickedly. "Lived next door to each other, give or take a couple of miles, but could MacRae ever catch 'im?" He cocked an eye at her. He'd known that Bill would have told her. "It were a game to Rory Grant," he assured her, "being chased by MacRae through the glens o' winter nights. There was sheep too, more 'n once my dogs have dug up sheep's guts way back there under Am Bodach. Foxes don't bury guts." He shook his head. "My, but Maisie were a great cook, still is for all she won't see eighty again, but 'course she had the very finest ingredients. I says to her one time when I come in from my lobster pots and a soft offshore wind blowin', I said as I could smell her roast the length of the loch – ah, there's nothing like the smell of a well-hung haunch of venison sizzling in the oven. And she said, cool as you please, that you could do wonders with a few turnips and herbs and a bit of scrag end, and then she asked me" – he hesitated and looked sideways at her – "asked me how the bairn were."

"You had a new baby?"

"Not the wife." He winked. " 'Twas one of the maids at the lodge had just been brought to bed."

"I see. And that was the last time you called attention to her cooking, or rather, what went into the pot. And now," she added idly, looking at the mountains on the far side of the water, "her son's put it all behind him and turned respectable. And Maisie? She's respectable too?"

"She always was!" He was amazed. Kate kept her face straight with an effort; the woman *knew* the deer were poached – and the sheep stolen, which was rather worse – but Hector was inconsistent and she'd touched a sore spot: "I were telling you about the *father*. Maisie had it hard; she brought that lad up alone all the time Rory were away at the War, but then he never done a hand's turn on the croft when he were home except to patch up the roof when the gales took another bit of thatch. Maisie were the crofter: it were her calved the cow and cut the hay and planted the tatties. Why, she even went out to lift the lobster pots. She ran that place better'n a man could an' then, an' then, when they bought the lodge, she ran that!"

"What did Rory do in the War?" Kate asked weakly.

"Merchant Navy. Convoys to Murmansk. And no knowing

what he got up to there." He was contemptuous, still preoccupied with the formidable Maisie.

"A woman in every port?"

"No, Rory weren't bothered about women – well, he wouldn't dare, would he? But there's always chances for picking up things in the services, aren't there?" He sniffed angrily.

"When did Rory die? I take it he is dead; no one's mentioned him being alive."

"He died around the time Neil married Poppy – her that ran off with the judge. You heard about that?" His eyes were eager again. He loved talking about women.

"Only that he'd been married. What happened?"

"Miss Gillean, that's what. Poppy couldn't abide another woman in the place, not one as – well, you know he should have married Miss Gillean?"

"Should?" What was this? More scandal?

"We all thought it was to be Miss Gillean, although his mother were close-mouthed about it. Then Poppy came to work there and Neil's a fool with women" – he caught himself up – "a fool with young girls, that is, not with ladies. That Poppy were no better than she should be – well, there you are, running off—" He floundered to a stop, obviously thinking that if Neil and Kate were close, then he'd insulted her.

"But Miss Gillean stayed on," she said calmly.

"Ach aye! She weren't bothered. A very well-mannered lady. She has her own little house in the grounds now. Some say she runs the place."

"And Neil never married again."

"Why should he? Who needs marriage? You're not married. I'm not." His eyes twinkled.

"You said you were married, Mr Stewart."

"I've been a widower these twelve year – but I'm not lonely. In the season there's always folk coming by on their way out to the point, and the lassies like to pass the time of day with an old crofter, maybe take a dram."

26

She ignored the cue. "You must have been a powerful man in your prime."

"Anywhere, any time." He actually flexed his biceps, but then she'd laid on the flattery with a trowel. "I'm still gey strong," he assured her.

"Did you climb too?" – quickly, a little desperately.

"Not like you mean. We used to go to the sea cliffs and gather birds' eggs but we never used these nails and belts and them coloured nylon ropes. We used stuff our dads had used. Sometimes they broke. I mind Willy MacRae, that was an uncle of Duncan's, that's how he died: fell all of three hundred feet onto the rocks at low tide."

"Nylon breaks too. Neil's rope could have broken that time on Ben Torboll."

"So they say. I was away to Oban that day but I know what folks said." He was dismissive, wanting to get back to more exciting matters. "I'll bring the bottle," he announced, lurching to his feet.

She sat with a large whisky in her hand and considered him. His eyes were bright, he'd probably had a drink inside before returning. It couldn't be long before he crowded her into a corner, literally as well as metaphorically. Breaking away from him would mean the end to any cooperation.

"Mr MacRae says you were first on the scene when the Flying Fortress crashed," she said, and it sounded like an accusation.

He flinched as if she'd hit him, then swallowed, ducking his head. He drained his glass and caught sight of the cat. "Away, you!" he shouted, bending to scoop up a handful of gravel. The action brought a cry of pain. The cat dropped fluidly from the wall into the street. Hector fell back, gasping.

Kate reached for the bottle, took the glass from his unresisting fingers and poured a small measure.

"You're damty free with a body's drink," he muttered.

"You need it." They were silent except for his heavy

breathing. The air was electric with tension. "There was a strong wind and flurries of snow," she murmured. "The cloud was down."

"Aye, the cloud was down." His voice was weak.

"When did it break?" No response. "It had to lift sometime for the wreck to be spotted."

"Must have done."

"Where was the diary?"

"I never saw the diary."

"Who did see it?"

"I don't know."

"Was one of them still warm?"

"That's a lie!" He was galvanised. "Who said that? I never touched 'un. They was all dead when we got there! It was the RAF had the moving of 'em, we just carried 'em down. Besides, we was together, Duncan and me, how *could* I have done anything?"

"Done what?"

"Nothing. I don't know. I've forgotten. It were over forty year since."

"Who was the person out in front of you?"

He stood up. She rose with him, and more quickly, wondering what was in his mind. He was glaring at her, a transformed character from the jolly old lecher of five minutes ago. She stepped to the garden gate in order to be in full view of the neighbours.

He picked up the bottle, tramped inside his cottage and slammed the door.

Below the summit of Am Bodach she found a piece of grey alloy, pitted as if with salt. Where was the rest of the wreckage: the other wing, the fuselage that had held so many young men? What were they like, these fellows who would be seventy, eighty years old now if they'd lived? They were returning to the States so probably they were about to be demobilised, and they'd be looking forward to

– what? Skyscrapers, Los Angeles and the HOLLYWOOD sign, Las Vegas; presumably people were homesick for such things.

She came on a small but carefully constructed cairn. Cemented in the stones was a plaque bearing the dead men's names: Scandinavian, Spanish, English (a Barber, a Smyth), Sullivan, others which had a flavour of eastern Europe. Their home states looked alien too, recorded in metal on a Scottish peak: Utah, Arizona, Montana. She sighed heavily and looked up at the ridge. Another thirty feet and they'd have cleared it.

"The wreck was removed," Dunbar told her. "It was unstable, too close to the edge. The Americans took it down with one of those massive choppers. They had to leave the wing in the gully, it's jammed hard."

They were sitting on the terrace, watching the shadows lengthen. She told him about the people she'd met during the day. She finished with Hector's outburst. "What's he afraid of, Alec?"

After a pause he said, "Don't pursue the matter. Forget about it."

"About what? You mean, forget about the plane crash? Why?"

"It may not be the diary that's missing at all; that's just gossip, probably a cover for something else – like – instruments from the cockpit? Clothing? Cameras? And who are the most likely suspects?" She was wide-eyed. He nodded. "Rescuers, locals, even police. Best advice: let it rest."

She rubbed her nose. "Well, I wasn't going to use it anyway." She sounded sulky. But she wasn't sulking – her brain was racing.

Three

M aisie Grant was small and spare with striking eyes: grey and clear under hooded lids. Her white hair was looped softly about her head, secured with tortoiseshell combs, and she wore a lavender blouse pinned at the throat with a topaz set in gold. "You'll be Miss Munro," she said, advancing down a flagged path between banks of irises. "Thank you for coming."

Kate had had no choice; Maisie had telephoned the hotel to leave a message that read more like a command than an invitation. "She's heard you're interviewing the gossips," Dunbar said. "She needs to set the record straight."

Her cottage was perched above the river: an old house, carefully restored. Kate was ushered through a dim dining room where an elegant table glowed like new chestnuts to a kitchen that was flooded with light, the door open to a rockery full of alpines, to birdsong and the sound of water talking in the river bed. A recipe book was on a stand beside a blue bowl of eggs with incredibly dark shells. A dresser held a dinner service in scarlet and gold.

"Do you use that?" Kate asked in awe.

"The Crown Derby? When I have guests. My son brings people over – those I knew from the old days, before I retired." She smiled. "I used to do the cooking at Armidil."

"I know. Everyone talks about your cooking." Watch it, Kate thought, remembering the butchered sheep, the venison.

"It's a hobby nowadays." Maisie moved to a counter. "Sit

30

down, my dear. Gardening's my main interest now that I have time for it. What are your hobbies?"

"Work." It came out more bluntly than she'd intended. "Well, mountaineering, but at the moment climbing's all part of the work."

"And you're interested in Neil." Maisie nodded. "I know all about you. It's the Torboll tragedy you're concentrating on – or are you after more than that?"

Kate refused to catch any double meaning and stayed resolutely on the surface: "The question came up; in fact, I raised it – a biography, but that's something he should do himself. I've seen one of his journals – the one with the Torboll rescue. If all of them are as detailed as that he's got loads of material." It wasn't enthusiastic but Maisie didn't seem to notice.

"That's what his publishers say." She was occupied with a coffee-making machine. Kate stared at the straight back. "Not *his* publishers." Maisie gave a deprecating little laugh. "I'm anticipating there; it's just that one of his American friends is in publishing and trying to persuade him to write a book."

"They would." Particularly if they hadn't seen the journals. "He's had an eventful life. And the illustrations will be superb." She had glimpsed Alpine photographs on the panelled walls of the dining room and guessed that any with a figure in the foreground was there because it was Neil.

They drank good coffee and Maisie enthused over his exploits while Kate wondered when they would get to the purpose of this visit. Maisie had ascertained within a few minutes that her interest in Neil was only professional. Perhaps she wasn't convinced? Kate waited to see what was to come when the eulogy ended.

"I'm boring you," Maisie said.

"No, not at all! But you seem to be giving me background for a biography. Do *you* want me to write it?" Kate's eyes were innocent.

Maisie's gaze wandered. "I get carried away," she confessed. "I'm that proud of the lad – hardly a lad any longer but there, they stay the same age: twenty years younger than yourself. He's still a lad to me."

Kate thought of the young girl arriving in Cullen with the man who looked like a tinker. "You've had an interesting life too," she pointed out. "What were you doing when you met your husband?"

Maisie studied her. "I was cook in a big house in the South. I was very young." She stopped. Kate raised an eyebrow. "And then I met my husband," Maisie said without expression, "and we married and came here."

"I passed your old house. It must be sad to see it falling into the nettles."

"Never! Nasty primitive place; all the water had to be carried before himself put in the pipes; there was no electricity, no indoor toilet – although I won't say I didn't enjoy working the croft, hard as it was, but my, not half as hard as the work we had to put into getting the lodge fit for guests!"

"No power tools then either, but I heard your husband could turn his hand to anything."

"Yes." She drew it out. "He was clever with his hands."

"Even Duncan says so," Kate blurted. Where was this conversation leading?

"Even Duncan," Maisie repeated softly. She poured more coffee. "MacRae's a local man," she observed. "We're incomers; we worked to get that hotel on its feet. Highlanders aren't all that industrious. The MacRaes and the Stewart lads were of an age with my Neil but they left the glen to find work, and the best of them never got no further than a sergeant of police in Aberdeen, whereas my son plays host to chief constables. You'll not get the truth out of those two old gossips. They're jealous as cats."

"Not of yourself. Hector's been carrying a torch for you since the day you arrived in Cullen."

"Nonsense!" But she couldn't resist a smile. "What else did he have to say?"

"Well, actually," – thinking it was time she took the initiative – "we discussed the plane crash: the Flying Fortress."

"Of course." Maisie's eyes glazed. "Stewart and MacRae were among the first to reach it. But I thought it was Ben Torboll you were interested in."

"I am, but I'm fascinated by the stories about the plane. Apparently something was missing from the wreck. The diary? No, it couldn't have been the diary, it had to be something valuable. At least, that's the inference. When I asked Hector some innocuous question about the crash he lost his temper."

"I'm not surprised." Maisie was unperturbed. "With them it would be the same as beachcombing: picking up something that would come in useful on the croft. It's not important. Most of them are dead anyway."

"Most of who?"

"The men who brought the bodies down. My Rory went up, and he's passed away; all the locals went, Sir Ian saw to that. He's dead too, along with most of his generation. The Lawries were great climbers; the younger ones come back, you know; the family still owns the land and a lot of the houses – for what they're worth." Maisie glanced round her kitchen smugly. "But they've got lovely homes in Edinburgh, even in London. I've kept in touch with Lady Lawrie and I stay with her now and again. But as for their places here, some of them's as primitive as that old blackhouse, if truth was told. No amenities, no road to some. Look at Dunnas! You can only get there in a four-wheel drive."

"That's the house on the point? It's occupied?"

"Never! Miss Bell's there now and again just. She's Sir Ian's niece. It was her father used to take Neil climbing. Neil would be eighteen then, rising nineteen. They were the first mountaineers he met and it came at just the right time for him: a young man, in Cullen, nothing to do, and we kept him hard at it modernising the hotel, bringing it up

to scratch. He deserved a bit of fun in his leisure time." And
she was off again: Neil guiding the guests in Switzerland,
forging friendships, nowadays spending his holidays in Alaska,
Canada, the Rocky Mountains. Kate came to the conclusion
that she'd been right first time: she'd been summoned here so
that Maisie could discover her intentions, whether she was a
gold-digger. Satisfied she had no designs on Neil, she could
now indulge herself spinning these secondhand accounts of
great climbs. But she was shrewd, and had seen once that
her visitor was bored; Kate tried not to show it now. All
the same Maisie had divulged one snippet of information:
the name of someone else who'd known Neil when he was
young. Not that she wanted more on his background but a
woman who had been around when he started climbing might
well have accurate memories of the plane crash too: accurate
and objective, which was more than could be said of Hector
Stewart.

Hector's door was open when she passed again and she
glimpsed a form at a window but she ignored it. Beyond
the old blackhouse the road deteriorated to the remains of
hardcore interspersed with dried mud and potholes. There was
the imprint of wide tyres in the dust. She came to the Turkey
Burn and slowed for a sight of Torboll at the head of the glen.
The road, a track now, climbed to the open moor after crossing
the stream and now the views were wide, from Am Bodach to
the uninhabited country east of the loch. There was no road
on the far side, only abandoned crofts in bays where the burns
came down from a high plateau.

A mile past the Turkey Burn the track had been washed away
and the vehicle she was following had taken to the heather. She
left the van and started to walk.

Dunnas remained hidden until she was almost on it. There
was a cove this side of the point and in the bottom, sheltered
from westerly gales and only a few yards above the high-
water mark, was a cottage. It was squat and solid with tiny

dormer windows and huge square chimney stacks. It had been whitewashed but not for a long time, and there was a sag in the roof slates. A dusty Land Cruiser was parked under the gable-end.

A gull screamed. A bulky figure stood up from a rock on the shore and started to plod through the sand. Miss Bell was large but with an aura of power about her. She had cropped grey hair and sharp eyes behind spectacles with big round rims in red plastic. She wore khaki trousers and a thick navy guernsey.

"Want to buy it?" she asked, nodding at the house and extending a brown hand.

"The access road's not much cop," Kate said.

"That's an advantage: keeps the trippers at bay. Come in and have some coffee." She led the way towards the cottage. "I was expecting you. Ha!" – catching Kate's startled glance – "You've been around long enough to know you can't move a yard in the Highlands without the whole village knowing where you went, how long you stayed there, not to speak of who you were with." She grinned like a leather gargoyle; she must have been seventy if she was a day. "You camp down the coast road," she went on, "so you won't know that Duncan MacRae has lobster pots round the point here. He called in today, brought me a couple of lobsters and the local gossip. How're you making out with Neil Grant?"

"My God!" Kate recovered and said coldly, "I expected the family to be the epitome of good manners. Family as in Mafia."

"Temper! I'm the black sheep. My father was an artist and a maverick; I take after him. What d'you want from me? The lowdown on Neil? Wait. The coffee! Sit down."

They were in a dim and cluttered living room. Kate subsided on a kitchen chair. Prints of mountains were stuck unframed on wood-lined walls. "You were all climbers?" she asked.

"Virtually all of us. The Lawries too. My mother was a Lawrie: Uncle Ian's sister." She brought mugs to the table.

Both were chipped. Kate tried to turn hers unobtrusively but Miss Bell noticed and grinned.

"Why are you doing this biography?" she asked.

"Duncan screwed up." Kate was smug. "I'm not interested in a biography. He has to do it himself."

"Research too much for you? I've had a sight of the famous journals, d'you see. Isn't it odd how brilliant climbers turn out to be such turgid writers? Present company excepted, I'm sure. But if you're not interested in Neil – or are you?" Her eyes gleamed.

"We're talking climbing here." Kate was stiff. "Maisie Grant said you started him off, you or your father."

Miss Bell shrugged, evidently disappointed; she'd been hoping for something indiscreet. "Papa showed him a few tricks: how to handle rope, laybacks, hand-jamming techniques and so on, but the boy was a natural climber. You'll have met the type. What I want to know is what you said to Hector Stewart. Duncan says you upset him."

"I asked him about the plane crash: the Flying Fortress. Why would Hector delight in telling my photographer all about it, and blow his top when I asked the obvious question?"

"What was that?"

"Was anyone alive when he reached the crash."

"Wrong question. Did you ask if anything was missing?"

"No. Should I have done? With hindsight he could have thought I was implying that. So what was missing? Oh, I did mention the diary."

"No!" Miss Bell was contemptuous. "That diary never existed. What was missing was a very expensive camera: a Leica."

"Ah. There have been vague hints."

"It was nearly fifty years ago." The tone was loaded. "They're all dead now."

"Hector isn't dead."

"Best thing to do is forget about it. No proof anyway. Could have been one of the RAF. Have some more coffee."

36

Kate passed her mug across. "How do you know about it? He'd never have talked – I mean, whoever . . . er . . . appropriated it."

"Someone came over from the States: a relative of one of the victims. The camera wasn't among the dead man's effects and the family wanted it, as much for the film as anything: the last memento of him. And this man wanted to go up there and take photographs of the site. His name was Royal: Glenn Royal, not an easy name to forget. MacRae took him up, not to the crash – he was wearing high heels – just as far as the lochan. Showed him the wing hanging in the gully."

"High heels?"

"Duncan's words. They'd be cowboy boots. The chap was from Montana: cattle country."

"Why didn't he go to the police?"

"He did. He reported it at Strathmor and so far as I know nothing came of it." Miss Bell paused. "You can't use it," she added quietly.

"I'm not going to." Kate jerked to attention. "Why should I? It has nothing to do with the accident on Ben Torboll."

"But you're intrigued by the plane crash." The old eyes were keen behind the glasses. "I think you're considering another book. Am I right?"

Kate said slowly, thinking her way into it, "Even leaving out the rumours: the diary, the person ahead of the rescuers" – Miss Bell raised an eyebrow – "even the myth that someone could have survived . . . if you discount all that stuff and consider only the facts, the truth, it would make an epic story. Tracing the victims back to their roots . . . the names on the memorial plaque are extraordinary: Arizona, Montana . . . and this chap who came over was from Montana, wherever that is. I'd start with him."

"Are you serious about this?"

"Why not? I've written one book – almost finished now. What do you think?"

"I think that if you were to give me your word not to

mention the camera then I might be able to get you off to a good start."

"I did wonder. You were here when it crashed."

"No. We came up in April. By that time the wreckage had been removed; there were only odd bits of debris left, and that wing in the gully. It was the thing to do that year: to visit the site. One of the maids from the lodge came with us when we went up. Cried her eyes out. Almost had me doing it."

Kate was silent, absorbing this. Miss Bell elaborated. "My papa and Uncle Ian took everyone climbing: my brothers and me, the Lawrie cousins, the servants if any of 'em expressed an interest. The child had only been at the lodge a short time, probably getting over an unhappy love affair. I found her sitting on the scree hugging a piece of metal to her breast and sobbing as if her heart would break. She kept saying, 'Oh miss, I can't stop, I'm so sorry.' I couldn't get anything else out of her. Curious. None of us was affected, but then she was very young. And insecure. She left the lodge shortly afterwards, disappeared in the night. Uncle Ian was worried because I'd told him about her crying on Am Bodach. They thought she might have gone back there but she was seen catching the Glasgow bus in Strathmor, so we knew she was safe; she wasn't on the hill anyway. Funny how I remember it so clearly, but then it was an event in our lives: the aircraft crash. Now what's going on in your head?"

"Did she leave an address?"

"Oh yes? You're sharp. That was odd too. She gave an address when she came but when they tried to trace her, to make sure she was all right and to send her wages on, they discovered there was no such street. It was Glasgow, I think. That child was hiding something but – one thing – she wasn't a thief, so far as we know. Nothing was missing – well, nothing from the lodge." Miss Bell glanced towards the stairs. "And what did go missing could have had no connection with her."

"You lost something? Out here?"

"Food." Surprisingly Miss Bell winked. "I was friendly with the chap in charge of the rescue team and the RAF were issued with the most divine tinned sausages. He gave me a whole crate! Ridiculous, wasn't it? We had all the game we could eat and I preferred tinned sausages. My mother called them our iron rations, kept them under the stairs there for emergencies. But someone else liked them too. We lost six tins that winter."

"Someone broke in – that winter the plane crashed?"

"I wouldn't say *break*. In those days any of these windows could be opened with a knife. I keep them wedged now, against campers and so on."

"You think the maid lived here for a while?"

"No. I said that she was seen catching the bus the morning after she left the lodge. This was someone else. The crofters were very poor in those days." They were silent, evidently the same thought in both their minds. Miss Bell voiced it: "Although some did well enough out of Uncle Ian's deer and salmon, even" – her voice sank – "even the sheep, some people said. Neil jokes among his guests about his father's prowess with the deer, but sheep are never mentioned. There's a limit – and old Linklater would have a fit. It's not so long ago that sheep-stealing was a capital offence."

Kate's mind was on other concerns. "What was her name?"

Miss Bell was disconcerted. "I've forgotten. Aunt Anne would know. She's Uncle Ian's widow. I'm going home to Edinburgh in a few days so I can find out. Let me have your number."

"It's not that important. If she married she's changed her name – and she could be anywhere. At least with Glenn Royal, you know he comes from Montana."

"Or came. He's probably dead. And d'you know the size of Montana? However, we may be able to narrow it down a bit. Leave it with me and I'll see what I can do. I'll come to Armidil tomorrow evening. How's that suit you?"

*   *   *

"A pleasant enough girl," Maisie said, stroking the fine wool of the cardigan Neil had brought back from Edinburgh.

He frowned. "Where did you meet her?"

"I invited her here. I like to meet your friends."

"You mean you like to inspect my ladies. I only climbed with her, Mother."

She nodded, trying on the cardigan. "Does it suit?"

"Perfectly. Blue's your colour."

"She's pleasant enough," she repeated. "She knows how to conduct herself, but she's after something."

He raised his eyebrows. "Or someone."

"Not in that way. She's inquisitive."

"Writers are. Any author who stays with us is full of questions. They never say anything about themselves but they'll turn you inside out in an evening."

"She's not that clever – and I didn't tell her any more than she'd picked up from MacRae and Stewart, less in fact." Her tone was sombre. "She's talking to everyone; she's interested in the plane crash."

Neil stared at her. "She reckons," Maisie went on deliberately, "something went missing from the wreck and that Hector was the thief." She amended it slightly: "That is the impression she has."

"What did you tell her?"

"That nearly everyone who went up there is dead, including your father, and any left alive are just a lot of old gossips. They were always jealous of us: the MacRaes and the Stewarts."

"You shouldn't have encouraged Stewart."

"When did I ever" – she caught his expression – "That's not nice, son."

"You've got no sense of humour. Now go upstairs and see yourself in the mirror. That cardigan makes you look stunning. And don't worry about Kate Munro. She's trying to establish herself as an author and I'm in a position to help her. I've not decided how to handle it yet; she'd like to do my biography but we'll see."

"You do it. If she was to write it she'd want to know everything: the croft, me being in service, your father."

"There's nothing to hurt. You were a cook, Dad was a superlative poacher – and don't look like that, it's history – and it makes a good story. We lived in a blackhouse until Auntie Rose died. We worked our way up from nothing. The old class system's gone, Mother; we're a meritocracy now and by those standards we're upper class. We've got nothing to be ashamed of, just the opposite. I'll handle Kate, trust me."

"Just you watch yourself. You're far too easy where a pretty face is concerned."

"They're drinking Dom Perignon," Linklater growled. "Being a bit obvious, isn't he?" He was fascinated by Neil and Kate tonight, neither of whom seemed aware that they were the focus of attention in the dining room. "Is he having an affair with her?"

"It won't work out." Dunbar helped himself to asparagus. "He's old enough to be her grandfather."

"Nonsense, he's your age! And he's rich."

"You mean he can feed her lobster thermidor instead of her eating baked beans in her tent. She doesn't care."

"You may be right." Linklater reached for his glass. "But if it isn't his money that impresses her, what is it?"

"She's not impressed. She's drunk."

He was exaggerating. Kate was excited and a little wild, clumsily trying to parry Neil's questions concerning her day. He knew she'd talked to his mother, and Maisie must have told him she'd visited Duncan and Hector. It appeared that he didn't know she'd seen Madeleine Bell, but he'd find out, no doubt about that.

Her efforts to stall him were undermined by the champagne, and Neil was assiduous in keeping her glass topped up. She guessed that he was afraid she'd cause embarrassment in the village and she knew she must reassure him at some point, but she resented his attempts to bully her. She let him stew for a while, noting that he was becoming increasingly flushed, aware of his frustration when, emulating Maisie, she diverted him with yet another question about the Alps, the Rockies, Alaska. Finally he could take it no longer – and he abandoned finesse.

"Why are you frightened of me?" he blurted.

Her eyes were wide. "Frightened of you? Why should I be?"

"Because you've been pumping the crofters. Why couldn't you come to me?"

There were a number of responses to that, the obvious one being that she needed material about his early days from other people, but they both knew that wasn't essential for one chapter on one rescue. "You're mad because I've been asking about the plane crash," she said coldly. "There's been a cover-up, hasn't there?"

He stared at her. "Go on." He was grim.

"The stolen Leica?" She shook her head. "Look, Neil, I'm not going to use it—"

"*Use* it?"

"I mean if I wrote a book about the plane crash. You've been away all day. I've been busy. I've just about finished my first book, I have to do a second; I need the money. I can't keep myself and run the van on what I make from newspapers and magazines; in fact I need new wheels—" She trailed off. She was gabbling, trying to conceal her knowledge of the man from Montana, not sure of her motivation there. Not use the missing Leica? She was having second thoughts about that; she wasn't bothered about the identity of the thief but she was enormously intrigued by a man who'd come thousands of miles for a camera.

"Is the book commissioned?" he asked.

"Not yet. It will be. My editor at Macmillan is a mountaineer. He'll commission it."

"You're going to hurt a lot of people, my mother among them."

42

"I told you: the camera won't be mentioned. In any event," she added nastily, "I'd think Hector would be more embarrassed than your mother."

"They're friendly. We're all close in the village. But it may not have been Hector, did you think of that? Could have been any of them." He held her eye, saw a thought there. "Have you contacted the RAF?"

"Not yet."

"Don't. Remember the diary? It was suggested the RAF suppressed it. You don't want to run foul of the Ministry of Defence."

"You're not saying they'd actually try to stop me investigating this crash?"

"They could even stop you writing the book. They could ruin you." He beamed, back to his avuncular role. "Just keep clear of them – and the police if it comes to that. Confine yourself to the rescuers—"

"They're dead. And the ones that aren't won't talk. And you're no help; you were only a kid, and your father wouldn't have told you anything—" She looked away, appalled. His father could have been the thief.

"We'll have coffee upstairs," he said firmly, catching her at a disadvantage, rising and coming round to draw out her chair. He was well mannered when he remembered to be; she appreciated that.

"What do you think of it?" she asked as they mounted the stairs. "It would be a faction: the true story rather dramatised, from when they left the States until – well, until they returned – in body bags. Oh, how sad; I can't do it like that."

"They didn't start from the States," he told her gently, "but from East Anglia somewhere. They were going home."

"I mean, when they left their home towns to join up – I suppose they'd have been conscripted in those days. They came from all over America. I was on Am Bodach and I found the memorial plaque" – her voice broke – "so desolate, you know? Sunshine: there shouldn't be a feeling in sunshine

43

and yet – I know why the rumours started, about a presence. Something's still there."

He said nothing. When they entered his sitting room he crossed to the stereo and selected a record. Music started to play – rather saccharine, she thought. She perched primly on the arm of a chair. The room was quiet, softly lit, intimate. She'd made a mistake, she'd said too much, exposed herself. She shouldn't be here.

"Brandy," he announced, going to a sideboard.

"No thanks. I'm driving."

"You could have fooled me." He turned his back and when he faced her again he had two balloon glasses in his hands.

She stood up. The atmosphere was tense. "I thought we were going to talk – about my book."

"We're going to."

"I don't want a drink."

"Yes you do." He was smiling: suggestive, confident, macho.

"I said no."

"But you meant yes."

"You're drunk. And that's a charitable way of putting it."

"What have I done? You've had a good meal – you enjoyed your dinner, didn't you?"

"I wouldn't have if I'd known I was expected to pay for it."

"For Christ's sake, what d'you think I asked you up here for? To seduce you?"

"You'd have a job; the state you're in attempted rape would be more like it." She raised her hands, repelling him. "Okay, I made a mistake. Now I'm remedying it. Am I getting through to you?"

"Shit." He put the snifters on the sideboard and advanced. "I've been thinking about this evening for two days, Kate. Don't you know how I feel about you? Have you no idea?" He was sweating prodigiously and his face seemed to have swollen.

She sighed and shook her head. "Goodnight, Neil."

"I – listen—" She was making for the door. He plunged after her and stood in front of it. "I want you – to stay. To help you."

"Help me with what?" She spat it out.

"With your book."

"It's finished."

"I mean the next one. Or I can read the proofs of the first."

"You! Read my proofs?"

He glared at her, his head lowered like a bull's. The implication was obvious. "I want my journal back."

"I'll drop it off tomorrow."

She waited for him to move, her head up. No way would she touch him, she had enough sense not to do that.

"See you do."

He walked away, leaving her to open the door.

Four

"I want you to do something for me," Kate said. "It's a bit delicate."

Dunbar had been lacing his boots when she arrived at the hotel after breakfast. She'd left the journal on the counter in the residents' bar and emerged to announce that she would accompany him on his walk (the colonel was visiting an old army chum in Oban). Now they were sitting on turf above the cliffs on the eastern shore of the loch. Below them water sucked in hidden caves. Auks were coming in to their nesting ledges. "Razorbills," Dunbar murmured, adding in the same tone, "I noticed you didn't want to return the journal personally."

"The point is I feel rather crowded." He said nothing. "I need my space." She bit her lip; he'd been in the dining room last night when she was making a fool of herself over the champagne. "I don't want to come in the bar tonight," she went on peevishly, "and the trouble is, I agreed to meet Madeleine Bell there."

Dunbar waited; she'd tell him as much as she wanted him to know. Questions were superfluous. "She may have an address for me," Kate went on, looking across the water to Torboll and Am Bodach, clear as a bell this morning, the broken wing showing up quite plainly. "At least I hope she has. I'm going to write a book about the Flying Fortress."

His jaw dropped. She turned and studied him. "It has to be written, Alec." She was defiant. "Madeleine's in favour. I'm telling you this in confidence; I don't want Neil to know. He's fiercely opposed – he'd stop me if he could. You know

46

why, don't you? Everyone must know. About the Leica?" Dunbar nodded. "I promised Madeleine I wouldn't use it," she continued, "and she trusts me. She's going to try to locate Glenn Royal."

"I see. But he's in the States – if he's still alive."

"And I'm going to find him. I need him to put me in touch with the other relatives. I don't know what Madeleine's doing today but if she does find out something, would you take the message when she comes in this evening – without Neil knowing? Please, Alec; it means everything to me."

"And nothing to be written about the camera?"

"Cross my heart. It's forgotten."

"What else did Madeleine tell you?"

"What else?"

"You didn't get the story of the stolen Leica from the crofters or from Neil. It had to be Madeleine."

"Do you remember the maid from the lodge who went up to the site of the crash?"

"I wasn't here but I heard about it."

"What was her name?"

"I've no idea. I see how your mind's working. I always wondered if she could have been in love with a chap who died in the crash."

"I considered that, but why should she make a mystery of it? She gave a false address to the Lawries, she disappeared in the night – but she was seen next day, catching a bus, so she went voluntarily. What was she hiding?"

"You tell me. You're the investigator."

"How sweet of you. There could be a connection; the girl was at the lodge for such a short time that the motive for taking the job could have been just to get up to the wreck. Could there have been a diary after all? Was that what she was after?" Dunbar made no response. She went on, following the thread: "A diary would be very significant if someone survived the crash."

"No one did."

"How can you say that? Have you seen the autopsy reports?"

"No, but I've talked—" He looked away, avoiding her intense stare. "I did hear something," he admitted, "that someone – reached the wreck ahead of the rescue team."

"That old story? There's something in it after all?" Her voice dropped. "You have to tell me the rest, Alec."

"Yes, I think I do." He sighed. "There was a chap camping on the coast road – where you're camped actually – and he'd been there a while, waiting for the weather to clear. He had no wireless and he didn't come in to Cullen. The cloud was down much of the time and it was snowing. On his last morning he decided he must do something, whatever the weather. He was about to emigrate, d'you see, and this would be his last day in the Highlands.

"So he went up, into cloud – a white-out – and that's how he stumbled on the wreck."

Kate was wide-eyed. "He didn't know a plane was missing? He came on a Flying Fortress – God! What a dreadful shock! All those bodies."

"Exactly, but this is my point. They were all dead. He went to each one, he counted them all, twenty-seven, and every one of them was dead."

"You've talked to him." It wasn't a question and he didn't accept it as such. "Was he a doctor?" she asked sceptically.

"As a matter of fact, he was. A GP. There was no mistake about it: no one lived after the impact." He threw her a quick glance.

"How long after the crash was he there?"

"I think it was two days."

A thought struck her. "That was how they found the wreck! He reported it." She stared across the water, then turned on him. "Why wasn't anyone else told? The authorities kept it quiet . . . Oh, I get it: the cover-up was because a lone climber found the wreck when the professionals failed. But what about the newspapers? Didn't they find him?"

"Pratt's not the chap to make waves; with him emigrating

48

in a day or two, he'd feel that once he'd reported the wreck his duty was done, not to mention missing his boat if he had to attend the inquests."

"Pratt. So you know him. Where does the stolen Leica fit, and the maid from the lodge?"

"There's no connection. She couldn't have stolen the Leica because by the time she came to Armidil everything had been removed, even most of the wreckage."

"I'd like to meet Pratt."

"And ask him if it was he who picked it up? Come *on*, Kate!"

"No. What I'd ask him is: was one of the bodies warm?"

He gasped. "Couldn't have been," he snapped, recovering. "He'd have stayed and tried to do something."

"I said warm, not alive. He didn't stay anyway. He went down and reported it."

"I assure you they were all dead. He's always maintained that."

"You know where he is."

He frowned at the water. A puffin appeared on a ledge. Kate saw it but Dunbar was lost in thought.

"I suppose you're committed to this book," he said at last. Her head moved in the slightest gesture of assent. "He's in this country," he admitted. "He's bought a house—" He checked. "If he tells you himself, will you drop the story?"

"I'll drop that part – or I'll say they were all killed on impact. Can you arrange a meeting?"

He glanced at the sky and sniffed. "Weather's changing. We'll go back now. I'll see what he has to say."

Bartholomew Pratt had bought a house above Loch Harport, looking out to the Cuillins of Skye. He was not much over five feet in height, a diminutive troll with a corrugated face. He had white hair and a neat white beard and he wore new breeches still stiff from the factory, sandals and no socks. On his yellow

T-shirt was a coiled rattlesnake with the legend DON'T MESS WITH ME. I WAS HERE FIRST.

Kate had left Armidil immediately after Dunbar's successful telephone call. She was anxious to put as much distance between herself and the hotel before Neil returned. Dunbar said he'd gone out dressed for the hill. After last night Neil was an unknown quantity.

Dr Pratt had agreed to see her at eleven the following day – which was just as well; even pushing the old van as hard as it would go, it was evening before she drove off the ferry and started the last leg of the journey across Skye.

She slept in the heather, woke to wash in a burn and at eleven turned in at the gate of a modern house with no distinguishing features until this little man ushered her into his living room. One wall was mostly glass. Below them was the pewter expanse of the loch while beyond the water and the brown moors cloud was creeping along the Cuillin Ridge like mist caught on a dinosaur's spine.

They sat down. He asked if she'd climbed here and she referred to her harder routes. There was a pause. He opened his mouth and closed it again. He flashed her an artificial smile. "Your move," he said. "You solicited a meeting."

She had rehearsed this. "The most important question is: was one of the bodies still warm?"

"No." He was equally prompt, unfazed. Dunbar would have briefed him, had probably talked at length while she was on the road. "They'd all been dead for some time. They'd had two nights of intense cold, remember, on top of massive internal injuries and bleeding."

"Originally I wondered why the police allowed you to leave – was it next day?"

"I left the area that afternoon. Originally? You've worked it out."

"I guessed. You reported it anonymously."

He looked mischievous. "I wasn't bothered so much about the authorities as the Press. I had a job waiting for me in British

Columbia. I wasn't needed here; I'd done my bit, reporting the wreck. Besides—"

"Yes?"

He shrugged. "There was a complication. You suggested to Dunbar that someone might have survived the crash. The answer to that is yes and no. It's possible that one chap lived for a while, but he was dead when I reached him. He was rigid, but then they all were. Snow was driving in through gaps in the fuselage."

"Why one particular man?"

"He had a diary under his hand."

She was speechless. "Dunbar warned me," he went on. "He says there's a camera missing too. I didn't see a camera but I could have missed it; there was a lot of snow about. I had to wipe it off the victims. It would have drifted back of course, it covered my tracks too."

"So how did you spot the diary?"

"It was on his lap, and he had a pencil in his hand. Cadaveric spasm, you know? A tight grip at the moment of death. It was a propelling pencil."

"What was the last entry in the diary?"

"Yes, I was curious about that: wanting to know if he wrote before or after the crash – but it was no good. He'd haemorrhaged from the mouth and spattered the page, two pages actually, both blank. That is, only one word was visible: 'Chick'. It puzzled me. Why refer to a chicken in a diary, and the capital 'C'? Later, living in Canada, I guessed it was 'Chuck'. A message presumably: 'Tell Chuck—' And then he died."

A breeze lifted papers on a desk. Dr Pratt stood up. At the side of the living room another window looked towards the open sea. "Here it comes," he said, with the satisfaction of one who has read the weather signs correctly.

Kate joined him and looked between two headlands – clear as glass and gold where dry grass caught the sun – to an opaque bank of rain. "No diary was found," she said. "At least, that's the story."

"The RAF wouldn't have wanted it known that someone survived, if only briefly. The Press would have blown it up, made headlines about the team's incompetence in not finding the wreck sooner."

"You said he'd have died anyway."

"Ah yes, but then there's the camera." He shook his head. "This was a poor country in the forties."

Kate felt deflated, the mystery having dissolved into a clutter of petty thefts: camera, diary, a propelling pencil. Was there anything left to talk about? "Have you been in touch with Alec Dunbar all along?" she asked.

"No, I'm virtually another generation. But there's our club, and the membership list. He knew where to find me. He phoned me recently, when you started to show an interest in the Flying Fortress. You know, there's never been any secret about my finding the wreck, not a close secret. People in the club knew; they just didn't talk about it."

"A gentleman's agreement. So Alec thought my writing about the crash would revive interest and then the media would discover you."

"Particularly when you got this notion into your head that someone survived and that this was connected with the theft of the camera. The tabloids would go into a feeding frenzy if you put that in your book."

Bill Hoggart trudged into Strathmor just in time to see a blue Transit turn down a side street. He came to the corner and saw it stopping outside a shop. Kate got out, pulling on her cagoule. It was raining hard and had been for two days. He plodded down the street, heaved his rucksack in the back of the van and climbed into the passenger seat.

Kate, emerging with a bag of groceries, stopped short at sight of the figure in the cab. He wound down the window and grinned at her. "Hi! It's only me."

She opened the driver's door, swearing at him. "For a moment there I thought I was going to be mugged."

"A mugger would be waiting for you in the back. You should lock your doors. I keep telling you."

"Where's the bike?"

"I had a spill: came round a bend and there were cows all over the road. I left it at a farm and hitched here. Can we go back for it? Only a few miles."

"I'm knackered. I was on Skye this morning, and then I had a puncture in Glen Shiel. What are you doing here anyway? You're supposed to be developing my prints."

"I've brought the proofs. Let's find a bar and you can tell me the score. What were you doing on Skye?"

They sat in a quiet bar and she brought him up to date, mentioning Neil only in passing and saying nothing of that ridiculous scene in his flat. She told him about Glenn Royal and the missing Leica, which amused him, but he was puzzled when she recounted Dr Pratt's story. It seemed to explain – as far as it went – the missing diary and the ghostly presence ahead of the rescuers. "But it *doesn't* explain the ghost," he argued. "The team didn't go up there until Pratt had come down and reported finding the wreck—"

"Obviously they saw his tracks—"

"I thought there weren't any tracks."

"That's the *rumour*. Since Pratt was there he had to leave the odd footprint, like in the lee of a boulder where the snow wouldn't drift over it."

"And there's the diary. What happened to that?"

"Ah! The RAF is covering up. I phoned Andy MacLeod in the local team; he's been cooperative with information for the rescue book but he's a dead loss on the Flying Fortress. He says those old Incident Reports will be with the Ministry of Defence now if they haven't been destroyed. The man who was in charge of the team is dead, and as for the other members, those who are still alive, he has no idea where they are. I felt he was trying to stall me. So I came to the police here and they told me to apply to the chief constable – which I wouldn't. I'd never convince him I wasn't interested in the missing camera, and that's what everyone's scared of. I could get more from the States: relatives first, then official reports." She paused. "I've got Glenn Royal's address," she added, her eyes shining.

Dr Pratt had been most accommodating, insisting she use his telephone. She had asked him to contact Dunbar, and that was a prudent move because Neil answered and wanted to know who was calling. She took the phone only when Dunbar came on the line. Yes, he said, he'd seen Madeleine Bell and she had given him Royal's address. What had happened was that the American had kept in touch with the police sergeant in Strathmor and they'd exchanged Christmas cards. After the sergeant died his daughter had continued the tradition until Royal's cards stopped and she assumed he'd died too. However, she'd kept the last envelope, thinking she ought to write to someone over there, but not knowing whom. She never did.

"The postmark was Great Something, the rest illegible," Kate told Bill. "But there was a return address: Slaughter Creek, Arletta, Montana."

"You're going to write?"

"No, I'm going there. If he's dead people will put me on to his relatives – and they'll lead me to others. Relatives get together after multiple tragedies."

"Why don't you try to find the maid from the lodge?"

"She'd be hell to trace. Madeleine's going back to Edinburgh and she did say she'd ask her aunt – that's Lady Lawrie – for the girl's name, but I doubt it's still the same, she's probably married." Her tone lightened. "I called my publisher. They want me to go up to London and discuss this idea. My editor thinks it's brilliant and, of course, I can give him the old book, the rescue one." She was dismissive, she'd lost interest in that. "So I'm away just as soon as—" She stopped. "As soon as what?" she asked herself. There could be problems with Neil if she returned with Bill – the old chap was bad enough when she was on her own, for goodness' sake. She went on, "I've got my sleeping bag and pack with me, and my boots – what more do I need? I can take off from here."

"Hell, woman, I've got no wheels. Or do I come with you?"

"You stay here." She thought about that. "You can have the van while I'm away. We'll go and fetch your bike now, put it in the back, then I'll hitch to Glasgow and go on from there. I have to pick up my passport and things. What you do is go down to the camp in the wood, wait for a break in the weather, then run up Am Bodach and get me some shots of that memorial plaque – and while you're about it, take some long shots of Bodach from Torboll – and the wing, don't forget the wing in the gully."

"Well, thanks a lot." He begrudged her taking over his life but it was certainly to his advantage. He could get his bike to Glasgow this way and he had a dry place to sleep while he waited for the weather to improve. But he didn't like taking orders, and he showed it.

She glanced at him. "I'll send you a cheque as soon as I get some more cash for the old book."

"I'm not asking for money."

"Call it running expenses. You need a new wheel or new forks? Listen, man, the way this idea's shaping up your share for the pictures will buy you a new bike!"

That was nonsense, all the same he had to go along with her plan; if he didn't and she was set on leaving tonight, he'd have to go to Glasgow with her, and she'd be in a foul temper because she needed pictures of Am Bodach, and they must go to Cullen to pick up her tent.

"At least you'll have transport this way," she pointed out. "I'm not going to enjoy hitching across Rannoch Moor on a wet night."

Later, however, when they'd driven back to retrieve the bike, she had him drive her to the next village where there was a café. Drivers of fish lorries pulled in there for a meal on the night run to Glasgow. She'd get a lift with one of them, she said.

*   *   *

At one o'clock in the morning Bill was on his last reserves
of energy as he came slowly down the coast road towards
their old camp. She'd made him promise to take care. "You
remind me of my mother," he'd said nastily – but when
he came to the bends there was no question of speed. The
cloud was down almost to sea level, swirling through his
headlight beams.

It was a wild night. The burns were high, in places splashing
across the road, and the wind was blowing a gale. June, he
thought, and wished he were going to America. He guessed
he'd get mired trying to reach the tent but he didn't care so
long as he was off the road. He'd dig the van out in the morning
after a night's kip. He was so tired that nothing mattered now
except to get his head down.

The burn beside the wood was full of white water. As he
eased across the bridge he could hear the boulders trundling
down the bed. The cloud was too thick to see the trees. He
turned up the rutted track, crawling in bottom gear, then
accelerated for the gradient, but the surface was slime and
the tyres worn. After a few yards the van crabbed sideways and
stalled. He was off the road and tolerably level. He reached for
his cagoule and worked his way into it, putting up the hood.

He switched off the lights and opened the door, to be met
by the roar of the flooded burn and the sweep of trees in full
foliage lashed by wind. It would be just his luck to fall in the
burn when all he wanted was a leak. He turned and, opening
the door again, reached in the glove compartment for a torch,
wishing the interior light wasn't broken. God, it was dark!

He pulled back and suddenly there was light: blinding,
exploding. There were crashes – more crashes, something
human – a human noise – a gasp, a groan . . . Then nothing.

America

Five

"There's nothing at Slaughter Creek could interest you. There was a ferry once and the house is still lived in, but the guy there, Old Copper, he never had no kin in the Army; no way could he be connected with your plane crash."

Kate breathed deeply and turned to the window. After half an hour she had the librarian's measure: friendly, lonely, and delighted at the sudden appearance of a Scottish author in this dead-end community sixty miles from a proper town.

The library was housed in an old shop, the books arranged on the original shelves, the window fronting on a wide stretch of dust that was Arletta's main street. The door was open, the insect screen closed. There was no air conditioning and the library, on the shady side of the street, was dark and warm, like a womb. Outside, beyond the glass, the American West drowsed through the brilliant silence of a summer's afternoon.

"I'm interested in Glenn Royal," Kate said.

Barbara Lomas was middle-aged, single, emotional. Every emotion showed. Now she was amazed. "Glenn died a year or two back. Why should you – I'm sorry, none of my business." But her eyes were avid.

"His cousin died in the crash." Kate was insistent. "Glenn went to Scotland to see where it happened and he kept in touch with one of the local policemen. That's how I know his address. Who's Old Copper?"

"His brother of course." Barbara was puzzled. "I never knew they had a cousin in the Army. You sure you're not mistaken?"

59

"Would you know? Forty-five years ago?"

"Well, maybe not." She was delighted at the compliment. "I didn't even know that Glenn had been to Scotland. I didn't—" She stopped and bit her lip.

Kate looked idly along a shelf of books. "You'd be much younger than him, of course."

"Oh, more'n ten years, not that that made any—" Again the woman checked, to resume in a lighter tone: "People were much stricter in those days. I've lived here all my life; we have a ranch, my brother runs it now. I moved into town, see a bit of life. When I was growing up we were seven miles from town and our nearest neighbours were two miles away. You went everywhere on a horse, and if there wasn't a horse to spare you stayed put. Arletta was a different world. I ran this store when it *was* a store; we sold everything: dry goods, groceries, meat. That's how I come to be running the library; I stayed on when I gave up the store. The supermarkets in the city put me out of business, and folk getting cars. I'm not a trained librarian and I'm not paid no more'n peanuts but it's a service, isn't it?"

"So you knew the Royal brothers as customers when you ran the store."

"That was all." It came pat but in the face of Kate's surprise, restraint broke down. Barbara shook her head forcefully. "My mother would never have allowed me to go down there. They had no womenfolk: two old bachelors – young bachelors then, of course – that made it worse. No, no way. I was a young girl. Mind you," – her voice dropped and she threw a glance at the open door – "some went. I knew. The kids would know, wouldn't they? Got eyes everywhere. I tell you, there are some old ladies in this town—" She drew herself up. "There. I'm gossiping. But you can guess, can't you?"

"You wouldn't expect young men to live like priests." Remote communities were the same everywhere, Western Scotland or Western America.

"I just remembered!" Barbara exclaimed. "I said Glenn never went to Scotland but there was a Scotch girl came here: a very

60

pretty lady with a neat accent – like yours, in fact. My mother said she was pregnant. She visited with the Royals."

Kate's mind lurched. "When did she come here?"

"I can't – wait! If my mother told me she was pregnant that could mean I was old enough for such talk but not old enough to see for myself." Barbara beamed. "I recall I started to use her shade of lipstick after." She looked round the library. "Lipsticks were kept there," – she pointed – "I had to be working here already so I'd be around fifteen, sixteen. That would make it forty-nine or 1950. Who is this woman?"

"I don't know." Which was true – although Glenn Royal at the crash site, the maid from Armidil: there was the link. "You don't remember her name?"

"I don't recall that I ever heard it."

"What about Old Copper? Would he talk to me?"

"Oh, my Lord! You're never going down there?"

"What's wrong with him? Surely he's too old to be much of a threat."

"He's turned seventy but he's still active enough for *that*. You take your life in your hands if you visit with him. That Scotch girl, she didn't stay but one night. Maybe she never—" She gasped and her hand flew to her mouth.

"Maybe she never left?" Kate was cool.

Barbara grinned weakly. "I've always been known for my big mouth. Of course she came out: same way as she went in, with Billy Newman. He was the blacksmith but he bought a load of army Jeeps at the end of the War and he changed over to automobiles. The girl hired him for the trip." She paused. "But that can't be right; Billy wouldn't never have stayed down to Slaughter overnight. I guess one of the Royals brought her out next morning and she went on with Billy."

"Went on – where?"

"She'd go to Great Falls. That's our nearest city."

"Is Billy still at the garage?"

"No, he moved south years ago." She reverted to the more immediate matter. "If you're set on going down there you let

61

me know what time to expect you back. And you'll have to drop by Grace Bierman's – she owns the land. 'Fact, the brothers worked for her when she ran her cattle down there below the big cliffs. Old Copper still does odd jobs about the place. That Grace," – she shook her head – "she collects weird folk and no mistake. That's how the Royals come to be on the river; the old ferry house is Bierman property."

"How do I get to it?"

"For Heaven's sakes, you can't go tonight! It's near six o'clock. It'll take you upwards of an hour to the Bierman place and you'll need to stop and visit with Grace. The sun'd be going down by the time you reached Slaughter. You'd never find it. You don't want to be out in the coulees in the dark. The breaks swarm with snakes."

Oh come on, Kate thought. Aloud she said, "What's the coulees?"

Barbara shook her head in exaggerated despair. "In the morning I'll draw you a map."

The tarmac ended at Arletta and the old ferry road was graded. Graded meant a dirt road made by some kind of blade that had pushed the earth into low banks on either side. The surface was rough and Kate's Jeep, bought cheap in Chicago, wasn't in the best condition. The gear lever seemed loose in its seating, she'd need to check it at a garage on her return.

The land was flat and featureless, thin grass clumped with what she took for sage. This must be what they called a prairie. She came to the start of a track: two ruts running out into infinity. A hand-painted board was nailed to a post. THE TIEGENS, it read.

She stopped. She could see those ruts for miles, disappearing and reappearing beyond incipient swells, and there wasn't a sign of humanity, only the board. A sound perhaps? A dog's bark would carry a long distance in this thin atmosphere. She switched off and climbed down into the dust. The silence was profound; there wasn't the breath of a zephyr through the low vegetation, not even the cheep of a bird. She stepped away from the jeep and looked around, intimidated. It was as if the land were no more than a skin and all the rest of the world was sky. There were a few little fine-weather clouds, very high, but nowhere, anywhere, was there a hint of a mountain. This wasn't her country.

She drove on and after interminable miles she came to another track. There was no board but the dust was marked by tyres. A woman lived out here, on her own – well, not quite alone; Barbara had said there was a hired hand, said it with the kind of tight-lipped smile that implied she could say a lot more. A message was being conveyed but Kate was unable to decipher it and Barbara had changed the subject.

She had insisted that Kate sleep in her guest room. Her house was next door to the library. Kate had been fed beef from the family ranch and plied with Budweiser, hospitality that could have had ulterior motives: to oil her tongue or dull her curiosity. In the event her eyes started to close after only two beers, and she'd learned nothing more than that Grace Bierman employed a man, two if you counted Old Copper Royal, and that she was *very* old, whatever that meant.

It meant she was on the edge of senility. She was a wizened little woman in denim trousers, pale hair hacked short, her eyes milky with cataracts. Kate, creeping down the potholed track in the Jeep, seeing the small figure in front of the ramshackle house, had been seized with diffidence. How would she be received by this person living at the back of beyond: a stranger appearing without warning, with God knew what purpose?

Grace Bierman regarded her approach without expression. "I've been waiting for you," she said.

"You're not on the phone!"

"I pray for visitors every night."

"I don't wonder. I'm Kate Munro. Barbara Lomas sent me, from the library." She looked round at the barns that dwarfed the house, at the corrals and the ancient implements overgrown with weeds. "How long have you lived here?"

"I was born here. Come inside. We'll have some tea."

The ranch house was only a cabin really but its living room was large, with a number of internal doors, only one of which was open. It revealed a kitchen alcove with crockery everywhere: stacked on shelves and draining board, a pile on a wooden bench. None looked clean but then the dust coated everything.

"You keep the door closed for the dust?" Kate observed. The room was stifling in the heat and Mrs Bierman had shut the outer door as well as its screen.

"Not really. But the snakes get in if you don't."

"You should keep a mongoose."

"Down south they have ringtail cats. The men kill the rattlers here but they keep coming back. You gotta kill the mate too, or he'll come in the night and have his vengeance."

"You have hired hands?"

"Chesler looks after things but that Royal: I never see him from one month's end to the other. There's two young bulls I want to sell but they can't find 'em. Maybe they been bit or they fell in the river, the banks give way without warning. I need a new well dug, so the money'd come in handy. The water's turning brackish. I forgot the tea."

She went to the kitchen, limping slightly, and opened a refrigerator with old-fashioned moulded corners.

"You do have electricity!" Kate exclaimed. "I didn't see any poles."

"The fridge runs on kerosene. It makes the food taste."

The tea was ice-cold, in a red plastic tumbler. Kate put it down after tasting it. "So you don't live alone," she observed brightly, and looked meaningly at the closed doors. "You have the hired men for company."

"Royal's five miles away, on the river." There was a pause during which Mrs Bierman sipped her tea and stared at the window, draped with several layers of net. "The boy frightens me," she said.

"The younger generation. They have different values." There

was no problem getting the old lady to talk; the difficulty could lie in steering her, but would she remember the Scottish girl?

"He wants this place," came the monotone. "He's waiting for me to die. Maybe he won't wait. When I came off my horse last fall he didn't help me. I crawled home and he never lifted a finger. I'd have starved 'cept Royal come by and he looked after me till I mended. That Chesler took off for Great Falls."

"Why do you keep him on?"

"He won't go."

"Ask Royal for help."

"Royal's terrified of him."

"Where's Chesler now?"

"He's supposed to be looking for the bulls."

"What do you think he's doing?"

Mrs Bierman's mouth twisted in a sneer but her eyes didn't change. "He'll be after a woman."

"Where?"

"You name it. No woman's safe from Wayne Chesler."

"I'd better look out for myself then."

"He won't bother you." The clouded eyes stared at the visitor. Kate shifted uncomfortably, wondering what they saw, wondering what was going on in this jumpy brain. "He won't be interested in you," Mrs Bierman said. "He'll see your power soon as he sets eyes on you. You got nothing to fear."

"Weak men can be dangerous."

"True, and this one—"

The door opened, letting in a flood of sunshine. A man entered: young, slim, graceful, in faded Levis and pointed boots, wearing a ball cap. He had the face of a beautiful ravaged youth: pouting, delinquent, with circles under his eyes.

"Hi!" He nodded to her as if they were acquainted. "You're driving the right rig for this country. That so, Ma?"

"Nothing's no good in the wet." Mrs Bierman brought a jug of tea from the fridge. She looked at Kate's untouched drink but made no comment. "And the snow," she said. "People die out here in the winter and no one knows."

"The coyotes get them," Chesler said. "Saves us the trouble of burying them." He regarded Kate keenly, then he smiled. It was the full drooping lips that made him appear delinquent. His smile was enchanting, and he exuded sex. His eyes went from her to one of the closed doors and back. "So," he said softly, "how can we help you?"

Kate was expressionless. "I want to talk to Copper Royal," she said.

"I'll take you down there."

"She can manage herself." Mrs Bierman was suddenly aggressive. "She can't go wrong. The Australian didn't."

"Texas," Chesler said. "He was from Fort Worth, Ma. A hunter," he told Kate. "He was after a lion."

Kate stood up. "If you'll just set me on the right road. I'll call in on the way back, Mrs Bierman, and tell you how it went." How what went? The woman had shown no curiosity. Chesler was a different kettle of fish; she felt sure he was going to try to discover why she wanted to see Copper Royal.

He followed her out to the Jeep. "Don't take no notice of Ma," he told her quietly. "She's confused. You got business with Old Copper?"

She regarded him equably. "Should that be your concern?"

"If it touches Ma, yes. Copper works for her – and I look after her." He met her eyes squarely.

"My business with Royal doesn't involve Mrs Bierman." She opened the Jeep door, got in, reached for the ignition and checked. "You haven't shown me the way."

He indicated a track running between two barns. There were horses in a corral, a pick-up, dusty like everything else. Even her pale blue Jeep was furred with dust.

He delivered a parting shot. "Old Copper can be awkward when he's drinking. If he don't show, don't hang around, and don't get down from your Jeep unless he do show. He's got a hound he's trained to go for the throat. And see you come back before nightfall – you don't want to be coming up them coulees in the dark."

"I'm armed," Kate said, and had the satisfaction of seeing surprise give way to suspicion. She wondered if it was this one who was dangerous, not Old Copper.

The track was fenced with wire strung between posts that were merely tree branches. On the other side black steers with white faces stood around in the sage. Kate glanced in the mirror. Chesler hadn't insisted he accompany her but would he follow? Not now. He'd have second thoughts after that last statement. I should be armed, she thought, if only for the snakes and coyotes, not to mention the lions. She giggled, then she sobered. A killer dog. Now there was something. She started to look for sticks, for old fence posts, anything that could be used as a weapon against an animal trained to go for the throat. There was the tyre iron – that would do.

The fences stopped and now the land on either side looked as if it had been cultivated: weeds interspersed with straggles of barley. Surely Wayne Chesler could do better for himself than wait to take over this ranch, by fair means or foul? He had the looks to attract a prosperous ranch widow . . . Poor Mrs Bierman, didn't she have – Christ! She slammed her foot on the brake.

The ground had opened like an earthquake fissure. Below, pale brown walls, crumbly but vertical, plunged for hundreds of feet, the bottom out of sight. It was a titanic chasm; a few hundred yards ahead it turned at an angle, the lips of the gorge gaping like an old wound, turned again – and beyond the mouth of that last stretch was an opaque mass the colour of milk chocolate: the Missouri River.

She opened the door carefully even though it was on the side away from the abyss. She moved round the front of the Jeep and studied the terrain. The cliffs looked as if they had been formed from petrified dust. Angular chunks lay in the bed of a dry watercourse that must be seven, perhaps eight hundred feet below. No wonder she'd been warned to be out of here before dark. So this was a coulee: impressive scenery but she had no intention of going any closer. It was unlikely that anyone ever went there, in the bottom. There was nothing to eat so cattle would stay on the grassy shelves now visible along the river bank. These were broad, perhaps half a mile of level ground before it started to rise towards the cliffs. A fringe of trees lined the river, in places broadening to woodland. The light was flat, without shadows; the sun had gone behind clouds but it was still warm, even humid. Away to the north a long hill rose to a flattened cone and on its left a shower hung like grey lace.

The track, which had been level for miles, started to dip. The ground fell away on the left as well, not precipitously – although a truck would roll for hundreds of feet if it went over. She thought about four-wheel drive, but it was a Jeep, built for this kind of gradient. She changed down, blessed the smoothness of the ruts – no potholes here – and glanced ahead to see the track running straight for buildings on the edge of a wood. After the uninhabited miles and the wild coulee this looked like the essence of civilisation, but lonely, incredibly isolated now that there was no longer a ferry.

There were a number of cabins and a two-storey house. A few small barns were scattered in a random fashion and there were the inevitable corrals. A pick-up stood outside the house and two horses grazed in the sage, lifting their heads to observe the approach of the Jeep. Kate's eyes were everywhere, watching for the hound.

She came to a halt beside the pick-up, switched off the engine and waited. The dog must be chained but why didn't it bark? She looked at the house, seeing now that it was less delapidated than the cabins, none of which had windows, merely empty sockets, and all were without doors. The house, on the other hand, had a solid door, now closed, and glazed windows, at least in the upper storey; she couldn't see if the lower windows had glass in them because they were screened. The shingled roof had weathered to shades of grey, the boarded walls were a deep chestnut.

She touched the horn. Nothing happened. No dog, no sound. Yes, there was. She jerked round at the sound of soft steps but it was only the horses approaching. She relaxed and yawned. Chesler could have been kidding about the dog, but he could have been speaking the truth when he said Old Copper was awkward when drunk. What should she do now? Go in and wake him, or wait? *You don't want to be in the coulees after dark.* Well, she knew the danger now, and the Jeep's headlights were adequate, moreover there was no reason to go in the coulees. She thought about spending the night down here and approaching the old fellow in the morning when he'd be sober, or more sober than now. She looked at the wood – no; she'd like to sleep close to the Jeep. She'd drive along the shelf and spend the night a discreet distance from the house. Old Copper wouldn't know. If he hadn't heard the horn he didn't know she was outside at this moment. Sod it! Just her luck to have business with an alcoholic. She pressed the horn hard. The horses whirled and thundered away. She glared at the closed door thinking, too late, that he might come out blasting with a shotgun.

The echoes died. The horses had stopped and stood with high heads, watching her. She got down, reached under her seat and grabbed the tyre iron. She strode across to the door and hammered on it. "Mr Royal!" she shouted. "I want to speak to you."

She hefted the iron, ready for the dog, baring her teeth. There was no sound from the house. She swallowed and, very gently, she turned the handle. The door opened a crack.

"Mr Royal! Copper Royal!"

There was a scurrying in the depths and she slammed the door shut, appalled. After a moment she knew it hadn't been a dog, more like rats.

She opened the door again, the tyre iron poised. The place seemed to be waiting. The door opened on a passage that ran to the back of the house where a room was faintly lit by a window. The floor of the passage was bare boards, strewn with old hay and rat droppings. Doors were open on either side.

A glance in the room on the right revealed a pot-bellied stove and two kitchen chairs, back to back, supporting a western saddle. Ropes and harness hung on the walls where lath and plaster had fallen away to reveal the boards. The smell was overpowering: of horses and greasy leather, musty grain and something rotting, like meat. It occurred to her that the hound could have died, a thought that was strengthened in the room across the passage where floorboards had collapsed leaving a jagged hole. She went back to the Jeep for her head-torch.

The open air was sweet. She stood for a moment looking at the river. She hadn't studied it until now; all her attention had been on the house. The water was disconcertingly quiet, a few feet below the top of the bank and sliding past with a speed that was awe-inspiring. It gave the impression of tremendous depth except that here and there whole trees must be caught on submerged bars, tips of roots or broken trunks protruding. The only sound came from the mutter of water round these snags. The river was broad, and loaded with silt.

Returning, she shone her torch into the hole in the room on the left and saw rubbish just below the floorboards: empty cans, some shreds of paper.

The last room on the ground floor was the kitchen and there the stench was ghastly. Putting off the evil moment, rationalising that the most likely place for Old Copper to be was in bed, she climbed the stairs. Two treads were missing. She came out on a landing. There was no rail above the stairwell. The place was full of death traps.

There were two small rooms at the back, empty, a large one in front. Old Copper's bed was there: a single iron frame, a palliasse, a dirty sleeping bag. Clothes hung from nails, a pair of Levis and a blue shirt on a wire hanger above high boots, almost new.

She crossed to the window and stared at the river. A slippery bank, an old drunk – who couldn't swim? Was there any family to inform or was she the only person who would regret his death? He could have known the identity of the girl who had arrived in Arletta after the crash, who had come down here, to the old ferry, and spent the night. Was it possible that, in looking for Glenn Royal, she had found the Scottish maid? Found her? She could be more difficult to trace in America than in Scotland. Where had the girl slept? And what happened to her? She did leave, surely? Had Barbara lied? Miserably Kate remembered the cabins behind the house.

She went outside, glancing in the pick-up as she passed. The keys were in the ignition. Behind the seats was a gun on a rack.

She explored the cabins and the barns but found no sign of Old Copper, nor of anyone else. There was a skeleton, remotely canine but ancient and long-legged, perhaps a coyote's bones. And in the least decrepit cabin there was another iron bedstead. Glenn could have occupied this and after he died his brother removed his possessions. Could Glenn have fallen in the river too? If that was where they obtained their water . . . There were no sinks or taps in the cabins but there could be in the house. She couldn't put off entering that kitchen any longer – the source of the smell had to be traced.

In the middle of the kitchen was a table with two six-packs of Coors beer, one carton containing three unopened cans, empty ones standing about. Two chairs were pushed back from the table and there was a pressure lamp, its glass cold. Taps showed dully above a sink containing dirty dishes and an uncovered saucepan. There was an explosion of flies as Kate advanced. Something in the pan seethed with maggots.

She recoiled, tripped and fell. As she stood up, reminding herself to slow down, not to panic (it was only a piece of meat) she felt solid metal under her hand. A heavy ring was set in a trap door. A well perhaps, even a cellar.

The door was hinged. She heaved it upright and lowered it to the floor. There was enough light to see a gleam of water. She switched on her headlamp. Her first reaction was that the well had been plugged with rocks and water was shining between the stones, but then objects took shape: not stones but something human, alive, moving. A face stared at her with blind eyes. And then she saw the movement was rats.

71

Six

A weak board in the passage sank under her weight. Instinctively she stepped sideways and continued towards the open front door. She stopped before she reached it and tried to make sense of the scene beyond. The pick-up had moved.

It had been parked to the left, looking out. She had placed the Jeep directly in front of the house. The pick-up was now on the right. Vaguely she was aware of possibilities: she'd suffered a black-out or was dreaming or had gone mad. Deep in shock she moved forward and saw there was another pick-up – on the left. Reason returned, but reluctantly. Someone else was here.

She didn't recognise the second vehicle – pick-ups resembled each other, but because there had been one at the ranch and this was Bierman land the conclusion was obvious. She couldn't have contrived a better dampener for his machismo than the one she was about to produce.

He came swaggering round the corner of the house, unfazed by her appearance, his eyes intent. His lips stretched: hardly a smile, more like a rider to his thoughts. "How was it for you?" he asked softly, and then he did smile.

She felt relaxed and empty. He couldn't shock her more than she'd been shocked. She said the first thing that came into her head: "With a dead man?" She saw again the eye sockets, the stained bone. She stepped down from the door sill, meaning only to reach fresh air, but she kept lurching towards him, saw his consternation, and then he appeared to sway, and the trees with him. She felt pressure: on her elbows, her waist, her spine. The sky wheeled.

After a while she moved her head, saw the chestnut boards of the house above her and sat up slowly. Suddenly Chesler was there, his eyes wild. She was totally disorientated, and the thought of rape was automatic. He stooped to her, groping savagely, and then he was gone. He'd torn the headband of her torch out of her hair. Not raping but robbing. She giggled hysterically.

She didn't know how long she was left on her own. She glanced at her watch but a moment later she'd forgotten what it read. She had time to regain some equilibrium, to get to her feet and walk carefully to the Jeep which, being solid and familiar, seemed a kind of sanctuary. She drank some bottled water and leaned against the passenger seat watching the house. The germ of a thought sprouted, then swelled monstrously. Old Copper had been *put* in the well – because the trap door had been closed on him – by someone else. Chesler? She straightened, staggered, and pawed her way round the truck to the driver's door seeing, as she climbed behind the wheel, that Chesler's pick-up was too close, she'd have to side-swipe it as she took off. But the Jeep was solid as a buffalo; she'd make it.

The engine fired. As she crashed into second gear Chesler came leaping out of the doorway. She surged forward, twisting the wheel, and hit the corner of the pick-up, thrusting it aside. The Jeep scraped along the other truck with a screech of metal, came clear and then she hit the ruts. She grabbed the gear lever – and it turned flaccid in her hand. She floored the accelerator. The engine roared and movement slowed to the treacle progress of a nightmare. She had no power. The gear lever seemed to be disconnected.

The Jeep came to a halt. If he approached the passenger door, she'd make a run for the trees, she'd swim the river, anything. If she was the only person who knew he'd murdered Old Copper he had to kill her.

He came to the driver's door, now in no hurry. The window was open, she had one hand on the steering wheel, the other still grasping the gear lever. He raised an eyebrow. "What happened?" he asked.

"It came away in my hand."

That wasn't what he'd meant. "Did you push him in the well or shoot him first? 'Course, either way you had to push him in."

"He's been dead for days."

"But you were here before today."

She gaped at him, then closed her mouth and thought about her response, looking away, afraid he'd see what she was thinking. He was setting her up for the fall guy, saying she'd come down here before today and killed Old Copper – because the fellow had come on to her? Ridiculous of course, she could prove she hadn't reached Arletta before yesterday; he hadn't thought it through. She'd go along with him for the moment; what she wanted most of all right now was to be handed over to the police, anything to get away from him. Protests were in order but she must be circumspect, must declare her innocence without accusing him.

"How could I have been here before today?" she asked dully. "The only way in is past the ranch."

"That's where you're wrong." He looked at the cliffs downriver. "There's a way across Tiegen land." He was needling her – he knew she hadn't been here before today.

She followed his gaze and saw that the cliffs were indented by what must be the mouths of coulees like the one she'd seen this morning. Morning? It was an age ago.

Her throat was dry. She twisted in her seat, remembered that she'd told him she was armed, and froze.

"You go ahead." He was amiable. "You ain't got no gun."

He knew. He must have looked in the Jeep when he arrived, while she was in that ghastly kitchen.

"Did I faint?" Keep talking. Aim for a normal atmosphere. Lull him into a false sense of security. Where was she dredging this advice from?

"I guess. He don't look pretty. Give me some of that water."

She passed him the bottle, not daring to make eye contact. She tried to pick out a break in the cliffs where another track came down to the river. Without the Jeep she'd have to get away from him on foot. She'd never make it to either of the pick-ups before he'd be on her. She sensed that he was waiting for something: for her to take some action that would give him an excuse for violence? Panic triggered violence; she must stay calm. She could see a gun on the rack in his pick-up. There was the other one in Old Copper's truck but again she'd never reach them before he caught her. There had to be a way out of this. What were his weak points, what was he *about*? Sex. Greed. Could he be bribed?

"What happened to this gear lever?" she asked helplessly.

"The shift? It broke." The tone was careless; his thoughts were elsewhere.

"Shit! I paid two thousand for this rig."

"They shoulda paid you to take it off of their hands."

"That's what I'm thinking. I'm going to get a Suzuki."

"So why d'you buy this heap?"

"It was cheap." He still wasn't giving her his attention, not in the immediate sense. He could be considering a staged accident, like putting her in the river. She might not be able to outrun him but she might incapacitate him . . . The tyre iron was in the well in front of the passenger seat. She'd dropped it there when she came back to the truck for her torch, when she'd decided there was nothing alive in the house other than rats, so there was no further use for a weapon. There was now. She exhaled heavily.

"God, it's hot in here. I need some air." She put her hand on the door and he stepped back automatically.

She leaned against the wing and took deep breaths. "If we dropped more stones in there on top of him no one would know. We could go away and forget about it." 'We' implying they were in this together now.

His eyes bored into hers. "What was it you wanted to see him about?"

75

The truth came easily in familiar words while her mind plotted how best to reach the tyre iron. "His brother came to Scotland years ago, asking questions about his cousin who was killed in a plane crash. A Flying Fortress. I'm writing a book about the crash."

He was suddenly interested. "What was wrong with it? Sabotage?"

"It was an accident. The weird bit came afterwards; someone was at the wreck ahead of the rescuers – at least, that's the story. There were lots of rumours. Glenn Royal must have heard them, seen them reported in a newspaper, something like that, and came to Scotland to investigate."

"Glenn left here to go to Scotland? What was in it for him?"

"It is odd, isn't it?" She was chummy, ingenuous. "And when he came back, he was followed by a Scottish girl—" She trailed off, surprised at her own words. The girl *followed* Glenn?

"She came down here?" He was amused. "So what happened to her? I know them Royals – leastways, Old Copper – and his brother were the same, Ma says. That girl coulda ended in the river after they finished with her. Now why didn't Ma tell me about the girl? Maybe she thought it would give me ideas." He looked at her without expression. "Like the river were a good place to dump someone you got no more use for."

"She spent one night here and went back to Arletta and hired a car at the garage. Barbara Lomas is asking around to find out where the driver took her and she'll let me know the result this evening. I'm staying with Barbara," she added carelessly.

"I don't think so." That smile – no longer enchanting – and the knowing eyes.

"What – Oh, I see what you've got in mind!" Her eyes too wide, her grin a rictus. "Not here," she gasped. "Let's get away from this house." He frowned, suspicious of the sudden capitulation. "Beyond the horses?" she suggested, meaning it to sound light but she was desperate, too desperate. She gestured at the hard earth and shrivelled cactus. "Hold on, we'll use my sleeping bag."

Before he could move she'd rushed to the passenger door and reached behind the seat. As she pulled out the bag folds of it fell in the well. She gathered them up and her hand closed on the tyre iron. She stepped back, tried to look coy and realised he was very close. "Here!" she cried, "You carry it." And thrust the bag at him.

It was light yet cumbersome, enveloping him, but he'd seen her face harden and, like an animal, sensed danger. He raised a hand, swathed in feathers, and the iron made scarcely an impact, but in throwing up his arm he'd exposed his groin, and Kate kicked like a mule.

He screamed and sank to his knees, clutching himself. She ran straight for the trees on the bank. She was in trainers, and he was in cowboy boots. By the time he recovered she should be out of shotgun range.

There was a game trail in the trees, running more or less parallel with the river. Here he might overtake her if he took off his boots. She still had the tyre iron but it would be useless against a gun so she threw it away. After a few hundred yards she stopped and listened, hearing the soft call of a bird and the ripple of water. The river showed through the tree trunks: very fast with whirlpools quietly circling. No escape route there.

She ran on, padding through the dust, stopping when she caught the sound of an engine. He was driving along the shelf. He knew where she was, but not exactly where. If the trees ended he'd be waiting – either there or at the foot of the Tiegen track.

He didn't know she was a climber. If he was expecting her to try to escape by one of the two tracks, the way out was to climb the cliffs, however improbable, however dangerous. She had nothing to lose; what was one more murder to a killer?

There was a glint of metal through the trees. She slipped behind a trunk and crouched, peering through the undergrowth. The pick-up passed. She started to work her way towards the open ground.

The terrain was very rough: holes masked by rank grass and

stuff like cow parsley. Brambles tore at her skin. She broke clear, staggered into a glade where cattle had been – here were their droppings – and there was a sound that was totally alien yet immediately identified. She leapt sideways, crashing into a bush, and stopped, pinpointing the menace unerringly.

What she had taken for a cow pat was moving: plump coils rippling backwards, a fat, wide-cheeked head weaving and feinting, the dark tongue never still, the tail, curiously upright, a blur of rattles.

The warning stopped. She held her breath then carefully, one heel behind the other, she retreated, catching on thorns and slowly tearing herself free, heedless of the pain. As she put space between herself and the rattlesnake, she was looking for a way round it, a clear way where she could see what was on the ground. High above, away from the river, she glimpsed pale rock. She shielded her face with her hands and plunged through the undergrowth, trusting that the noise would scare the snakes.

She came to the edge of the trees and looked along the shelf. There was no sign of the pick-up. She sighed with relief and turned to the cliffs.

She was lucky; she'd emerged at a point close to the mouth of a coulee, and that looked innocuous enough – a V-shaped depression with a dip in the middle that would be a watercourse in the wet but that now offered access to the coulee proper. There had to be gullies up there leading to the plateau; whether they could be scaled was a different matter. There was an object on the skyline: a post probably, not Chesler; he couldn't have reached that point in the time.

She started to walk across the open ground. Behind her an engine came to life. Half a mile away the truck emerged from the trees and started after her. She ran like a deer but the engine note didn't change – he was taking his time, convinced that she was heading into a box from which there was no escape. She slowed and glanced back. He didn't blow his horn or shout but kept coming at little more than a walking pace. She jumped down to the sandy ribbon of the draw and slowed further to a brisk walk.

The pick-up came to the dry watercourse and stopped. Chesler got down and when she looked again he was leaning against the wing of the truck. He went to the open door and reached inside, moving with difficulty. He was still feeling the effects of that kick.

She continued up the draw. Behind her Chesler started to follow but now he was carrying a gun. Suddenly Kate remembered that this was the West, where men shot big game, not grouse. He was carrying a rifle, not a shotgun, and she was well within range – he could pick her off at his leisure. She had one slim chance – if he intended rape he wouldn't kill her till afterwards. On the other hand rape might be too painful in his condition. She had to get out of range as quickly as possible.

She was helped by the tortuous line of the coulee, zig-zagging at sharp angles, and there was block scree in the bottom which must hide her at intervals. But if she wasn't a sitting duck while she was in the bottom, she'd be fully exposed when she had to start climbing. However, she had no choice, there was no going back.

It was hot in the bottom, the rocks retaining all the heat of the day even when they were in the shade. The rift turned and she was full in the glare of the sun. Ahead the cliffs appeared, not plunging all the way but with steep slopes below them, slabby rock showing through a skin of soil. Here and there huge chunks like table tops were poised on the slant. She climbed over boulders, clumsily and too fast, barking her shins, but Chesler would be much slower in his smooth-soled boots, encumbered with the rifle, and hurting.

She came to a break in the beige rocks, an oasis of grass and little thorny trees and fresh animal droppings, like those of sheep. Small deer, she thought, seeing their prints in the dust, or antelope. They were moving ahead of her. Hope leapt as she realised they might show her the way out of this place. Now she had to look out for the animals; she didn't expect an escape route to be obvious. She glanced back. There was no sign of Chesler.

The sides of the gorge started to contract and steepen. She had been climbing the draw steadily and now there were only a hundred feet or so between her and the base of the cliffs. At close quarters these were overpowering, no less so on the sunlit side than in the gloom. Dust motes floated under shadowed overhangs as if the rock were disintegrating before her eyes. Her throat was dry and she felt light-headed in the terrible heat. The only consolation was that Chesler must be in a worse state.

The stupendous walls closed in and squeezed the slopes to nothing; only on the left was there a kind of cove containing the last of the soil, the end of vegetation. After this it was all vertical rock, apparently impossible. Where had the antelope gone?

The bay was in shadow but softly lit by sunshine reflected from the facing wall. A pale spot moved up the slope. Kate rubbed grit from her eyes and saw another: five or six of them. Now she could distinguish their forms and they were moving with purpose; she might be driving them but there was no panic, they knew where they were going – and they were heading deliberately for the cliffs.

There was a dull thud from below: a rock moving, not a shot. She looked down to see Chesler about half a mile behind. She started after the antelope. Stones fell from above, and they fell free. She glanced up and saw that where the water would drop in a long fall in the wet, flash floods had worn a kind of staircase down the cliff. Unstable rock overhung on either side but in the centre the rock was dark, suggesting it was less friable – not firm, but it might be climbed. The antelope were going up the side in bounds, sticking like limpets to unseen holds and springing to the next with the grace of cats. But they weren't cats and they weren't antelope; they had massive curled horns – wild sheep? It was immaterial, they were showing her the way. She threw one look back but she couldn't see Chesler. Out of the corner of her eye she was aware of an obstruction on the skyline. What she'd thought was a post was a man, big and solid, and he, like Chesler, was carrying a gun.

She daren't shout to him for help as it would betray her position to Chesler and it was possible that, on the shadowed side of the coulee, he hadn't yet seen her. She wondered if the man on top was watching her. He could be the neighbouring rancher, Tiegen. Another possibility occurred to her. They could be in it together – the murder of Old Copper; if so both needed to silence her.

There was nothing she could do but go on. The sheep had vanished. She hoped that meant the angle relented eventually. From a distance she had calculated that the staircase pitch was about a hundred feet high and it had looked as if above that there were the kind of earthy slopes that one might scramble up with care.

At the bottom of the cliff was a scoop which would be a pool in the rains and above this was a wall about ten feet high that she avoided by means of a diagonal ledge rising under a shaky overhang. The sheep would have negotiated the ledge with ease but she had to go on all-fours, her back cringing from the rock, terrified that the lot would come down to crush her if she so much as scraped it.

Above the wall the rock reared in steeply sloping treads and long rises, the latter scored with cracks. These she climbed by hand-jamming: placing her fist in the crack, twisting the hand and pulling up on the jam. Chesler wouldn't know about hand-jamming and would be forced out to the loose flanks, which was how the sheep had got up in careless leaps – that was where they'd knocked down the stones. But animals could move continuously, and they could leap uphill. A human being has to stop, to survey the rock and plan the next move. So Kate worked her way up the fall-line relying on expertise until she came to a bare slab that steepened to the vertical, and there were no holds at all, not even cracks for hand-jamming.

She was very close to the top of the pitch, that was obvious from the extent of the drop: nearly a hundred feet to the dry

81

scoop. On the far side of the slab, about six feet away, was a kind of miniature balcony and, in shade but outlined against sunlit rock, a tuft of hair was caught in a fissure.

Halfway across the slab there must be a pocket, an incipient wrinkle. Could she jump across, touching down for one moment on that tiny hold?

"Stop right there!" someone shouted.

Chesler wanted her alive, not smashed at the foot of the cliff. She saw him then, saw the rifle pointing straight at her. She thought of shouting that there was a witness, glanced up and saw the other man – and he, too, was bringing up his rifle. They were both going to shoot her! To hell with them, she'd die climbing.

She gauged her distance, marked the landing, and jumped. One foot came down on the wrinkle – she'd meant it to be a light step but she was compelled to spring off that foot to gain extra impetus.

The report of the rifle wasn't stunning because she was forewarned; blocking it out, concentrating fiercely on balance, she landed, both feet on the balcony, wet hands grasping gritty rock. There was no time to recover; she was up and away, scrambling over blocks, some of which rocked under her weight, finding an earthy trail, following it, easing to level ground, running – a huge boulder ahead – round it – flinging herself to the ground, panting, exhausted, skinned and bruised but unwounded.

Chesler couldn't follow and he knew he hadn't hit her. Now he'd go back to the truck and join the fellow on top – if they were acting together. Cautiously she peered round the boulder until she could see the skyline. There was no sign of the second man.

There was no more rock above, only earth slopes to the rim. She couldn't see Chesler below so he must have moved in close to the cliff after all. She scrambled diagonally up the slope in the opposite direction from where the man had been standing on top. She kept glancing at the skyline but he didn't reappear.

Once she thought she heard the sound of an engine but it was too far away to pose a threat.

She clawed her way up the last few feet to the rim and wriggled over the edge on her front. Lying there, she looked back and listened. There was no sound and nothing moved as far as she could see. Even the river, miles away, seemed to be stationary. At the mouth of the coulee a small square object would be Chesler's pick-up. She squirmed back from the edge and she didn't get to her feet until she knew there was no chance of her being seen from below. She looked around. There was no sign of the stranger. Now the priority was to reach the road, any road.

Arletta lay to the south-west. The sun, setting behind smouldering clouds, was something north of west. She started to walk, keeping the sun on her right. When it was gone she'd steer by the pole star.

The ground appeared level, both at a distance and close at hand. She hadn't been walking long when she came to a fence. She squeezed through the wire and shortly afterwards she saw the skeleton of a windmill gleam in the afterglow. She had been trying to ignore her thirst but she was aware that she was growing weak, and that if she didn't drink soon she'd become irrational. She eyed the windmill resignedly, thinking it was probably broken and with a bone-dry tank below. Then she smelled cattle and, peering through swollen eyelids, saw dark forms and heard the squelch of hooves in mud.

She staggered forward, sank in ground that was deep and wet, filling her trainers, flung herself at a low trough and collapsed to her knees, her face in water, gulping like a fish.

After a while she made her way to the tank that fed the troughs and drank cleaner water, and it was there that, without warning, she was struck from behind and thought, Christ! I've been horned by a cow! And then she thought it was a bullet, and gave up, accepting the end. A dog started to give tongue with a deep bay.

Seven

Kate turned, to be slammed back against the tank. As something slobbered over her face, she realised that the impact was soft, not the hard stab of a bullet or a horn. A dog. There were two of them: this one effusive, the other standing off and summoning help.

After a moment the sage was silhouetted against a glow, then the lights themselves appeared. They advanced, holding her like a rabbit in their beams. She stared back without expression. The dogs left her, their job done.

The truck stopped as close as the mud allowed. She moved forward.

"Hold it there," a voice said. "Turn around."

She did so, showing that she wasn't even carrying a knife.

"Where's your truck?" The voice was elderly and definitely not friendly.

"Mr Tiegen?" She tried to sound cool, aware of the figure she cut, her arms scratched and caked with blood, her shirt in rags, mud to her knees. "My Jeep's in the bottom," she called above the sound of the engine. "It broke down and I had to come out on foot. Mrs Bierman knows I'm here."

"Who was doing the shooting?"

"I – I heard a shot." She hesitated, then risked part of the truth. "There was a man on top with a rifle."

"I scared him off. Couldn't catch him though. He's after the bighorns." There was a pause. He went on, carefully not asking a question: "So you was visiting with Old Copper."

"Mrs Bierman sent me down there." She floundered out

84

of the mud and approached the driver's door. She knew he wouldn't believe her story, not the whole of it anyway; might even think she was a nutter and drive off. She'd tell just enough to persuade him to take her to Arletta.

"You're nowheres near the Bierman track," he said accusingly.

"I got lost."

"You sure did. You come up my track – because you wasn't about to take a lift with Old Copper." There was amusement in the tone. He was in no hurry, studying her in the glow from the headlights. "So you're a friend of Grace Bierman," he mused. "You'll be wanting to be taken there."

"No. I have to go straight back to Arletta. I'm staying with Barbara Lomas. She'll be worried; I promised I'd be back before dark."

"You're English."

"Scottish." She added, presenting it like a bribe: "I'll tell you why I'm here as we drive. I'm about exhausted."

"Get in."

She went to walk round to the passenger's side, staggered, put out a hand and recoiled from the hot radiator. She climbed in stiffly.

"You're in a bad way," he said. "You could stay the night at our place. Call Barbara, let her know where you are."

There was no point in argument. Action was what was needed and for that she had to be fit. Food and drink would be great, except that they'd make her sleepy, and she wasn't sure of this guy yet. He might not be Tiegen, or if he was he could be poaching himself. On his own land? Shooting out of season then.

He drove slowly, seeming to know the best line by instinct although he wasn't on a track. The hounds kept pace alongside. In the light from the dashboard she considered his profile: beaky, a strong jaw, scrawny neck, eyes shadowed by the hat brim. He shifted in his seat. "There's his tracks again," he muttered. "I'll catch him one of these nights. The dogs heard him pass. We're a mile from the road but they heard him."

"You're only a mile from the highway?"

"No. I mean the ranch road as serves Grace Bierman and us."

"So this guy had to pass Grace's place."

"Not that neither. He's driving a Cherokee, can go off-road if he doesn't want to be seen, like we're doing now: cut across the sage. And you never saw no one, nor a truck?"

"Wayne Chesler's in the bottom," she said cautiously.

"Why didn't you come out with him when your Jeep broke down?"

"What girl would get in a truck with Chesler?"

"Can't say I blame you. I thought he were up to no good. Come over to our place around noon to use the phone. Spoke to a girl. That wouldn't be you?" Just a hint of a question this time.

"Hell, no!"

"Just askin'. Because you was down there when he was, in the bottom. He told this girl to meet him, same place, same time. Said he'd got a present for her. You want to be careful of these cowboys. And Old Copper Royal: he had a reputation for the ladies when he was young. You want to watch him too."

"You shouldn't never have gone down there on your own, book or no book," Jetta Tiegen said, filling Kate's coffee mug yet again. "Them old pastures swarm with rattlesnakes."

"Two-legged 'uns as well," Tiegen put in.

Jetta snorted derision. "That Old Copper! No self-respecting woman – but you weren't to know. If Tiegen hadn't found you you'd have been out all night on your own."

"She can take care of herself." Tiegen was jocular. "Way she looked in my headlights, she were fit to throttle them hounds and then come at me."

"I didn't know who you were," Kate said, and poured the dregs of a glass of bourbon into her coffee. She felt good, relaxing in the comfortable clutter of the Tiegens' kitchen, finally convinced that neither of these people was ill-disposed towards her. On the contrary, Tiegen was now clumsily concerned, refilling her tumbler with a whisky that was as rough as himself, but welcome. His wife looked tough too, bustling about her kitchen in stained Levis and old trainers, making steak sandwiches, brewing coffee, trying to persuade her to take a shower. "Later," Kate had pleaded. "Let me drink first." Meaning coffee, but Tiegen brought out the bourbon and kept her tumbler topped up while she told the familiar story about the plane crash, and one of the victims a cousin to the Royals. They hadn't known the Royals had a relative who was killed in a plane crash and were as amazed as Barbara Lomas to hear that Glenn had visited Scotland.

They'd phoned Arletta but could get no reply from Barbara's house. She'd be in the library, they said, and that wasn't on the phone.

Now they watched her in a loaded silence. Suddenly both Tiegens spoke, stopped, glanced at each other. Tiegen said, "They give you a bad time?"

Jetta's mouth opened and closed.

"Who?" Kate asked, too innocently.

"One or other of 'em," he said. "You got your wits about you, I can see that. You're not used to these parts but even a stranger'd take one look at a trail up them cliffs, full in the sun, and prefer to accept a ride. No one'd hike out unless he had to."

Kate looked away. "He – made his intentions clear," she muttered.

"Which one? Or both? They didn't—" He stopped, glaring at her in consternation.

"Hush now," Jetta soothed. "Let her be. She's had a hard time." She sighed and tried to change the subject. "Grace Bierman should never be living in that place on her own. She oughta sell up and buy a house somewhere that she can be looked after properly – but there, she don't know her mind's going. And as for that Chesler!" The tone was fierce.

"She's old and confused," Tiegen said. "But he's not interested."

"Of course he's interested! Not in the same way as with the girls—" She stopped, embarrassed.

"He says he looks after her," Kate said.

"Never!" Jetta breathed. "He's that sure of himself? It's weird, the way he's wormed himself in there."

"Nothing weird about it." Tiegen was grim. "It's straightforward enough. There's never been any doubt in my mind he was after the ranch. But what can you do? We're neighbours, not family."

Kate pushed her plate away. "I feel a new woman after that," she announced. She drained her coffee and stood up. "You will run me back, won't you, Mr Tiegen?"

"Of course we will," Jetta said comfortably, "that is, if you're sure you won't stay. We'll both come with you." She could be thinking that something unpleasant had happened at the old ferry, and the last thing Kate would want was to be alone with another man in the night.

"*Did* he rape you?" Barbara Lomas asked.

"Can we wait for the police?" Kate leaned back on the sofa. "He – attacked me, threatened, yes, but I'm so knackered my eyes won't stay open. I can't tell it all twice."

"You need to bathe those eyes. You been out too long in the sun. You shouldn't have gone down there on your own." She wasn't much concerned, her attitude suggesting that Kate was dramatising. "You should be in bed," she went on and, resentfully: "But I guess you have to wait now; you should have told them to come out in the morning after you'd had a good night's sleep."

Barbara had people in the library when the Tiegens dropped Kate in Arletta so she'd not been present when Kate called the sheriff's office from the house. To report a murder, she'd said, and then amended it to 'a death'. A man took down her particulars and told her to stay where she was, someone would be with her shortly. He didn't seem concerned either.

When Barbara closed the library they sat in her bright living room and drank beer. Kate was still thirsty. She'd told Barbara no more than she'd told the Tiegens: that when she went down to the ferry house Chesler had been there, that her Jeep had broken down and she'd come out on foot rather than ride with him. At the close of this obviously edited account she'd asked sharply – demanded – that the curtains be drawn. Barbara did so, and it was then she'd asked if Kate had been raped.

It was dark, her neck hurt, people were talking. She tried to turn over but she couldn't. So it was one of those dreams. Now she had to will herself awake but first, what was the dream? Men's voices, deep and low: ". . . English . . . shouldn't . . . touch of the sun . . . how much has she had to drink?" And a woman, quick and angry: ". . . look at her! . . . face . . . arms covered in blood!"

Her eyes wouldn't open. She was terrified. She grimaced and forced her eyelids apart with her fingers. She was looking through slits, but at least she wasn't blind.

Two men were standing across the living room, contemplating her as if she were something in a hospital bed, but they were in immaculate khaki, not white. God, she thought, they've sent in the Army, and giggled. They responded like friendly dogs: a smile, a nod, both affable, the one blond and crew-cut, the other dark with a moustache.

Barbara appeared, holding a wet cloth. "Here, wipe your eyes – they're swollen like plums."

Kate did as she was told, glad of the chance to orientate herself. The police had probably told Barbara what she'd said on the phone. The woman looked annoyed, still convinced her guest was way over the top.

"I could do with more coffee," Kate said.

"Take your time." Crew-cut was amiable. "We'll all have coffee. No sweat."

The men sat down. Barbara busied herself with the coffee. Kate had a premonition of how this was going to go. She felt vulnerable and dispirited. She tried to rally her forces; there was a job to be done. She started with the worst item. "There's a body in a well at the old ferry," she told them, knowing she sounded defiant. The premonition wasn't far out; the men weren't surprised, merely attentive. Barbara looked resigned.

"I'm Sam," Crew-cut said. "And my partner here, he's Al. You're Kate, right? Now Kate, what does this body look like?"

"Not much. There's not much of it left. A rat crawled out of an eye socket so I didn't look closely." There was a weighty silence. "He's clothed," she added.

"How d'you know it's a man?"

"I don't." The question surprised her. "It's Old Copper Royal's place so I assumed it was him. His pick-up's outside, and I'd been looking for him. I thought I'd found him."

Al's expression changed. "His pick-up's there?"

"That's how I came to be in the house. I wouldn't have gone in otherwise. I thought he might have had an accident."

"Where is this well?" Sam asked.

"There's a trap door in the floor of the kitchen. It was closed. That's why I said on the phone it was murder. If it had been an accident he wouldn't have closed the trap door."

"Must be dark in the bottom of a well," Al said.

"It's been plugged with rocks, and I had a flashlight. He's only about six feet down – less, although I didn't measure it."

Eyes sharpened. Barbara frowned a warning: don't antagonise them.

"What did you do after you found this – body?" Sam asked pleasantly.

"I went outside and Wayne Chesler was there. He'd followed me down."

Sam looked at Barbara. "Grace Bierman's hired hand," she explained. "The old ferry is Bierman's cow camp."

90

He turned back to Kate. "And what did he have to say about the body?"

"Well, actually he asked me what happened." She started to talk fast. "Then he accused me of killing Old Copper – which I pointed out to him was impossible, the condition the body was in, so he said this wasn't my first visit to the ferry. Then he got nasty and I tried to get away in my Jeep and the gear lever came out of its socket, so I kneed him, and he chased me through the woods – no, he drove along the outside of the woods while I was on the river bank. There was a rattlesnake – am I going too fast?"

"We're with you so far," Sam said genially.

Barbara asked suddenly, "Did you get bit by the rattler?"

"No, I'm just worn out, and I'm talking fast to get it over and go to bed. I'm not delirious or anything." She gulped some coffee and continued, "When Chesler had gone past in his pick-up I made a dash for a coulee but he'd been watching for me and chased me back into the cliffs."

"Is this the White Cliffs we're looking at?" Al asked. "Them big rocks below the old Slaughter Creek ferry?"

"You know this place?" Sam asked in surprise.

"I've hunted down there. They got bighorns back in them coulees."

"They're protected!" Barbara blurted. "That's a reserve specially for bighorn sheep."

"I were hunting deer," Al said with dignity. "Go on, ma'am, you were saying as Chesler chased you back into that coulee."

"And when I was climbing out of it he took a shot at me."

Barbara gasped. "He did!" She turned to the police in horror.

"What had he got?" Al asked.

"A rifle, I suppose. He had one in his pick-up."

Sam was disapproving. "You *had* kneed him."

Kate studied him. "Are you taking any of this seriously?"

"Well now, Kate" – his eyes narrowed – "we gotta dead body

down a well, we gotta cowboy shooting at you with a rifle, and
now we got you trying to climb the White Cliffs."

"Not trying. I did climb them. I came out at the head of that
coulee. You think I'd turn back . . . with Chesler shooting at
me?" And another guy on top, she thought, but didn't say so.
It would be gilding the lily.

"I know one thing," Sam said with finality. "No way did you
climb out of no coulee on the White Cliffs."

"Any news?" Kate asked, sitting down in the breakfast nook,
catching sight of the trees behind the house and frowning. But
the window was draped with two thicknesses of net, so she
should be safe. All the same she moved back a couple of feet.

"It's too early." Barbara turned from the stove. "How do you
like your eggs?"

"How you do them for yourself. They should have gone
down there last night." The police had said they couldn't do
anything until daylight. "They don't believe a word of what I
told them," Kate said. "Do you?"

Barbara kept her back turned for a long moment then she
pushed the pan aside and faced her guest. She said defiantly,
"About Old Copper – I mean, what you thought was a body
– you said there were stones in the well, and rats. But stones
could look awful like a skull, you know? And some of these
old-timers, they're not house-proud. He coulda thrown some
rags in there, even scraps of food" – she shuddered – "so there
would be rats."

"Right, I know what I saw and you don't, so you're making
sense in your terms. But if you're right, where's Old Copper?
I looked everywhere: in all the cabins and the barns. And his
pick-up's there."

"He could have been bit by a rattler or fell in the river – or
both of those. There are so many ways you can die by accident
down there. Maybe he *is* in the well but he fell in when he was
drunk."

"And closed the trap door after himself?"

Barbara turned back to the eggs. They said nothing until she put a loaded plate on the table and sat down, pouring coffee for both of them.

"Aren't you eating?" Kate asked.

"I ate hours ago. I've been up since six. You've had a good sleep." It was nine o'clock.

"I needed it."

"How are – your bruises?"

"I'm not bruised. I was scratched by thorns in the woods."

"I thought that . . . did Chesler . . . touch you?"

"Not at all, not even to hit me. And I wasn't raped."

"Oh. Good. But did you knee him?"

Kate sighed. "Everything I told the police was true. I left out one thing. There was another guy on top, and he was bringing his rifle up at the same time that Chesler shot at me."

"Oh, come on!" Barbara's shoulders dropped. "You really believe that," she breathed as Kate regarded her woodenly. "OK, you saw Tiegen on top, with a rifle, and he was sighting along the barrel. But he was using the telescopic sight like binoculars. He wasn't firing."

Kate was astounded. "I never thought of that! But it couldn't have been Tiegen or he'd have said. It must have been the man Tiegen said he thought was poaching, the guy he was after when he found me at the windmill. You're right: the man could have been using just the telescopic sight. But then so could Chesler! No, Chesler fired at me. I heard the report. So did Tiegen."

"So that's that sorted," Barbara said cheerfully, ignoring the last part. "The guy on top was a complete stranger and he didn't mean you any harm. He'd be interestd in you of course. Anyone would be: a woman in a coulee, on foot."

"I was climbing; I was near the top of the cliff at that point."

"You may have thought you were near the top . . . You shouldn't have said anything to the cops about a coulee; it was what convinced them that you were – er – mistaken."

"How do they think I got out of the coulee?" Barbara

wouldn't meet her eye. "They talked to you after I'd gone to bed, I can see they did. What did they say?"

Barbara swallowed. "They figure you got a touch of the sun: walking out in that heat; you're not used to it, and then, well, the Tiegens said you were dehydrated. And he gave you bourbon."

"They're saying I was drunk. True – to a point – except that by the time they arrived your coffee had sobered me up. And I wasn't drunk in the afternoon down on the river."

"But the White Cliffs can't be scaled, even by technical climbers."

Kate raised an eyebrow in despair. "If by that you mean proper rock climbers, that clinches the matter. I am a climber – but it makes no difference? And Chesler chasing me, and shooting at me?"

"Ah, there they think you started with the truth – I'm sorry," she quailed at Kate's expression but recovered and came back stoutly, "they don't believe he fired at you, and I – well, I figure you made a genuine mistake. Chesler had to be sighting at you, and at the same moment you heard a sonic boom, or a rock falling, like that." Kate glared. Barbara tried to ignore it and went on, "They think Chesler made a play for you and you *did* knee him like you said, and he turned mean and drove back to the ranch, leaving you to walk out. Maybe he didn't know your Jeep wouldn't start. They'll be stopping by the Bierman place on their way this morning and if it turns out he deliberately left you down there, they'll give him a going over, depend on it."

"And they'll ask him why he fired at me?"

"They think you're getting your own back at him. I guess they'll forget you ever said that."

"Because it might annoy Chesler and he's one of them and I'm a foreigner – and a woman. An hysterical woman. I see. I'm surprised they didn't suggest I led him on. No doubt they'll get around to it in time."

"They're only doing their job, Kate. They're country boys, not all that bright."

"You can say that again. Chesler's going to twist them round his little finger, like he's done with Grace Bierman. His word against mine. The sooner I get away from here the better. What am I going to do about my Jeep?"

The police solved that problem. They must have bestirred themselves, must have gone down to the river at first light because they were back in Arletta before noon, Al driving the Jeep.

Barbara had gone over to the library leaving Kate to follow after she'd made a phone call. She felt the need to hear a familiar voice, and the most comforting would be Bill Hoggart's. She didn't intend to unburden herself but she knew that if she did he'd believe her, at least he'd believe she'd managed to climb a hundred feet of loose rock. Nor would he have been surprised if she'd found a body at the foot of the cliff . . . but a body in a well? Never mind, she wasn't going to tell him, she only wanted to talk.

It was a forlorn hope; when she'd mastered the procedure for an overseas call there was no reply from Bill's flat. Kate was depressed. She had no documents, no transport, no friends, particularly no friends – not here anyway; even Barbara seemed to be against her, along with the police and Chesler. She was a crazy lady; at the least she'd caught a touch of the sun – but then she remembered thinking, yesterday evening before she came on the windmill, that if she didn't find water soon she'd become irrational. Was it possible she had been hallucinating already, had been for hours? If so, when had it started? She *had* climbed those cliffs; no way could she have imagined the intricacies of the route: the crucial slab, the incipient hold halfway across, the bighorn sheep – for Heaven's sake, she hadn't known bighorns existed until she came on them in the coulee! And the skull: she couldn't have dreamed that up, and the rats.

It was this line of thought that was crazy; as soon as the police saw the body they'd know she'd been speaking the truth. Chesler had seen it – and virtually accused her of murder – but then Chesler . . . She sank on a sofa, deeply troubled. He'd tell the police she'd been to the ferry house before yesterday – but she had alibis, receipts that would prove she'd been in New York or Chicago when Old Copper died. But all her papers were in the Jeep – which Chesler could push over a cliff, except that it was already at the foot of the cliffs. Oh Christ, he could have set it on fire!

She started again. There were people who would confirm she couldn't have been at Slaughter Creek when Old Copper died . . . At this point the Jeep came into view, like a character making a stage entrance, framed in the window behind layers of net. She sighed with relief – here was her means of escape from whatever Chesler might have in mind for her. But what had he told the police? She crossed slowly to the door.

Al eased himself from behind the wheel. "There's nothing wrong with it then," she said absently, noting the police car pulling in off the highway.

"All it was," Al was saying, "was this pin had come loose. You were lucky it hadn't dropped in the gear box, or your rig'd have to be towed out. You better take it to the garage; if it's done it once it can do it again. Get it fixed proper. Needs tuning too. It's running rough."

"I'll do that. Thanks for bringing it out for me." She looked from him to Sam who had approached and was observing her quizzically. "You went to the ferry house?" Raising her voice, resenting their casual attitude.

"Oh yes." Sam grinned wryly. "Can't blame you for thinking like you did. That smell's worse than a convention of skunks. Dead skunks. Best thing to do now is torch the place. That meat's been there a week at least."

"So you didn't get around to the well." She felt weak; she couldn't believe this; she'd left the trap door open – but Chesler could, would have closed it. "I left it open," she said: "the trap door."

"No, Kate; you closed it. But like you said, there was rats." Sam drew a deep breath. "Appreciate you bringing it to our attention even if you had to go a roundabout way to do it.

No one'd know what happened till he was missed and God knows when that'd be, the old lady in the state she's in. Poor old bugger. He musta been blind drunk."

"I agree. He closed the trap door after himself."

"Kate!" It was Al. He'd called her 'ma'am' last night. "There's no one in the well," he said gently.

She gaped, then snapped her jaw shut. "You said he was drunk. 'Poor bugger', you said." She glowered. "So where is he?"

"As to that, he has to be way downriver by now," Sam supplied. "Caught on a snag maybe. He wouldn't stand much of a chance even if he was sober and he could swim."

"We don't know he couldn't swim," Al pointed out. "Only that he was drunk. Mrs Bierman wasn't surprised, leastways she didn't show no surprise but then she didn't know – couldn't remember when she saw him last. Months, she thought, but there you go: coulda been last week. Chesler'll be able to tell us more."

"How do you know he was drunk?" Kate asked, going along with this crazy development.

"Why, beer on the table, and he'd been working for the Biermans for over forty years; he musta known every inch of that property. How could he put his truck in the river except he was drunk?"

"His pick-up's in the river?"

"You musta been confused with Chesler's," Al told her. "And you didn't see there was another in the water, justa bit of its roof showing, and close under the bank like that. With the driver's window rolled down, so we figure he climbed out and tried to make it and fell back in. Them banks is slimy like liquid glass."

"But you didn't ask Chesler about it?" Her voice was dangerously high.

"He's not around. Gone to Great Falls, Grace says, to see a woman." Al shook his head. "That old lady shouldn't be left on her own, state she's in, no knowing what she might do. Fell off her horse last fall, she'd a died there if Old Copper hadn't come along. You talked to her, saw what she's like. She's confused in her mind, we couldn't follow everything she said. Seemed to think we was after poachers. Who's this Texan?"

"What Texan?"

He made a dismissive gesture. "Nothing. She rambles. She should be in a home, somewhere she can be supervised. We'll visit with her again and talk to Wayne Chesler, find out if she's got relatives'll take her in, look after her. And when did Chesler see Old Copper last, like that. And what he has to say about leaving you to walk out. That's not the way we treat visitors in these parts: giving 'em sunstroke and dehydration – and that place alive with snakes." He seemed more concerned about that than an old cowboy drowned in the Missouri – except that he hadn't drowned, Kate thought grimly.

"They didn't arrest you then." Barbara was amused. She was dusting shelves in the library. "I saw them arrive but I knew you were fit enough to cope with them on your own. You look lost. What happened?"

Kate sat down at a table and said dully, "The body's gone. And his pick-up – which was outside the house – is in the river."

"*What!*"

"They say he drove into the water when he was drunk, tried to climb out and got swept away and drowned."

"He was a heavy drinker."

"You think I mistook stones in the well for a body. But if his pick-up was in the water when I arrived, whose pick-up was it outside the house?"

"Someone else's. Why, Chesler's of course!"

"I left him at the ranch. He'd have had to pass me on the track."

"Look, Kate, you don't know the country; he could have worked round ahead of you, taken a cut-off. Did you stop anywhere on the way?"

Kate said deliberately: "When I came out of the ferry house, after I'd looked down the well, there were two pick-ups, one either side of my Jeep. Are you saying I can't count?"

Barbara opened her mouth and shut it again. "That truck was moved," Kate said harshly. "And the body. And Wayne Chesler's disappeared: gone to see a woman in Great Falls according to the police. Grace said so. If you ask me he's gone for good."

Barbara flicked at a stack of books with her feather duster. After a while she turned and said quietly, "Are you still insisting he shot at you, that he chased you back into that coulee?"

"He definitely fired at me."

"Do you realise what you're saying?"

"I'm suggesting that the murderer didn't expect the body to be found so soon, didn't make allowances for a nosey foreigner going down there determined to have a word with Old Copper. When I got away and he knew I'd report the body to the police, he moved it, and the truck, and rigged it to look like an accident."

"Only Chesler and Grace knew you were there – except me and I don't count. Grace is confused, she couldn't be involved. So you're saying it had to be Chesler. That's wild. Don't you see? If he had killed the old guy he'd have tried to stop you going down there."

"He wanted me to go so he could set me up as the fall guy."

"Oh, Kate! Now you're onto a different scenario. That would have to mean he knew Old Copper was dead."

"And that's just what I'm saying."

Barbara gave a tight smile. "I don't think you should be here when he comes back from Great Falls. I think you ought to push on. Not that I wouldn't enjoy having you another night," she added hastily, "but once he finds you've been talking about him like this, he's going to come gunning for you."

"That's a great comfort."

Barbara licked her lips. "Did Al fix your Jeep?" she asked

99

brightly. "Is anything missing? It's been down there all night – but then if Old Copper drowned—"

Kate shook her head, bewildered. "That's curious; Chesler didn't take anything, just my torch. I looked. My money's there in my wallet, and travellers' cheques, passport; the police even picked up my sleeping bag that was on the ground. I suppose Chesler was in too much of a hurry – to catch me—" She trailed off, frowning. "Can they tune the Jeep in Arletta? And there's something about a pin that worked loose. That's why the gear lever came unstuck. And I need to buy a new tyre iron," she added.

"The guy at the garage can fix anything. I was visiting with him yesterday – remember? The Scotch girl? You asked me could I try to find out where she went . . . forty-five years ago" – emphasising how she'd put herself out for the visitor – "I tried to tell you last night but you were too tired to take notice."

"I'm sorry. I'd forgotten all about her." Kate was astonished. "Small wonder," she added darkly, "considering. So," – trying to summon interest in this trivial matter – "what did you find out?"

"Nothing that's much use. I don't know where she went but Randy – who has the garage now – he says Billy Newman retired to Arizona when he left Arletta. He was the guy who took the girl down to Slaughter Creek and then took her some place when Glenn brought her back. Randy gave me an address for Billy but it's six years old. He coulda moved on since. Did you ask Grace about the girl?" She was rooting in her handbag.

Kate stared at her. "It never occurred to me. So long ago, and her brain going . . . It doesn't matter now; this by-passes her." She took a piece of paper from Barbara. "Kingman. Where's that?"

"Just point your rig south and drive. When you come to Mexico you've gone too far. Arizona's the state before the border."

Eight

The road was almost empty of traffic and the land was flat for as far as she could see. As the Jeep rolled on – smoothly now, the garage had tuned it beautifully – Kate had the impression that time and space were disconnected, that the truck was stationary and only the road moved – backwards.

Late in the afternoon, as she followed the flight of a pale falcon that floated away from a power pole she glimpsed a frieze on the horizon: grey, irregular and unmistakable, a mountain range.

There was a sensation of relief. She'd felt vulnerable on this enormous level expanse, had eyed every pick-up warily. The police thought she'd been hallucinating but Chesler knew she wasn't, that she could expose him. He could be ahead and waiting in ambush now, but as soon as she reached the mountains she'd be on home ground and, irrational though it might seem, she felt that there she'd have the advantage. It *was* irrational, she had to admit that; if Chesler were to lie in wait and shoot at her as she passed, it was here that she was safest, where there was no cover. Mountains are full of hiding places. On the other hand, Chesler was a poor marksman. She'd been the perfect target, immobile as she studied that slab on the coulee's headwall, and yet she hadn't heard the bullet strike rock. He'd missed by miles. Of course he could be lucky next time.

She glanced in the mirror, saw the road was empty and pulled onto the shoulder without troubling to signal. She climbed down to stretch her legs. The land was rolling in long swells

101

now so that the road, visible for great distances ahead, seemed misaligned, stretches of it out of sight in the troughs. Behind her the crest of a swell was only a mile away. Scale could be judged by the size of a vehicle that came into sight and trundled towards her.

She rooted through the clutter on the passenger seat, found the map, lifted a hand and grinned as the other driver passed (everyone waved in Montana), but this guy wasn't interested, didn't even look, at least she didn't see his face turn towards her. The truck – rather posh, like a dark Range Rover – had smoked glass in all its windows.

Studying the map she saw that she could spend the night in Bozeman: she would go to a motel and do some telephoning. She considered the conversation. "Bill, I found a body in a well and the killer chased me and tried to shoot me as I climbed out of a . . . gorge, and then he got the body out of the well and put it in the river. The dead guy's truck too. The police think I'm hallucinating." So would Bill. There was another problem. Telephone lines could get crossed so the call could be overheard, could be reported, might be traced. The police had dismissed her as an hysterical tourist – for the moment – but if Old Copper washed up with a bullet in his skull, or some other injury indicating murder, Chesler's act of putting the body in the river could be part of some diabolical plot to incriminate her. I'm going to keep quiet about this, Kate thought; no point in telling him anyway, except for sympathy, and he's not going to give me that because he won't believe me. Men are all the same. It was a wild story. Even Madeleine Bell would find it incredible. She thought of Madeleine's cool friendly voice; she'd call her, see if she'd discovered the name of Lady Lawrie's maid. She'd be fascinated to learn of a Scottish girl turning up in Arletta not long after the plane crash, and pregnant at that . . .

She drove on, following the line of the Musselshell River, delighted to see its banks were lined with trees. She was sick of treeless country. She slowed down when a track left the highway, thinking it would be fun to follow those ruts, camp down there on the river bank – a safe bank this time – to sit by a fire in the sunset and watch for wild animals. A windshield flashed in the sun. Someone else had had the same idea. She pressed the accelerator and continued. Behind her a dust cloud rose and lengthened along the track from the river.

"*Kate!*" Madeleine Bell shrilled. "Kate, where are you?" Her voice, much too loud, could have come from the next room.

Kate was amused. "I'm in Bozeman, in Montana."

"You've led us a hell of a dance!"

"What's all the excitement about?"

"Kate," came the voice, low and urgent now, "don't you know what happened? At Cullen?"

Cross-legged on her bed, in a warm, dimly lit room, she was suddenly cold. "What happened?"

"Your friend. Bill Hoggart. You haven't heard?"

That tone, associated with a climber, could mean only one thing. "He had an accident," she said flatly.

"Oh my dear, I'm so sorry. But at least you're safe. At first we thought it was you."

There was no sense in this. "You might tell me what happened," Kate said miserably, dreading it, knowing she'd *see* him, sprawled like a dummy below the cliffs of Am Bodach.

"He fell in the burn," Madeleine said. "We had a bad storm after you left. He must have gone for water and the bank gave way. We—"

"No." Kate was definite. "Not Bill. He's somewhere else – like me. You thought it was me. I'm alive. So's Bill. He's gone home, I'll give you his number—"

"Kate! Listen, my dear. His body's been found . . . on the shore; the river carried him down. He'd been drinking, you see; he was in a bar in Strathmor with a woman. At first they thought you'd both been k— that is, had an accident climbing. Alec Dunbar had been down to your camp, found the van and with the motor bike inside: your van, Bill's bike (they assumed it was his) so you were both on the hill – they thought. They didn't know where to search so they were at sixes and sevens until one of the crofters spotted the body. Then they looked for you in the river but Alec realised there was something missing from your van, your rucksack for one. He phoned your publisher and that's when they discovered you were in the States. You never had been missing."

"It was me with him in Strathmor," Kate said absently, disregarding most of this, trying to remember how much, or how little they'd drunk that evening. "He didn't drink much," she said aloud, "or I wouldn't have let him drive. I lent him the van. I hitched home and went straight to London, then on to the States. Of course I thought he'd tell people . . . Where's he buried?"

"In Strathmor. Your van's there too, with the police. I'll tell them you'll collect it when you return. When might that be?"

"How do I know?" The shock had hit her and she was surly. "I'm on my way south now. I could come back—" Her voice died.

"No point, my dear. Stay there and get on with the job. Aunt Anne remembered the name of the maid. That woman has the memory of an elephant. It was Tina Cameron. Did you find Glenn Royal?"

"He's dead." After a pause Kate went on in a monotone, "A Scottish girl turned up at Arletta – at Glenn Royal's place – after the plane crash. No one can remember her name. She was pregnant."

"Ah. That would explain her reaction when we took her up to the crash site. She did know one of the victims."

"You reckon it's the same girl."

"Funny coincidence otherwise, isn't it?"

When she replaced the receiver Kate lay back on the bed. The sense of loss was foremost as she visualised his chunky features, the hard muscular body, glowing, vital . . . the way his fingers curled over the rock as he climbed up to her, the small careful feet balanced on holds above her head . . . and nothing left of the competence, the confidence, indeed nothing left of the good body, just something dead in a box in the ground.

She tried to change gear, to come out of this, to harden. He'd been no great shakes as a lover but that wasn't important; he was her friend, her climbing partner. She was furious that he should have been so careless; she could have accepted – well, accepted better – a fall when he'd been climbing solo, trying to get good pictures for her book. She could have blamed herself then, and that would have been some kind of atonement. She could have understood his going over the edge of the road in the van; he always took that road too fast on his motor bike, and he might not have remembered how thin her tyres were. She'd not reminded him . . . but that wasn't how he was killed. He'd walked into a flooded burn in the dark – and that was totally out of character. It was crazy. He had to be drunk, must have stopped at a bar after he left her. The stupid, *stupid* git.

She sat up and glared round the room. One lamp was lit where she'd tried to produce an illusion of cosiness in which to enjoy her phone call home. She needed a drink. She got off the bed and went out to find a liquor store.

She didn't take the Jeep. On the return, walking aimlessly, she surfaced to find herself on a street parallel with the main drag and, seeing the huge sign of her motel at the end of an alley, she tried to cut through, only to come up against a chain-link fence. She prospected over waste ground, found another space in use as a car park and started down the side of the neighbouring motel. As she did so, one of the cars pulled out of the line ahead of her and moved towards the highway: a big dark vehicle the size of a Range Rover with smoked windows.

Back in her room, the phone mute beside the bed, it all came back to her, or was there waiting. Madeleine: "You haven't heard?" She splashed bourbon into her plastic tooth mug and switched on the television.

A bright light, a loud voice but a sensation of distance . . .

"Cherokee," the voice said. "Drive it and see. Call in at your local dealer and test-drive the *big* Jeep. Cherokee: *the* native-American!"

She stared at the navy-blue vehicle on the screen. A Cherokee. Tiegen had said that the man – the poacher – he was looking for was driving one. And it had surely been a Cherokee that had passed her on the road, the one with smoked windows and the driver who didn't wave. And a Cherokee had pulled out ahead of her as she came through the car park of the neighbouring motel.

I'm paranoid, she thought; it's no more than coincidence: popular car, popular colour. But she couldn't rest. It was turned midnight; she'd been asleep for quite a while. She switched off the television set and pulled the curtains aside; it was only a step to the other car park.

She closed her door quietly, went along the cement balcony and down the steps, along the side of her motel and across the forecourt of its neighbour. A light burned in the empty office, traffic was passing on the main road. She realised that if this Cherokee had smoked windows she'd see nothing of its interior without a torch. A rifle would surely indicate that the driver was up to no good – but then he wouldn't leave it exposed to view.

She walked down the line of cars, all neatly parked, facing out, about twenty of them. There were long American saloons, a couple of Golfs, a pick-up (with Utah plates), another with Wyoming plates and a fibre-glass shell on the back, a Renegade Jeep, a white Bronco, a Mini Cooper in racing green and immaculate condition. There were no gaps and no Cherokee. As she thought: she was paranoid. The car she'd seen pulling out was probably a Japanese model anyway. She went back to her room, locked the door and undressed.

Lying awake she reasoned that she was no threat to the driver of the Cherokee even if he was the poacher. If he'd watched her on the White Cliffs it was through a scope so he knew she had no binoculars, knew there was no way she could identify him. She was haunted by shadows. And as she disposed of that shadow, another advanced. She couldn't face it, wouldn't, and she reached for the bourbon bottle, anything to drown the guilt. She should have brought Bill with her.

The Jeep was running through acres of golden sunflowers. Huge butterflies, swallow-tailed, black and white, sailed across the road. Resolutely she was trying to erase Bill's image with brilliant colours, with all the differences of the West. The sun was already high and she drove in shades. There was very little traffic – and never a sign of a Cherokee.

She entered a canyon and was immediately struck by familiarity: a clear, clean river in the bottom, steep craggy rock, and trees; it was a world away from the Missouri with its cliffs of petrified dust. She had found an alpine land on another continent. Never mind that there were no glaciers, the smell was the same: scent of resin spiked with flowers.

A bluebird caught the light against a shadowed pine, brighter than a gentian. This was better than the Alps – except for the climbing, but she wasn't here to climb, she was researching a book. Kingman, she thought: two more states to cross, perhaps a thousand miles of driving, but she didn't mind taking two days to drift through this gorgeous country. In fact, catching a glimpse of a dirt road heading up a timbered side canyon, she wouldn't mind stopping . . . She would have done had Bill been with her. She winced and stamped the accelerator. Block it out, concentrate on the book, enjoy the Rockies; you may never come this way again.

"What's that peak called?"

"Lone Mountain, ma'am. That's where the weirdos hang out. You didn't know? Where the mountain men took that jogger and held her in the back country until they was shot. A posse went after them and gunned them down like they was coyotes."

"The girl was shot?"

"No, she's still alive, far as I know." The garage man replaced the petrol cap and nodded sternly at Kate. "You drive with your doors locked. Woman on her own: asking for trouble."

Kate glanced round the forecourt, her eyes lingering on the few vehicles. "Perhaps I should buy a gun."

"You mean you don't carry one?" He was astonished.

The Alps were never like this, she thought, easing back to the highway, and then she remembered the accidents she'd investigated, and the occasional reaction of the police: did he fall or was he pushed? There was crime everywhere; the difference was that in the States people took it for granted, along with their defences against it. It was *normal* for women travelling alone to carry a gun?

The air was perceptibly cooler now although the sun shone brilliantly and the few clouds were merely fine floss about the big peaks. The road climbed to a plateau to run level through endless stands of tall pines. Nothing else was visible, only tree trunks and a gash of sky. She passed through West Yellowstone and started to climb Targhee Pass, her eyes widening as she saw a dark truck on the gradient ahead. She put her foot down and as the gap decreased identified it as a Cherokee.

Yesterday she would have been more prudent but yesterday she didn't know that Bill was dead. Anger came flooding back and was diverted; she would overtake and have a good look at the driver.

She started to pull out, saw that the side glass of the truck was smoked but that the driver's window was open. She saw a hand, a shirtsleeve – and suddenly the Cherokee was drawing away. She pressed the accelerator to the floor, clenching her teeth, willing the Jeep to keep up, but the Cherokee surged ahead like a sports car and, seeing something even faster looming in her mirror, she was forced to drop back, fuming.

She plodded up the pass suffering from reaction. He was a total stranger, a man who wasn't going to have a woman pass him in a little Jeep. Belatedly she realised that she hadn't noticed his registration number, only that he had Montana plates: red on white.

She crossed into Idaho, passed signs indicating new housing developments in the trees, and came down to the valley of the Snake River and an interstate. Evening found her in Utah, weary from driving the long straight roads. She spent the night in a shabby motel where the desert started outside the window of her room and a distant mountain range stood up like cardboard against an afterglow of kingfisher and jade.

Next morning it was back to the interstate, boring south for hundreds of miles: down the length of Utah, across a corner of Arizona into Nevada, turning left at Las Vegas and across the Colorado by way of the Hoover Dam, and back into Arizona. She came to Kingman and the heat was devastating. The address she had for Billy Newman turned out to be a trailer court on the edge of town, and he was no longer there.

He had moved south over a year ago, according to the polite German woman who managed the court and who gave Kate iced tea in her trailer. Billy liked the desert and didn't care for people; he was now camping at a place called Apache Creek. She couldn't miss it: south of Wickieup on the road to Phoenix.

Kate was depressed and curiously debilitated, not realising that she was suffering from the heat, and not drinking enough. She had left the flat deserts behind but not the high temperatures, and the dry air seemed to act like blotting paper, sucking up her body fluids.

She was mildly diverted by the vegetation. In Utah it had been nondescript scrub in a waste of sand. Here the ground was a maze of ravines and ridges covered with brush that was a foil for prickly pear and barrel cactus and weird chollas, while above the riot the majestic saguaro raised stumpy arms to the sun-bleached sky.

Apache Creek was a shallow stream with a gravel bottom. The campground was a scatter of recreational vehicles that appeared abandoned. When she switched off the engine the only sound was the call of a quail.

A man approached. He was in his forties; wire-rimmed spectacles, a trimmed beard, a bristling German Shepherd on a leash. Billy Newman, he said, was expecting her.

She gaped at him. He pointed upstream. "Go past the Winnebago with the TV mast and you'll see the trail between them tamarisks. You'll come to Billy's camp in less'n a mile. Don't take no side trails, just keep in his tracks. Put your rig in four-wheel drive before you start."

She got down and locked the hubs. "He's expecting me?" she repeated, her hand on the door.

He smiled slyly. How much did he know? How much did Billy know? Expecting her? Barbara Lomas thought Billy was still at Kingman – or was that a ploy? Had she known Billy had moved on, had she phoned here . . . Kate's eyes searched for telephone lines – and found them.

"Don't worry," the man said. "He's on your side."

She climbed behind the wheel. Would the police be waiting at Billy's camp? Should she turn and run now, when there was no one to stop her, only this guy with the Shepherd – and that couldn't reach her inside the Jeep . . .

"You drive up and visit with him," the man said. "You've come this far. You're looking for someone; Billy may be able to help you there."

He knew more than she did. Something exciting was waiting for her upstream. And possibly dangerous. Adrenalin surged; she had to know what Billy knew. She put the Jeep in gear and moved towards the tamarisks.

"'Course I were expecting you. It were on the TV, and I called Barbara Lomas. You been on the road for two, three days, you wouldn't know."

"Wouldn't know what?"

"You sit yourself down and I'll fetch us a beer. You look like you could use one. Folk not familiar with this country, they never drink enough. You get dehydrated."

Billy Newman was lean and spry, well into his seventies,

Kate calculated, neat in bib-and-brace overalls and a rusty black Stetson. He lived in a grove of cottonwoods; a small caravan and a battered pick-up stood in the shade.

"You haven't got TV," she observed, when he emerged from the caravan with cans of Budweiser.

"I was watching with Varick: him as sent you here."

She popped her can and drank deep, taking her time, preparing herself for new shocks. "What happened at Arletta?"

He settled himself on a log beside her. "River-runners found Old Copper washed up on a sandbar, what were left of him." He cocked an eye at her. "He were dead long before you come to Arletta – well, maybe not long, but several days. You met Ed Tiegen. He found Wayne Chesler in the bottom of a coulee – shot in the neck. Could have laid there for weeks without anyone knowing but Tiegen were looking for poachers, saw his pick-up in the bottom and went down to see what he was up to."

Kate was dumbfounded. "*Chesler* was shot? In the coulee?"

"Gang killing." Billy was prompt. "Poachers after bighorn. The cops are looking for a guy in a dark Cherokee. He was around when Chesler was down there to Slaughter Creek. When you was there." He returned her gaze calmly. "You was lucky not to get shot yourself. But you don't have nothing to worry about now; the cops know you was just an innocent passer-by." Having disposed of what he evidently considered trivial matters he changed tack. "Barbara says you're writing a book."

She was bewildered. Chesler shot? So who put Old Copper's body in the river and—

"And you want to know what happened to Miss Tina all that time ago."

"Tina?" Her voice rose. "Tina Cameron? It *was* her?"

"That's who you're looking for, isn't it?" He was impatient. "I drove her to Great Falls. She was looking for work and I told her as how she'd never survive a winter in the North; she should go to Texas or Arizona, I said, find a job waiting on tables, like that; in a diner, maybe a restaurant." He nodded at her. "She were a great looker, get a job any place."

"Did she tell you why she went to Glenn Royal?" Kate's voice was weak.

"Why should she? Not my business."

"Did you keep in touch?"

"No! No reason to." He was belligerent. After a moment he went on in a conciliatory tone, "My sister did maybe; she don't tell me everything." He stroked his chin and darted a glance at her. "I might be able to tell you more later."

She waited for him to elaborate and when he didn't she said, "This baby, I don't suppose Tina gave you a hint as to who the father was? I believe he died in the plane crash: the Flying Fortress. Barbara told you that's what my book's about?"

"Well now, I can fill in a few gaps for you there." Billy preened himself. "Tina were going to marry Chuck Sullivan and, you're right, he was killed in that crash. Chuck were a local boy but an orphan. Tina come to Arletta to find the folk that raised him but there was none of 'em left. She knew Glenn Royal were close to Chuck – not related – not his cousin like you told Barbara."

Wheels started to mesh: Tina, Glenn, Old Copper. "Why exactly did she come to Glenn?"

"You asked that before and I said: he was Chuck's buddy." He regarded her doubtfully. "You figure that wasn't enough to bring her to Arletta. You could be right, but that's what she told me, and I don't know no different. I just took her to Great Falls and put her on the bus on her ways south."

"Glenn never said anything to you about her?"

He shook his head. "None o' my business."

She felt he was about to clam up. "Did you know Glenn came to Scotland?"

He laughed. "You're misinformed there, ma'am. Glenn never left these United States in all his life."

"Never left Arletta?"

"I didn't say that. He worked on other ranches in the winter.

Montana cowboys come south when they're laid off, work on
ranches in Texas, Arizona, like that. Are you trying to tell me
he went to Scotland one time when he left Arletta?"

"It was just a thought. I wonder, could Tina have come here
to marry Glenn Royal?"

He was astonished. "You mean, so Chuck's baby would have
a daddy? If she did, she soon changed her mind. So would you if
you had to live way down to Slaughter Creek with Old Copper
as a brother-in-law! But she never needed a man to look after
her. She had a fine baby—" He stopped.

"So you did keep in touch."

"My sister told me. I keep in touch with my sister! She
was the midwife. That's why Tina went to Phoenix, be near
a friendly face when her time come. I sent her there." He was
proud of it. Tina had made quite an impression on him.

"You took her down to the ferry," Kate said slowly. "Did
you warn her about Old Copper?"

He looked uncomfortable. "Barbara gossips. Tina wouldn't
have come to no harm; she were Chuck's girl and Glenn'd
respect that. As for his brother, she were safe as long as Glenn
were by. Nothing happened down there; she'd have told me
if it had."

"A lot has happened there: to Old Copper, and Chesler.
Glenn died down there, presumably."

"He died natural. And Old Copper drove into the river,
drunk."

Kate said thoughtfully, "One woman goes there . . . looking
for information? Nothing happens." She paused. Billy's eyes
narrowed. "Forty-five years later," she went on, "another
woman goes down to the ferry, making inquiries about the
first. One man has just – died, another is shot – while she's
there." She stared at Billy. "They *are* poachers, aren't they?"

"Were. Them's dead."

"Not the one on top, the one Tiegen saw – and me: the guy
in the Cherokee."

He grinned. He was enjoying this. "I'll tell you where you

can buy a gun in Phoenix. Don't look like that! I was joking."
He stood up. "I'll come back with you, see if someone has
come up with more information." With that he stumped across
to his pick-up before she could press him to explain that last
remark.

'Someone' was Varick. He was standing in their path as the
trucks emerged from the tamarisks. Kate watched him at the
window of the pick-up, talking urgently. Billy got down and
came back to the Jeep. "Here's how you find Tina," he said.
"D'you have some paper?"

She passed him her notebook, her brain reeling. "I should
phone her first," she said. "It's only polite."

"I'll tell her you're on your way."

She was sure he would. Those telephone lines would be
humming before she was back on the highway.

"Shouldn't you give me her number in case I get lost – out
there in the desert?"

On a blank page he was shading in mountains, marking a
pass, muttering about a dirt road to the Bullion Valley under
the Skeleton Range: "You can't get lost. At Lobo stop and ask.
Anyone'll tell you."

She frowned, remembered her manners and thanked him,
nodding to Varick, including him. It was obvious that the camp
manager was party to the arrangements, relaying messages,
receiving them. If she were to ask whom they were in touch
with – Billy's sister or Tina direct, or Tina by way of the sister
– she'd get no satisfaction. A response perhaps but no answer.
It wasn't important anyway. As she drove back to the highway
Tina's importance receded before the startling revelation that
no one had shot at her on the White Cliffs of the Missouri. The
man on top had fired at – and killed – Chesler. And she'd seen
him do it. But if she represented a danger he'd have shot her
immediately afterwards; he'd had the opportunity. The reason
he didn't had to be because he knew she'd been too far away
to identify him.

Poachers, a poaching gang, thieves falling out over division of the spoils – or something. Perhaps the third man killed Old Copper too; it must have been he who went down to the ferry and put the body and the pick-up in the river. She thanked God Tiegen had seen that man, or rather his Cherokee, had known he'd been around for some days; that sighting left her in the clear. No question now that the police might think she was involved – perhaps as a member of the gang. On the other hand the authorities might well want to speak to her as a witness to the shot that killed Chesler but – she laughed aloud and stamped on the accelerator – everyone was convinced she'd regained the plateau by walking up a track, Bierman's or Tiegen's. No one could credit her with having climbed out of that coulee – no one except the gunman, and he wasn't going to come forward.

"Phoenix?" Madeleine was delighted. "Arizona? Have you found her?"

"She's about two hundred miles away, which is close in this country." Kate settled herself against the pillows on her motel bed and grinned at the familiar accent. "Tina had the baby and Billy Newman's sister was the midwife. They've kept in touch. Billy's the guy who drove her from Arletta to catch the bus south."

"Tina's still in Arizona?"

"At a place called Lobo. You reach it by turning right at Tucson. Can you believe it: all these outlandish places – and saguaro with everything. Like chips."

"Sa—oh, those huge cacti. Good. I'm relieved—" She checked and Kate swallowed unhappily, knowing Madeleine was relieved that the new country was proving a distraction. From Scotland the voice rushed on: "I telephoned everyone: Alec Dunbar, the police, Maisie, and told them your news. Aunt Anne will be tickled pink that you've found Tina. Give the child my best regards."

"Madeleine! She must be in her sixties."

"What was the baby? Boy or girl?"

"I've no idea. I've been thinking: when they were convinced

both Bill and I had had an accident why didn't they call my publisher straight away to find out where I was?"

There was a pause. "No one considered it," came Madeleine's voice, puzzled. "I mean, the problem was here – or rather, there – in Armidil, Cullen: it was immediate, you know? Naturally everyone was thinking it was your van so you were missing. It would never occur to anyone to phone London to find out where you were. They assumed – correctly – that Bill was in the area because his bike was in the van, but no one knew you'd lent it to him and that you had gone away." Silence. "Kate? Are you still there?"

"Yes, I'm here." She sat up. Something had flitted through her mind there and was gone.

Nine

S he slept late and it was eleven before she got away next morning. There was only one more stretch of interstate and then she would turn west: an exhilarating prospect because there didn't seem to be much in that direction other than desert and mountains.

She bought a shovel in Tucson, a torch, a tyre iron and a three-gallon container which the store owner, hearing she was going to Lobo, insisted she fill with water right there from his tap. It was a sensible precaution; she was drinking more now and feeling much better for it. She bought a straw hat too and, driving into the sun, the brim pulled low, wearing dark shades, a bottle of water to hand, she felt that she was coming to terms with this country, to some extent acclimatising to the heat.

She would never get used to the empty roads however, far emptier than in the Highlands. There were stretches where nothing was visible ahead nor in her rear-view mirror, and when a vehicle did appear it was like a mirage, with space between its wheels and the shimmering tar, a car trembling in air. She encountered the odd motor but nothing overtook her. Once or twice she glimpsed something pale behind her but following vehicles must have turned off on one of the mysterious tracks that occurred at long intervals.

For over fifty miles she had the road almost to herself until . . . there it was again, like a mote in the mirror, except that this was white. She was driving slowly, revelling in the backdrop of mountains, but the following car made no attempt to overtake. Enjoying the scenery like herself, she assumed. White trucks

117

were nothing to be concerned about; she would have been wary had it been a dark Cherokee, but that was history. Arletta was a thousand miles away.

The Jeep crested a rise and the road dipped, aiming for a dark smudge of woodland. The sun, westering now, held a golden tinge, and the shadows of the saguaro stretched long arms towards her. As she advanced she saw a cluster of adobe houses that looked as though they had crept in to the trees for sanctuary. There were no people in evidence.

There was an old store with a false front and boarded windows. A thin cow nosed in a trash can. A few pick-ups stood about but the houses could have been unoccupied with their blind windows and screened doors. The tarmac was drifted with sand as if the desert were moving in to take possession.

She had slowed to a crawl, alert for some sign of life, but the only movements came from the cow, the dust settling and the white car which appeared on the horizon behind her.

There was a kind of intersection: three dirt tracks taking off from the vicinity of the store, heading south and west, and a third that was no more than access to a builder's yard. The tarmac stopped at the intersection – Lobo was the end of the road.

Leftwards, on the southern route, she glimpsed washing on a line. Ask at Lobo, Billy Newman had said, his sketch, like the road, going no further. She guessed he had never been here. She drove down the road and stopped outside a shabby adobe, noting that the washing included a wide pair of Levis and several outsize T-shirts. A shadow moved behind unscreened glass.

While she waited for someone to appear – not getting down until she knew what kind of dog they kept, if any – the white truck passed the intersection heading west.

The screen door opened and a large fat man stood there, beaming at her. "Well," she exclaimed, much relieved, getting down and walking over. "It's good to find someone alive. I thought Lobo must be a ghost town."

He looked past her at the Jeep. "You alone?" he breathed, seemingly amazed.

She supposed lone women must be something of a novelty in Lobo but not to that extent, surely? There must be women engaged on field-work in the desert: botanists, geologists and so on.

"Quite alone." She was dismissive. "I'm looking for Tina Cameron's house."

"Oh, Tina. You want Tina. You're Scotch too?"

He had to ask? She considered the smooth fleshy face, seeing now that he was an overgrown boy, and pretty thick at that. "That's right," she said brightly, adopting the tone one uses to young children. "Which is her house?"

He hesitated, not meeting her eyes, seeming to consult the mountains. The sun had reached the horizon and was slipping like an orange balloon below a pinnacled ridge. He shook his head with finality. "Goin' dark. Best stay here the night." He edged back a fraction, indicating she should enter the house. His manner wasn't in the least threatening.

"Are you alone?" Kate asked, puzzled rather than wary.

"There's my mom." An ingenuous smile. "You're quite safe with me."

"Is your mom indoors now?"

"She's asleep. We'll have to be quiet. She don't like being woke."

"I'm sure she doesn't. What's your name?"

"Ozzie. Mom's Ruthie."

"And I'm looking for Tina. Where's her house, Ozzie?"

He pointed half-left at the mountains. "Down the valley a ways." He pondered. "You'll see her light after you've gone ten miles. You sure you won't come in, have a beer? Tina could be in town. And there's dogs." He held her eye. "Lions is out too, now the sun's gone."

He might not be persuasive but he was certainly inventive. "Another time," she said, smiling. "Tina's expecting me. Ten miles, you said."

119

He stepped down from the doorway, an ungainly youth with anxious eyes, probably no more than sixteen, but for all that she wouldn't care to be alone with him. She knew where she was with the Wayne Cheslers of her world, but not simple souls like Ozzie. He was like one of those powerful dogs that turn and savage children for no reason at all. He wasn't going to let her go easily either, persisting to the last moment, a big hand on her door even when she'd switched on the ignition, as if he'd hold the Jeep by force.

"You're a stranger in these parts," he said urgently. "There are bad people about." The doggy eyes were fearful as he glanced down the valley. "They shoot first, ask questions afterwards."

"I'm all right, Ozzie. You know where I am."

"Yeah, but—" His eyes shifted. Headlights showed back at the intersection, and approached slowly. "Now who's this?" He was suddenly authoritative. He dropped his hand, scowling fiercely. Kate put the Jeep in gear. "You remember now," he said absently. "Take care." But his mind wasn't on her.

She drove until the undulating ground concealed her lights from the hamlet, then she stopped and studied the map. She wished she'd listened more carefully to Billy's instructions. She remembered his mentioning the Skeleton Range; that must be the mountains immediately on her right, running parallel with the road, which was, in fact, no more than a dirt trail. He'd also said something about the Bullion Valley which must be where she was now, although it wasn't named on the official map. Some way down the valley the map marked a route taking off at right angles, crossing the Skeletons, otherwise there was nothing until a place called Montezuma Springs on the Mexican border, and that must be twenty miles ahead. When Ozzie referred to bad people he could have meant Mexicans, smugglers possibly, or people crossing the border illegally, looking for work. They couldn't represent a danger to herself. Tina lived here, and she must be on the road at night, at least

120

occasionally. Ozzie was trying to frighten her – or keep her in Lobo.

She drove on, her headlights momentarily illuminating banks, even quite high slopes, stony but vegetated, the discs of a huge prickly pear pale in the light, and saguaro like ribbed tree trunks. Occasionally she crossed a dry wash and was surprised to see tracks veering left and right, surprised and a little disturbed. She came to a fork and took the right-hand track, wanting to keep close to the mountains. There were no signposts, of course, as this wasn't tourist country; the only people who came here knew where they were going: to Montezuma Springs – or Mexico – or into the desert hunting. What did they hunt in the desert?

Another fork; again she kept right, uneasily aware that the track she was following was marked by only a few vehicles, too few. Ozzie had said she'd see Tina's light after she'd driven ten miles. She'd done eight and in this empty landscape a light should be visible for well over two miles. Providing it wasn't screened by something: trees, boulders, a hill. There were no lights anywhere – yes there were, far behind. She slumped in her seat. Those would be the lights of Lobo. But, wait a minute – these were nearer than eight miles.

She switched off her own lights, rationalising that she'd been about to do that anyway, the better to try to distinguish Tina's. She killed the engine too and got down, wondering whether she should stop the driver of the following vehicle and ask for directions, thinking that might not be a good idea. It could be Ozzie.

The lights were hidden now. The last of the afterglow had faded but the stars were brilliant. As her eyes became accustomed to the darkness she saw that she was in a depression more or less surrounded by low ridges, their scale apparent from the cacti fringing their crests, alien shapes against the stars.

A slope suddenly flared into brilliance, like land before a lighthouse beam, and as quickly reverted to darkness. Now she could hear the ragged sound of an engine interspersed with

121

thuds and rattles: some old pick-up going down to Montezuma Springs, and it was on the road! She'd taken a wrong turning. Amused, she moved a few steps along a bare wash to find it suddenly opening out to the valley. She could see the tail lights of the pick-up receding. And she heard the faint purr of another engine.

Her first thought was that this sound came from Tina's house and that Tina had a generator. She scanned the dark bulk of the mountains but there was no light, only the twin red glints of the pick-up. The murmur was close, almost on her. Instinctively she dropped flat on the sand, totally disorientated, thinking UFOs, the X Files . . .

It passed within a few yards. A small truck, gleaming in the starlight, dipped to cross the wash. Brake lights flared to show the logo of a bucking pony on the spare wheel. The truck was a Bronco. Without lights. *Bad people.* And she'd thought Ozzie retarded. Thank God her Jeep had been off the road, hidden. Faced with the reality, smugglers seemed less innocuous.

The driver of the pick-up couldn't be involved in crime because he wasn't bothered about showing lights; at that she wondered if the Bronco were more concerned about being seen by the pick-up than by Tina, since he must pass Tina's house. She shrugged, it wasn't her concern; all she had to do was keep well clear of whatever peculiar business was going on.

She returned to the Jeep and to pass the time while allowing the Bronco to get well away – and, incidentally, to make sure there were no more vehicles slinking south without lights – she went back to the map, recalling that there was a road of sorts branching off to cross the Skeleton Mountains. The other drivers could be making for that.

She opened the map fully, smoothing the folds, and saw Bullion Valley marked on the *other* side of the range. Ozzie, the bastard, had misdirected her. And he could be the driver of the old pick-up, following her. And the Bronco? Two villains on separate missions? But if Ozzie were in front, he would turn back when he realised she was no longer ahead of him and then he'd meet the Bronco. Perhaps the driver would send him scuttling for home. She'd had enough of this for one evening; she'd wait until the road was clear – of everyone – drive fast back to Lobo and head west for a town called Exito and a motel. Tina and the Bullion Valley could wait until tomorrow and daylight.

If she were on higher ground she might get some idea of what was happening on the road. Shielding the torch, alert for snakes, she picked her way past thorny plants to the crest of a miniature ridge. It was only thirty feet or so above the wash but it gave her a view down the valley.

A light was stationary in the south. A quarter of an hour ago she'd have thought it was at Tina's house, now she was wiser. After a while it seemed to be moving. She looked away and back. Definitely moving, and that wasn't all. As the vehicle advanced, another went south, tail lights blooming, the glow of its head-lights obvious. It was as if they had been together, the drivers communicating.

The lights approached. She backed down the ridge and watched from behind a shrubby cactus. She heard it before it reached the wash: the old engine, implements bouncing in the back as the driver dropped down the bank. If this was Ozzie back-tracking she must give him time to reach Lobo. She wondered how he had come to be in front when the Bronco had been approaching while she was talking to him – unless the Bronco driver had stopped and talked to Ozzie after she left; now that was an unpleasant thought.

She concentrated on the immediate moment, calculating that it would take the pick-up about half an hour to reach Lobo (on these tracks progress was slow). She stood up. There was a rustle close by. She froze momentarily, then stamped. She listened for the sound of flight. There was nothing. She would definitely spend the night in a motel.

She worked her way along the ridge until she could see to the north, towards Lobo. Someone else was coming down the road. She waited, her mind a blank but prudence dictating she should once again drop below the ridge. The lights approached and the vehicle crossed the wash: ragged engine, the tools clattering in the back. The same pick-up. Ozzie coming *back*?

She watched the glow and the tail lights drawing away, saw another vehicle coming north, watched them meet, stop, their headlights dimming. After a while both sets of lights flared and drew apart. The Bronco approached and crossed the wash, creeping at ten miles an hour. They were *patrolling*. They were looking for her. Moreover, they knew by the sudden extinction of her lights that she was hiding.

It didn't have to be personal. If they were involved in drugs they'd want to know what she was about, who she was with; they'd be afraid a new gang was muscling in on their territory. Now that they'd lost sight of her they would think their suspicions confirmed. Ozzie wouldn't be a very reliable member of a criminal gang – but then his stupidity could be a subterfuge. I'm getting out of this, she thought and, descending from the ridge, passed the Jeep and prospected beyond it, into the mountains.

Almost immediately she came on a cairn in the middle of a wide channel that must be a river in the rainy season. There were tyre tracks on sandy patches. Whether or not this was the mountain track it was going in the right direction, away from the valley. She went back to the Jeep, locked the hubs in four-wheel drive and, without lights, started up the river bed.

The summit ridge was too far away to judge scale so she didn't know how high she'd have to climb. At first the going was almost level, more gravel than sand, with intrusions of bedrock. At some point she'd need lights, but not yet; she was still visible from the valley.

Small trees on the banks of the watercourse were black against the stars. Weeds brushed the sump and her eyes played tricks, seeing bottomless pits ahead. She'd stamp on the brake, get down with the torch and find the pit was nothing more than a patch of low brush.

The gravel ran out and she was on bedrock. Suddenly she came to a jarring stop and the Jeep stalled.

Her chest hurt where she'd hit the steering wheel. After a while she climbed down, wincing, praying the truck wasn't damaged, and found one wheel flush against a rock step like a high kerb. Imprints of tyres marked the correct way up a steep rise.

She looked back the way she'd come but could see nothing more than the line of the watercourse fading into the void. She decided to risk her sidelights now, and was amazed at the increased visibility. She reversed and, following the tracks, put the Jeep at the rock, and he responded like a solid little horse. It amused her to find that she was endowing a vehicle with personality, and then she wondered if the solitude were getting to her.

If this track came down to the Bullion Valley she might spend the night with Tina after all, providing there were no unforeseen obstacles. The mountain was starting to close in now to form a canyon, a crooked canyon. Its walls gleamed in the light and the route in the bottom was turning, once acutely. She was surrounded by high ground and must be out of sight of the valley at last. She continued on dipped headlights, hurrying a little, anxious to get over the top. There was water on the track, trickling down a shallow staircase. The Jeep climbed, lurching and banging but steady, branches of some tall shrub whipping the closed windows.

She came to a level stretch, saw the reassuring marks of tyres in patches of soil, wondered if she could be past the worst, hoped so – and her lights illuminated the base of a slope that looked like Everest. Tracks were apparent, climbing diagonally. She had just time to remember that you should always take a slope direct before she saw that here it was impossible and, feeling light-headed, irresponsible, she surrendered to the Jeep.

The truck followed the faint marks on a surface like chalk, canted and slipped sideways. She clung to the wheel and

accelerated, topped the rise and levelled out. The Jeep dropped
its nose and stopped. She hugged the wheel, gasping.

After a few moments she lifted her head. A scatter of little
conifers showed in the lights and the track ran on deliberately as
if it knew exactly where it was going. She had arrived in a high
basin and she resumed the slow progress, suddenly aware of
how vulnerable she was, how small: an insect crawling across a
dark blanket. The dipped headlights revealed potholes and long
drifts of sand. There were the marks of hooves in the sand.

She passed the remains of a corral: wire sagging from posts
of knobbly pinyon branches. A windmill stood above a tank,
its vanes motionless in the breathless night. Way out on the flat
coyotes called.

The level ground ended at a kind of rock portal, the trail
squeezed into a narrow space: no wheel marks now, she
noticed, only the tracks of shod horses; but there was no
mistake about it: she was starting to descend.

The surface changed to deep gravel. Still in four-wheel drive
she was dropping down a hanging valley, low banks on either
side, the trail again taking the easiest line: a dry watercourse,
but this one was quite steep and the gravel deep.

She stopped on a harder patch and switched off the lights and
engine. When she got out the ambience had changed: there was
space ahead. She had crossed the divide and below, quite close,
was the Bullion Valley; she could see the next mountain range
humped on the far side.

There was no sign of anyone following and she was so tired
the memory of danger receded before the craving for sleep. She
wasn't thinking clearly. Ozzie – if it had been Ozzie – would
have given up long ago, and as for the Bronco, probably the
driver had never been interested in her. He could have been
hunting, driving up and down that road looking for antelope
or deer or lions.

The gravel ran out in another level basin, smaller this time,
hoofprints visible again. She followed the tracks dreamily,
considered changing to two-wheel drive, decided against it,

saw smooth sand ahead and ploughed to a halt. The engine roared and died.

She engaged reverse, felt the wheels spin, tried to rock – and dug in deeper. She was stuck. She dropped her head on her arms knowing that she could do no more tonight. She couldn't be more than a mile or so from the valley; she'd spend the night here and walk out in the morning.

The sand was soft, the relief of stretching out on it was bliss. In no time she was asleep.

The sun woke her, or rather its heat; she was sweating inside the sleeping bag. It was nine o'clock. She stood up naked, rejoicing in the solitude and the primitive aspect of the place – until she looked at the Jeep, up to its hubs in sand.

She dressed, drank some water, ate some crackers, packed passport and wallet, compass and map in her small rucksack and, seeing she'd got stuck in a wash, followed it auto-matically.

The sand had been a pocket, an intrusion. Within a few yards she was on rock and heading for a lip that threatened to be the edge of an escarpment but turned out to be no more than the top of a step a few feet high, not even steep. She walked down it without using her hands.

She was on the headwall of a miniature canyon: steps descending at a gentle angle under slopes stippled with saguaro and interspersed with isolated crags. Near the foot of the rock and before it gave way to one of those long gravel stretches there was a gleam of water. Beyond the gravel was a thicket of little trees and then a big shallow canyon. At that point there were rutted circles where vehicles had turned. With luck she might meet someone before she reached the valley, someone she could persuade to winch the Jeep out of the sand.

The air was dry and warm, the heat increasing. Her throat was parched, and she'd brought no water, but she could drink down there, at the pool . . . What was she thinking about? She was within a mile of the valley.

She trotted down the rock, beautiful smooth stuff, layered, folded and convoluted under the vegetated slopes, and she came to the water below a step: a small black pool about ten feet across, set in polished pearly rock that sloped so gently one could traverse round above it on scooped slabs. The surface of the water was littered with dead moths.

She moved to descend a slab at the side, then stopped and peered at the rock. There were no handholds, no footholds either; there was nothing. But there had been no holds higher up, the rock providing sufficient friction for rubber soles. This rock was different; it looked the same but it was smoother, more like limestone. It was only a matter of a few feet to the pool, however: ten feet? Twelve? If you slipped, you'd land among the dead moths. You'd have to keep your mouth closed but the water would be pleasantly cool and wet clothes a shield against the heat. She wondered how deep it was. She looked closer.

The pool had no rim. The rock sloped to it unbroken, steepening to the vertical. The water was jet-black and looked immeasurably deep. It had to be over six feet. If you fell in there was nothing on which to get a purchase in order to haul yourself out. The pool was a death trap at the bottom of a funnel.

She turned to the slabs. There was no technical difficulty, you didn't *need* holds; a good climber could walk round the hollow, perhaps rather fast, trusting to speed for impetus . . . She looked at the water again and she was terrified. Carefully she inched backwards, putting yards between her and the top of the last step before she dared to turn and start climbing back the way she'd come.

The Jeep squatted in the sand like an abandoned animal and, thinking of animals, she remembered the decrepit corral, the shod hooves. No horse had reached the top by walking round that ghastly pool. She prospected for the correct way and found it: on stony ground where hooves had left no mark but droppings indicated horses had come this way. She followed a faint line to a trail that zig-zagged down a slope to the big canyon where the trucks had parked. She thought a truck might be able to descend to this point although the angle was too steep for ascent. She returned to the Jeep, blessing the foresight that had prompted her to buy a shovel. She started to dig.

By mid-morning the heat was appalling, and she was getting nowhere; as fast as she shovelled the sand fell back. She needed some sacks for the tyres to get a grip. She needed a winch. She straightened her back and stared hopelessly at the sunken wheels. The silence was heavy. Behind her back there was a chink of metal.

She turned slowly, unable to believe that she was no longer alone. Two ponies stood a few yards away, heads up, ears pricked, more intrigued, it would seem, than their Indian riders: dark, immobile, expressionless.

"Hi," she said, leaning on the shovel, the picture of innocence and relief. "You don't know how pleased I am to see you." Trying to sound sincere as she absorbed their appearance: the older one, sitting low in the saddle, a thin wide mouth, high cheekbones, eyes large and deep as water. He wore Levis and a blue shirt, a baseball cap. The other was young enough to be his son: slender, tense under her stare, paler than the man, his features less broad and skin like brown silk. There was a single turquoise on a thong at his throat and he wore a scarlet sweatband. Both carried guns in scabbards on their saddles.

"Are you alone?" the man asked. The same question Ozzie had asked.

"Quite alone." She was cheerful. "I took a wrong turning. How do I get out of this?" Indicating the Jeep. "I'm visiting Tina Cameron. Do you know her?"

The man's pony rested a hind leg, its rider adjusting to the list. "Tell me about Tina Cameron," he said.

She knew it was a test. "She's Scottish – like me. She emigrated forty-five years ago and I've come to see her." She didn't want to explain her mission to this man; Tina might have concealed her past from the neighbours, if these were neighbours. She suspected that Bullion Valley didn't have many inhabitants.

"Has she family?" the man asked.

She hesitated. "I haven't met her – but she's expecting me," she added quickly. "A friend of hers, Billy Newman, who lives north of Phoenix, he talked to her yesterday; she told him to send me here." She sounded as if she were justifying herself. It wasn't because he seemed to possess authority but she was intimidated by those guns. It was time she took the initiative. "You don't trust me," she said. "You can look in the Jeep. I'm not armed. What harm can I do?"

The man glanced at the boy and they slid off their mounts and advanced, the man rolling slightly, the lad lissom as a young cat. She stood aside, glancing in surprise at the untethered ponies, their reins merely dropped to the ground.

They took the mats out of the Jeep and set them under the wheels; they fastened ropes to the chassis and their saddles and, with the boy at the ponies' heads, the man heaving at the rear of the truck, Kate steering, the Jeep came out like a dream, the ponies' hind quarters skittering as the engine revved.

"You've done this before," Kate cried, laughing.

The man nodded gravely. "Give me the keys."

"Why?"

"We're armed."

She gasped, and thought she understood. They had the whip hand. And it was no good trying to make a dash for it – those little horses could travel faster than a Jeep on this kind of ground. She handed him the keys without a word. She could be taciturn too, and she had the feeling he didn't intend her any harm. It was just that he wasn't sure of her: crossing the mountains, entering their valley by the back way.

The boy coiled the lariats and looped them over the saddle horns. "I'll drive," the man said calmly, giving her no choice. She squeezed across to the passenger side.

The trail wasn't all that steep but some of the turns could be negotiated only by backing up and taking a second lock. She was askance; the fellow went far too close to the edge. Neither of them had their seat belts fastened, the better to jump clear.

The boy came behind, the second pony following without being
led. She asked the Indian his name. "Talk later," he said.

They came down to the big canyon. He got out, unlocked the
hubs, whistled, and his mount came up like a dog. He took his
rifle from the scabbard and exchanged a few words with the
boy. The youngster cantered away and the man returned. "You
drive now," he said.

She moved across. He needed a gun for defence against *her*?
"So what's your name?" she asked coldly, putting the truck in
gear. The pony fell in behind.

"Lonzo."

"How did you train your horse to follow?"

"He won't leave me." Hardly an answer.

"Is that your son?"

"Uh huh."

"And his name?"

"Tony."

"Where's he gone?"

"Home."

It was like pulling teeth. She glanced at his profile as she
drove. He had fine features and he kept himself in good shape.
He smelled of sweat and horses – but she was suddenly aware
that she hadn't showered for some time herself. She couldn't
say he was rude, in fact she felt it was her questions that were
impertinent, although he had ordered her to give up her keys,
to drive . . . "It's your territory," she said aloud. "I suppose you
look on me as a trespasser." He made no response.

They passed the mouth of the little side canyon. "How deep is
the pool" – she jerked her head – "the deep water up there?"

"It's deep. Animals fall in. A lion drowned there last
summer."

They were now on a well-used track and the sun was high.
She glanced at her watch but it wasn't there. She bit back
a curse. She had known the bracelet was weak and now
she knew exactly when she had lost it: as she was digging
out the Jeep. She said nothing; she didn't trust him, not in

131

small matters. She would come back on her own and look for the watch.

Bullion Valley was wide, rough and, so far as she could see, uninhabited. Where the track ran into a dirt road he told her to turn right – which was a relief, for that way lay Exito and civilisation. South was Mexico; at least he wasn't taking her across the border. *Taking* her? This wasn't a kidnapping; he had no reason to think she had relatives rich enough to pay a ransom. No, not kidnap; for all his reticence he had an air of intelligence.

"Turn here," he said again, startling her. She eyed him warily, and the rifle between his knees. She turned.

The ground was hilly and covered with vegetation, the track between outcrops marked by tyres and horses. "Do you treat all your visitors like this?" she asked, surprised that she wasn't afraid. She liked the guy – which was crazy; she had no idea of his intentions. There was no reason to like him, this bloody country was playing hell with her feelings: the heat, space, being alone.

Structures appeared, hardly buildings: old trailers, mobile homes raised on cinder blocks, sheds walled and patched with wood in different peeling colours, their windows unglazed. There were corrals, a few thin hens, a mule in the shade of a cottonwood. A woman, slim, straight-backed, black hair to her waist, was walking away from them. She glanced back, and passed behind a shed. A second woman, very old, appeared at the door of one of the trailers and came down the steps, supported by the kind of aluminium stick supplied by hospitals. She wore a long dark skirt and a crimson blouse with sleeves to her wrists. Thick creamy hair was strained back from broad cheeks and steel-rimmed spectacles. She was smiling and nodding. "Hi!" she called. "Hi, miss!"

"Your mother?" Kate asked pleasantly.

"Uh huh. Wait, will you?"

A good sign: he was asking, not telling, but he leaned over, switched off the engine and pocketed the keys. He left the Jeep then and, turning to his mother, moved away. He seemed to be less sure of himself suddenly.

The old woman returned to the trailer and climbed inside. Lonzo whistled and the pony trotted up to him. He replaced the rifle in the scabbard and mounted before coming over to the driver's window. "I'm going to fetch Tina," he told her. "You stay with my mother. I'll not be long."

"Why can't I come with you?"

The deep eyes regarded her thoughtfully. "I don't know who you are."

"But you'd trust your mother with me?"

The wide mouth stretched to a smile. He was beautiful. She glared at him. The pony wheeled and was gone in a scatter of dust.

"Come, miss," the old woman called. Now she was giving the orders. "Come in the shade. Drink tea."

Kate shrugged, suddenly – amazingly – amused. She moved towards the trailer. It was surprisingly roomy. A short passage opened into a living room with spindly furniture that looked as if it had come from a sale of bankrupt stock. There was a bookshelf made of bricks and planks. Large coloured beakers, probably containing iced tea, stood on a table. She was expected. Tony must have called in to say his father was on the way with a guest. "What happened to Tony?" she asked.

The old woman closed a drawer and turned. "Tony, miss?"

"Don't call me miss. My name is Kate."

The faded eyes twinkled. "I'm Lucy. Tina will be here shortly." The tone was no longer senile.

"Has Tony gone to fetch her?"

"I guess. Drink some tea. You need it."

Kate picked up a beaker and sipped obediently. It was liquid if nothing else and would replace some of the lost sweat – although even Scottish peasants laced cold tea with milk – or whisky. She sighed and her eye fell on the bookshelf. She

133

moved closer. There was a large dictionary, Hillerman paper-backs, a field guide to reptiles and amphibians, a collection of old leather-bound copies of the *American Anthropologist,* a stack of newspapers . . .

"Lonzo's books," came from behind her.

"I'm not surprised."

She looked out of the window. No net curtains here. The Jeep stood in the sun, presenting its illusion of being animate. If you didn't know how to hot-wire, was there another method of starting an engine without a key?

"Don't go." It was a command, not a request.

She turned. The old woman was polishing a pistol on the hem of her blouse, the barrel aimed straight at Kate. Lucy caught her look. "Excuse me!" She pointed it at the floor, stroking the butt. "He keeps it loaded," she said chattily.

Kate swallowed. "Why are you holding me here? Is this a kidnap?"

Lucy was amused, her eyes crinkling. "Kidnap," she repeated, shaking her head, her hand steady on the pistol. "Tina will laugh. Not long to wait now."

"Then I might as well sit down—" but as she turned to find a chair there was movement beyond the window and a police car stopped beside the Jeep.

Kate went quickly to the doorway, Lucy making no attempt to intercept her. A lean tanned fellow emerged from the car and regarded her with interest. He was in uniform, and alone.

"Hi, Whit," Lucy called, and crowded Kate down the steps. One hand was concealed in the folds of her skirt.

"She's got a pistol," Kate said sharply.

The cop watched the old woman approach, without her stick now. He raised an eyebrow, she sketched a gesture with empty hands. "She's not armed," she said, indicating Kate.

He nodded and his attention returned to the visitor. "Have they been looking after you, ma'am?" He was the soul of courtesy.

"They're taken my keys and this old lady's got a loaded pistol in the trailer. That's looking after me?"

"They took your keys to keep you for me." She glowered, furious at what could be an innuendo. "They think you're a scout for a drugs gang," he went on. "It was only common sense to hand you over to the Law." He was speaking absently, absorbing every detail of her, from her trainers to her hat, her unwashed face. She was acutely conscious of her greasy hair and she caught a whiff of her own smell. She flushed.

"You don't appear to be a drugs scout," he said gravely, and she looked more closely at him, searching for the reason for his interest – no way could he think she was involved with drugs. She couldn't place him, even physically; there was an exotic cast to his features – perhaps he had Indian blood – brown eyes, however, not black. But that bonehead cut was all wrong with grey hair, however thick . . . like a pelt. She wondered what it felt like. He seemed young to be grey. In his forties?

"You have to be a writer," he said, as if confirming something.

"How did you know?"

"You're checking out my appearance like a homicide detective."

"You were doing the same. Where are my keys?"

He took them from his pocket and handed them to her. She gaped. "A genuine mistake," he said. "You're free to go." But he was waiting – this exchange wasn't finished.

"Thank you." The remark wasn't loaded, merely lightly weighted. "Where can I find Tina Cameron? Lucy" – she looked round but the old Indian had disappeared – "she said Tina would come here, to me. Mrs Cameron, I should say. I don't know her."

"You're visiting her."

"You met Lonzo. He must have told you. I'm not thick, Mr— What do I call you?"

"Whit."

"And the rest?"

"Call me Whit."

He was as bad as the Indians. "Where's your base – Whit?" Trying to be authoritative.

"Exito, ma'am." A pause, then gently: "Usually it's the cops who ask the questions."

"Only when they're interrogating criminals." The silence stretched. His eyes took over. "I'm not a criminal," she blurted.

"Someone might think you were."

Her hand went to her throat, wandered as if to loosen her shirt, desisted; she was blushing again.

"I'd like to hear your story," he said quietly.

She saw an escape route; there was no reason to think that he had been referring to two men murdered on the Missouri. "Someone – I thought someone was following me from Lobo," she said. "An overweight boy called Ozzie – a pick-up came after me down that other valley" – she gestured at the mountains – "and the driver met up with a white Bronco that had followed . . . that I thought had followed me from Tucson, and they started to patrol – God, this sounds wild – they had to be hunting, weren't they?"

"Ozzie can scare strangers," he said.

"You don't know where you are with boys like that – and in the dark – and everyone carrying guns. That scares me. Even *her*!" She glared at the trailer.

"It's a different country. What were you doing in that valley? You should have come west from Lobo."

"Ozzie told me to take the road to Montezuma Springs; he said that was the Bullion Valley."

"He did? I'll have a word with Ozzie Gilsdorf. So you came over the Skeletons in the dark." His face lit up. "You slept out on top?"

"Why not?" She was belligerent.

"Tina's going to love you."

"You do know her then."

"Everyone knows everyone else in the desert. If you follow me I'll take you to her. Keep back a bit so's you don't have to eat my dust. Or close the windows. But a lady as slept on the Skeletons won't be about to drive with the air-conditioning on." His smile was a caress.

Following him, hanging back for the breeze to waft away the dust, first she basked in the awareness of his admiration despite the fact that she smelled, then she was angry because she'd thrown caution to the winds, side-tracked by a hard body and warm eyes. He drove slowly and even that was a kind of sexual consideration – the man was coming on to her. It was a good thing she wasn't attracted herself: stupid haircut, old guy trying to look young, a cop with no rank, probably been on the lowest level all his working life. But he knew Tina. She hoped she hadn't run into Tina's partner. That would be an anti-climax. The woman she was seeking should have done better for herself. The end was in sight and she started to dread that she was going to find a slut in a tacky desert shack.

Ten

The approach to Tina's house was similar to the Indians' bleak access track except that there were power poles. The police car went down to the main 'road', turned right and right again towards another depression in the mountains. The trail snaked past sheaths of yucca knives and a riot of prickly pear and other plants with thorns or spines, impenetrable to anything higher than a lizard.

Trees appeared ahead and the track climbed a knoll and curved, spiralling. Kate came suddenly on the police car stopped in a grove facing a wall of chequered shade, gold where the sun penetrated the foliage. There were screens set in the wall that must mask open windows because someone inside was singing with superb confidence. It was a moment before she realised that the sound didn't come from a living throat but a good stereo.

A rottweiler came padding between the little trees to slobber over Whit. "Good boy," he crooned, rubbing its ears. "You can get down," he told Kate. "Hamish here is harmless. Ignore the other guy, let him make the running."

"What kind—" Kate began suspiciously, her hand on the door, following his glance to a corner of the wall. A doberman stood there, head up, legs planted, silent where the rottweiler snuffled and grunted, waiting for her to leave the Jeep. She did so, patting his head, watching the doberman warily. Whit took a grip on its collar and led the way through the grove.

They passed more screened windows and turned a corner to find another mud-coloured wall with a stone stairway, its risers set with ceramic tiles. At the top was a wooden deck: a balcony with wicker garden furniture. This side of the house was virtually all glass, most sections open and screened, but through the closed panels there were glimpses of blond wood floors, a bed corner, a magnificent china dragon on a window sill.

The view was of a jungly canyon and a skyline frctted with rock the same colour as the house. Quail called, a cardinal flashed scarlet through the bushes, there was a smell of baking bread.

"Hi, there," came a woman's voice, and Kate wondered if she'd been mistaken about the singer after all. The music had stopped but the voice lilted like a bird. "My, but you took your time getting here." There was still the trace of a Scottish accent but the woman turning to them with floured hands would no longer look at home in a Highland glen, not after decades of desert sun.

She had short silver hair with a soft wave but otherwise Tina Cameron was brown as a hazel nut from her head to her bare feet. This was one desert dweller who wasn't bothered about skin cancer. Her blue shift was sleeveless but no pale skin showed anywhere. At first sight she appeared plump but when she moved – holding out a hand, scattering flour – muscles rippled on the naked arms.

"But now you are here, welcome to the desert." Grey eyes observed Kate keenly, the wide mouth stretched. Suddenly music exploded from speakers.

"Turn it off, sweetie!" Tina shouted, and Whit moved to a corner of the big open-plan space beyond the kitchen area. Silence flooded back. "Away in and sit down," Tina ordered. "I'll be with you in a moment. Put the kettle on, Whit."

Kate said, "Can I use your bathroom?" She had seen the furniture: sofas and chairs in pale leather, pastel cushions, books, blinds in some straw-like material so primitive they were elegant. "I'm filthy," she added pointedly. "I can't touch anything."

"Take a shower, honey. There are towels in the closet – show her, Whit."

Kate didn't move for a moment. She stood just inside the kitchen, revelling in a draught that was marginally cooler than the hot shade on the deck. She was trying to reconcile this little round woman with the girl who had charmed an American GI and Billy Newman, possibly the Royal brothers.

"Run along now," Tina urged. "Tea will be brewed time you finish."

When Kate emerged from the shower she found her clothes gone and in their place a kimono in heavy cream silk, its touch on clean skin dusted with Chanel talc suggesting indecency despite the fact that she was fully covered.

This was obviously Tina's bathroom; there was no evidence of its being used by a man, nor was there in the bedroom, but it was possible, she thought, that old people didn't sleep together in a hot climate.

She had never been in a room like this: a bedspread – more silk – with a sheen like mother-of-pearl, a television set, a dressing table in pale wood. The scent, like the talc, was Chanel No. 5. The hairbrush was real bristles, and there was a clutch of expensive lipsticks. Louvred doors must conceal ranks of clothes. There was one picture, a large photograph in monochrome. She moved closer and Am Bodach materialised, stark under snow.

She returned to the living room. No one was about. She started to check the books.

"Why, that suits you down to the ground," Tina cried, bouncing into the kitchen from the deck. "I put your things in the washer. Now we'll have tea."

She brought it on a tray: everything in bone china, and lump sugar with silver tongs. Kate beamed. There were only two cups. "What happened to Whit?" she asked.

"He's away to Lobo to give that Ozzie Gilsdorf a dressing down. The idea: telling you the wrong valley! Your arrival's disrupted him – Whit, I mean." She smiled to show no criticism was intended. "No big deal. He's just not used to pretty girls invading his territory." She poured tea smoothly, using a silver strainer. "Milk? Full cream, I'm afraid, not that you have to worry. And I make the shortbread with butter; we like our creature comforts. But you're not pretty," she went on in the same tone. "'Pretty' is soap opera stuff. You're – different." She chuckled engagingly. "You can tell I live alone, can't you? If you weren't here I'd be talking to the dogs."

Kate gulped down her tea, confused.

"I should have given you a beaker," Tina said. "Let me top you up."

"Where does Whit live?"

"He works out of Exito. Heavens, you'd not expect him to live with me, surely? He's got his own apartment in town: quite large, too big for him now. He lost his wife two years ago. A brain tumour. Isn't that sad in a young woman? Well, young to me, she was thirty-eight. They had no children; perhaps that's as well. I'm sure it is. But a sweet girl, I was very fond of her."

"Why – you were friendly with her?"

"Honey, one usually is friendly with a daughter-in-law." Tina was gently reproving. She sensed shock and peered at her guest. "No!" she cried. "You never thought he was my boyfriend!"

"Of course I didn't." Kate was furious at herself. "I thought he was a . . . an old lecher. He was coming on to me. He's the *baby*? Your baby?"

"Well, I stopped thinking of him as my baby some time back, but he's no lecher, dear; like I said, he's bowled over by a new face."

"Jesus!" Kate slumped back on the sofa, exposing a length of thigh, her brain replaying the events of the immediate past, now viewed from a different angle. "He might have told me," she said sulkily.

"I guess he had more important things on his mind. He had to reassure Lonzo and his family – they're very touchy – he also had to make sure you are who you say you are, no ulterior motives. We only have Billy's story, you see, him and Barbara Lomas."

"So you've been in touch with Arletta too."

"At second hand, by way of Billy." Tina was serious now, and careful. "You left a rather delicate situation behind you in Montana," she pointed out. "Do you want to talk about it?"

"Why not? I've got nothing to hide. In fact, I told the truth: to Barbara Lomas and the police there." She grinned. "No one believed me. That's how I managed to get away without being . . . apprehended? Maybe you'll believe me."

She told it as it happened: from Barbara Lomas sending her to Grace Bierman, to her leaving Arletta, and all that happened between. It wasn't a monologue, Tina interrupting from the first. "I don't recall Grace Bierman," she said, "but I remember the Royals of course."

"That's why you were there," Kate said pointedly: "to look up Glenn Royal."

Tina's eyes clouded. "He was Chuck's buddy. You know about Chuck? Yes, but that's my story; let's have yours first. So you went down to the old ferry to find the Royals."

"Barbara had told me that Glenn was dead." She went on to tell how she'd found Old Copper's body, of the arrival of Chesler.

"Wait a minute," Tina interrupted, "we know the police version from Barbara, but she told Billy that you said you found the body in a well where the police reported it was in the river. Now who's right?"

"Both. There *was* a body in the well. It was moved and put in the river. I was not hallucinating. There was a trap door in the kitchen floor; I can remember lifting it. There was a heavy ring set in it; it had to be heavy because of the weight of the door. I needed all my strength to lift it. I couldn't have imagined that."

"All right, but if Old Copper fell in by accident, like if he was drunk, could he have pulled the door down on himself as he tried to climb out?"

142

"No way. The trap folded right back so it lay flat on the floor when it was open. Besides, the body was moved. Why would anyone do that except the killer? And his pick-up was there when I arrived but that too was put in the water."

"When?"

"After Chesler was shot." She reverted to Chesler's sudden appearance at the ferry and subsequent events: her flight through the woods, the rattlesnake, near panic, the wild thought that she might climb the cliffs . . .

Tina was puzzled. "Why were you so scared of this guy? You make it sound like you were running for your life. You know: like when you thought Ozzie followed you last night? Whit told me. Ozzie Gilsdorf wouldn't hurt a fly – although it was very naughty of him to send you out on the Montezuma road."

"Huh!" Kate was sceptical but she let it go. "I'd kneed Chesler," she pointed out. "He was going to pay me back for that: knock me about maybe if it hurt too much to rape me. But I'd found the body, don't forget, and I thought he was the killer, could be anyway. You would, wouldn't you? Both men worked on that ranch. But any woman who knees a fellow isn't going to hang around afterwards. I didn't; I climbed those cliffs." She had relived that climb many times and she could visualise it as she spoke. In her mind's eye, in her narrative, she reached the top, staggered across the grassland in the fading light, found the water tank – and Tiegen's hounds found her. She leaned back on the cushions overcome with fatigue.

Tina rose and went to a sideboard. She came back with a bottle of Talisker and glasses. "You're a rock climber," she stated, pouring the whisky with a generous hand. "People climb those sheer buttes in Monument Valley; I guess the Missouri cliffs would be child's play to an expert."

Kate snorted. "I'm not Monument Valley standard but you have the right idea. The police didn't, which is why they thought I'd got a touch of the sun. That, and the body not being in the well when they reached the ferry house. And the pick-up in the river."

143

"So who moved the body?"

"It had to be the guy who was on top. I thought someone shot at me but that had to be him: he fired at Chesler just as I made the hard move. I jumped, there was a report, and I kept going, fast, grabbing the rock, rushing it. By the time I risked a look back Chesler was out of sight. I thought he'd moved in to the foot of the cliff; it never occurred to me he'd been shot, probably dropped behind a boulder."

"Could you still see the other guy?"

"No. He'd disappeared too. I did think I heard an engine at some point, and Tiegen, the rancher who found me, he said there was a Cherokee about, had been around for some time. I've remembered something else. Tiegen said that that same day Chesler came to his ranch to use his telephone and he called a woman and told her to meet him: same place, same time. And Grace Bierman told the police he was with a woman. If they were a poaching gang – Chesler, Old Copper, the Cherokee driver – Chesler could have been phoning the Cherokee guy, pretending he was talking to a woman. Now how would he do that? Telephone the guy, unless the chap was holed up somewhere?"

"Mobile phone, honey. And Chesler was calling him – a pre-arranged call, in code? – to tell him someone had gone down to the ferry and would . . . might find Old Copper's body?"

"And the body had to be moved, set it up to look like an accident. But Chesler must have made that call before he came down to the ferry, and it wasn't until he met me that he knew I'd found the body. Afterwards he had no chance to telephone before he was killed."

"He knew you were going down to the ferry house. You called at the ranch."

Kate's eyes closed. "I wondered if there was a link," she murmured.

"A link with what?" Tina was sharp.

"Between our visits: yours and mine."

"After a forty-five year interval? That's wild!"

A Wreath of Dead Moths

"Why did you go down there? What was it between you
and Glenn Royal? Am I being impertinent? Blame it on the
whisky."

"Glenn was Chuck's pal, dear. I'd come to the States to have
the baby; naturally the first person I'd go to was Glenn. That
was always the idea: we'd make a home near Arletta, raise a
family on a little ranch—" She trailed away and stood up. "We
won't talk about that old stuff. You're nearly asleep. You go
and lie down for an hour or so while I fix a meal. Or sleep as
long as you like, there's no rush."

Dim light, a sense of deep silence, a weight on her feet. She was
shackled, she was trapped – an avalanche? "No," she gasped
and tried to turn. The restraint lifted, only to be transferred
to her thighs. She reached down and felt a hard furry skull.
"Hamish?" He licked her hand.

She slid away from him and sat up, reaching for the kimono.
She looked in vain for her watch and remembered it was lost
in the sand. A piano was playing quietly. A pan clattered.

She was in Tina's guest room. She washed her face in the
integral bathroom and ran wet fingers through her hair. Her
clean clothes were neatly folded on a wicker stool. She dressed
slowly, recalling the recent conversation – which had consisted
mostly of her own account, punctuated by Tina's queries and
observations. Now it was time for Tina's story.

There could be snags. Whit was on the deck outside the
kitchen, pounding something in a mortar. "I woke you?" he
asked, all concern. Tina, pausing as she shredded lettuce,
raised her eyebrows. Embarrassed, certain he would have been
acquainted with her gaffe, she tried to control her face. "You
didn't wake me," she said. "Hamish did. He's a ton weight."

"You were sleeping with Hamish?" he asked politely.

"There must be a witty comeback to that" – she was recovering her poise – "but I'm not in your class. Did you find Ozzie?"

"I didn't." He picked cardamon husks out of the mortar.
"He's away hunting coyotes."

145

"He saw you coming; you should have had someone at the back door of his house."

"I guess you're right. Where's the salad dressing, Mom?"

"I'll see to it. You fix Kate a drink. How about margaritas? Special occasion."

The blinds in the living room had been raised and they looked out on rough ground rising to the rock ridge; in the lowering sun the saguaro were golden pencils above the shadowed undergrowth.

"Lovely," Kate breathed. "Exquisite."

"The best time of day," he agreed, doing things at the sideboard. The piano played languidly. I could live here, she thought, Scotland forgotten. Whit approached and handed her something in a wide glass, the rim frosty. She sipped warily and wondered why she should be wary. He waited, watching her.

"It's different," she said. "I'm not much of a connoisseur. Why the salt?"

"I don't know. It's how you drink a margarita."

She turned back to the canyon. "Before I reached here," she said dreamily, "I'd anticipated another mobile home, like Lonzo's."

"The only difference is money. Did you see Lonzo's books? Mom's reading is lighter."

If Tina heard she was paying no attention. "What is it about the Indians?" Kate asked. "Your mother said you had to reassure them. About me?"

"They didn't know she was expecting you. And when you come in the back way, over the Skeletons – a lone woman in a Jeep with Illinois plates – Lonzo was suspicious. So he sent for me. Why Illinois plates anyway?"

"I flew to Chicago and bought the Jeep there." She added resentfully, "Lucy was holding a pistol on me."

"Keeping you at the camp until I arrived."

"Who's the younger woman with long black hair?"

"Maria." He glanced towards the kitchen. "She's . . . a visitor."

A Wreath of Dead Moths

"She's an illegal," Tina said firmly, coming into the living room, carrying a glass. "We can trust Kate, sweetie." She grinned wickedly. "She doesn't want the Montana cops to catch up with her."

"*Mom!*"

"My little joke." Kate stared from one to the other. "Two things you should know, Kate," Tina went on. "The first is that Maria – who is Lonzo's wife, and Tony's mother of course – she's an illegal alien. She's Mexican and she's been here sixteen years and she passes for Indian. There was an amnesty for illegals but I couldn't persuade her to register, however much she trusts me. We know each other well; she's helped in the house since she came here. She wouldn't register because she was scared of something going wrong, of being deported; terrified of having to leave Lonzo and Tony. She'd be scared of you; you could have been a government official."

"Whit is a government official."

Tina went on as if Kate hadn't spoken: "The other thing you should know is that this country, close to the border, is alive with drug-runners and illegals being smuggled north. Any stranger is suspect, and that's the general view. Specifically Lonzo would think of Maria and not give you the benefit of any doubt. Anyway you were on their land. They were here first."

Kate's eyes widened. "'Don't mess with me. I was here first.' Dr Pratt," she explained: "A rattler on his T-shirt and those words. Dr Pratt. Does the name mean anything?"

"No," Tina said. "Should it?"

"He went up to the site of the plane crash."

"Oh." Tina was enlightened. "He was staying with the Lawries. I don't recall—"

"No, he was alone." Kate stopped, appalled. If someone lived for a while after the crash it could have been Chuck. Tina was watching her closely. "He didn't go up with a party," Kate said wildly. "He came on the crash weeks later." Her eyes were jumpy.

147

Tina licked her lips. "This is going to spoil our meal," she said heavily. "I suggest we eat now, talk afterwards."

Kate thought: whenever the conversation comes round to her, to her past, she steers it away. This time it was a relief. She glanced at Whit and saw he was regarding his mother quizzically, or it could have been with concern.

They ate ratatouille and a green salad. Kate asked where the vegetables came from. Tina shopped once a week, in Exito; she would do so tomorrow, she said. Kate volunteered, and was stopped short. Tina guessed the thought. "You're staying here," she said firmly. "You don't think I'd let a fellow Scot go to a motel? We have to hear all about Glasgow and Edinburgh."

Kate doubted that. Tina was after something more than news of cities she'd left nearly half a century ago.

After the salad, there was fruit and a cheeseboard. Tina apologised because fancy cheeses had to be kept in the fridge. "Don't apologise," Kate said, helping herself to Brie. "This is the first cheeseboard I've seen since Armidil." She remembered that dinner at the hotel, Neil and his old man's obsession. She caught Whit's eye. He wasn't old, merely prematurely grey and, actually, grey looked good with that tan.

"I was trained well," Tina was saying. "Have some more claret."

It was the first time she'd referred to her time in service – and as yet there'd been no mention of Kate's book. Billy Newman would have told her about that, or Barbara via Billy. It should be mentioned. Kate tried to think of a way to approach the subject but Tina forestalled her: "I guess the old people at Armidil – Sir Ian and Lady Lawrie – they've passed away?"

"The lodge was sold after you were there. Lady Lawrie's still alive. She lives in Edinburgh and Maisie Grant visits her occasionally. It was the Grants who bought Armidil and turned it into a hotel. They still own it."

"Did the maids stay on? But of course, all that will be long before your time. Why, you weren't even born!"

"I'm sure they didn't. The Grants ran the place as Bed and

Breakfast at first, and they did everything themselves. They built it up from nothing; it's an institution among mountaineers now."

"So there'll be no one I remember." Tina wasn't interested in Armidil as an hotel. "I was there such a short time anyway."

"Madeleine Bell remembers you. She has a holiday cottage out on the point. It was she who put me on to you. She was in the party when you climbed to . . . climbed Am Bodach."

"Ah yes, a large young lady. Very sympathetic." Tina glanced at their plates. "We'll have coffee on the deck. Is the bug light on, Whit?"

Here we go again, Kate thought; perhaps she doesn't want to talk about those days with Whit around. Right, she'd talk about herself, fill some gaps in that direction.

"This business in Montana," she said bluntly once they were settled with their coffee, the deck softly lit, the bug light at a distance, drawing the insects away. "What's the police thinking on that? Am I in the clear?"

"From what Mom says, you are, and I'm inclined to go along with her." Whit was relaxed, his tone reassuring, even amused. "I don't see you as a killer." He went on, serious now: "I don't know what the police thinking is; I know what the media said and what Billy had from Barbara Lomas. The difference is that, according to you, Old Copper didn't drown, and the guy who's still alive could have killed him and Chesler. But he's a killer whether it's your story or the police version, which is a gang killing and an old drunk drowned in the river. They were looking for the Cherokee but they have to've given up because anyone in his right mind knows the guy will be rid of it by now. Your name hasn't been mentioned. My guess is that those two cops never reported meeting you. What was there to say: that you were at the old ferry, your Jeep broke down, you walked out and got a touch of the sun? You're a distraction. Country cops like things simple. Of course, one of the gang survived and is on the loose but that's Montana's problem, nothing to do with you."

Kate thought about the Cherokee on the road to Bozeman, about the white Bronco, Ozzie, the Indians. "I suppose I'm neurotic," she confessed. "This country has me disorientated."

"You're not neurotic," Tina said.

Kate was about to say something about its being an occupational hazard with writers when Whit put down his cup and stood up. "You're away, sweetie?" Tina wasn't surprised. "There's coffee in the flask."

"I'll see you tomorrow." He turned to Kate. "You'll be around a while. I'll show you the desert. I'm looking forward to it." And with that he was gone, the dogs trotting after him down the steps.

"He can't be on nights as well as days," Kate protested.

"Special duty." Tina was casual. "He'll go home tonight but first he'll take a run down to the border. Smugglers are looking for a new route, and our valley would be ideal – or so they think."

"A route for a drugs run?"

"Probably that too but Whit's thinking more in terms of illegals: truckloads of 'em being brought north by conmen who take the money and drop their passengers out in the desert: keep walking, they're told, and they'll see the lights of the town in a few minutes. That's what happened a couple of weeks ago: poor guys walked all night, sun came up, and they were out in the middle of an enormous desert."

"That's monstrous! What happened to them?"

"They all died. They were drinking hair oil at the end."

"Why, for God's sake?"

"It's liquid. Thirst drives them mad. So now that route's closed and they're looking for an alternative."

"And Whit's out there on his own—"

"Oh no. Lonzo and Tony will be around."

Kate absorbed this in silence. After a while she said, "Maria's illegal."

"In her case the amnesty would be a formality. And it isn't the aliens Whit's against – we're on their side – it's the traffic,

150

and the scum who run it. Well, scum when they drop them in the desert. I feel the same way about the Mexicans as I do about the Indians. Come to that" – Tina sat up straight, her voice rising – "come to that, so should you. What about the Highlanders and the clearances?"

"What?" Kate was bemused. "The clearances?"

"Native peoples." Tina was impatient: "Robbed of their land by invaders. Great landowners and huge flocks of sheep displacing peasants. When the Europeans arrived this whole country was inhabited, even the deserts. America wasn't a new land to be exploited, it was an old country with its own people already. We appropriated it. We can't ever make up for that but we don't have to make it worse. Whit's been raised properly; if he turns a blind eye to Maria's status and he don't hear a rifle shot out of season it's because he's got a fine sense of responsibility. The Indians were here first."

Kate was dazed by the tirade but Tina's emotions were mercurial. "Tell me about Dr Pratt," she said calmly, catching her guest off-balance.

"Well" – Kate began slowly, recovering as she went – "when I started to get interested in the Flying Fortress and I saw there was a book in it – Billy must have told you about the book?" Tina nodded, her eyes unblinking. Kate resumed: "I spoke to local people: the crofters, Dr Pratt, Madeleine Bell . . . she's not thick, you know; she guessed you had a personal interest; she's thrilled I've found you, asked to be remembered to you." She was frantically trying to avoid Pratt and his discovery of twenty-seven bodies but Tina cut through her waffling like a knife.

"And the doctor? What did he have to say?"

Kate said quietly: "It should be a comfort to you. It was instantaneous . . . all of them."

"Dr Pratt said that?"

"Yes."

"He was there just afterwards?"

"No, much later—" She saw her mistake and cast around for a diversion. "Tina, why did Glenn Royal go to Cullen?"

151

"He didn't!" In the silence the cicadas shrilled, and the dogs came scuffing up the steps. "Who told you that?" Tina asked.

"Several people. He didn't make a secret of it, not on that side of the Atlantic anyway, in fact, he kept in touch with the local policeman. When I came to the States I was following Glenn, not you. I had no idea you were over here. The policeman's daughter gave Madeleine Glenn's address." Kate frowned. "Did he go to Scotland after you met, or did you meet him over there and followed him back—"

"I didn't—" It was fierce but cut off short. Tina went on, too casually: "I met Glenn first at Arletta. I didn't keep in touch with him. Obviously he came to Scotland to visit the crash site. Because his best friend died there."

They stared at each other, Tina defiant, Kate's face blank. "I'm embarrassing you," she murmured.

"No, not at all. You're wondering why I came to Arletta and left after just one night. Chuck had written Glenn asking him to find him a small property – as a tenant of course – so we'd have somewhere to live when I joined him. He'd told Glenn about me; that's why I went straight to Slaughter Creek. I needed to find work and a place to have the baby. I saw right away that Arletta was impossible – those prairies in winter! But then Billy Newman told me about Arizona, how it was always warm and there were lots of rich people, plenty of work and his sister a midwife in Phoenix . . ." Her voice faded, came back. "I don't know why Glenn came to Scotland," she said, looking exhausted, "except his friend was killed there."

"Was it you who told him about the Leica? He told the police that's what he was looking for."

Tina had been staring out at the night. Her head came round slowly. "Run that one past me again."

"A camera, very expensive? He said he was looking for a Leica that belonged to his relative. He told people he was Chuck's cousin. Did Chuck own a Leica?"

There was a long pause. "Probably," Tina said. "He'd been

152

in Europe. He could have acquired one. Are you going to put that in your book?"

"No. It must have been stolen by one of the rescuers, and that's not nice. I'm not going to publicise it."

"They were no relation." Tina was preoccupied. "He was Chuck's best friend, is all. It's not important either, is it? I mean, there's nothing sinister about the camera. Let's forget it; Glenn shouldn't have mentioned it to anyone. What will have happened is that if Chuck did own an expensive camera, he could have told Glenn but not me because he'd . . . like looted it, and knew I'd disapprove."

"That must be the explanation." But Kate was thinking it wasn't adequate to explain why a cowhand should have gone all that way at phenomenal expense, and never told his best friend's lover. "So what did you do when you left Montana?" she asked chummily. "You were very young, pregnant, all alone; how did you cope?"

Tina sighed deeply and relaxed. Apparently this was something she didn't mind talking about. "I wasn't trained for anything except service, so that's what I did. Rich folk in Phoenix loved having a Scottish maid, still do, I guess. I worked my way up, travelled the state, had a number of situations . . . You'll be wondering how a maid could save enough to build a house like this, but me, I kept changing places until I found a gentleman who was an investment counsellor, among other things. He gave me sound advice and I started to invest. You might say he educated me about money, and I found I had a head for it. I looked after him when he was widowed and until he died. He left me a few dollars and some nice pieces of furniture, some pretty ornaments, but by then I had a tidy sum myself. So I built this place. Whit and me, we both love the desert. There. A dull story, and not at all what you were expecting, I'm afraid."

"You looked after Whit yourself?"

"That's why I moved around, until I found someone who was happy to accept the two of us. No way would I have farmed him out."

Kate said carefully, "Do you mind talking about Chuck?"

"No, dear, I was telling Whit about his daddy soon as he was old enough to understand." Her eyes were soft, remembering. "We met in a dance hall in London. He was on furlough, I was in service in Mayfair." She smiled. "He was the only man I truly loved. Isn't that amazing?"

Not really, she hadn't done much since. Over forty years of domestic service! Kate winced.

"He felt the same way," Tina went on. "And so thrilled about the baby. We were to be married soon as I joined him in Montana."

Kate shifted uncomfortably, she hadn't expected confidences to go this far.

"It was a long time ago," Tina said, as if excusing herself. "I still grieve." They were silent and in the canyon the cicadas were still. "You can never go back," came the calm tones. "Not to where you were before it happened. Life changes. You accept it of course; if you didn't you'd go mad or kill yourself. And I had Whit."

"You didn't take anyone into your confidence – I mean, before he was born, when you discovered you were pregnant?"

Tina gave a snort of derision. "My mum and dad would have thrown me out; only bad girls had babies out of wedlock in those days. No, no one knew except Chuck until Billy Newman, and I only told him because he had a sister who was a midwife, and that was just what I needed at that time, in a strange country. We're still in touch, the Newmans and me."

"Didn't you tell Glenn Royal?"

"No. No point, I wasn't staying. Glenn was all right but I didn't take to his brother. I got out of there next morning, soon as I could. Glenn took me to Arletta and Billy – but you know the rest."

Not by a long chalk, Kate thought, although what she didn't know came before Billy Newman, even before the States. What had Tina told Glenn Royal that had sent him over

154

five thousand miles to look at an aircraft wreck? And he hadn't even done that, according to Madeleine who'd said that Duncan Stewart took him only as far as the corrie below the suspended wing.

Eleven

"You don't take notes," Tina said. "How can you remember everything?"

They were enjoying a late breakfast: homemade croissants and Cooper's Oxford marmalade. Under the projecting roof the shade was balmy and there wasn't a breath of breeze.

"I make notes," Kate said. "I've been working in the bedroom."

"You should use a tape recorder."

"It's an idea, although I didn't with my last book. That was on climbing accidents and I photocopied all the reports. If you're bothered about accuracy I'll send you a draft of the part that concerns you and Chuck – though all I know about him is what you tell me." Tina wouldn't meet her eye. "You *are* bothered," Kate said.

"I guess that after forty-five years it doesn't matter, and in today's climate . . . But Whit *is* illegitimate, honey."

"That worries him?" Kate was incredulous.

"No, I said: it was so long ago – but I'll take you up on that suggestion; I'd like to see what you've written before it's published." She paused, then asked politely, "Who are you going to visit when you leave here?"

"I've hardly given it a thought. Originally I'd expected that once I got started I'd be handed on from one relative to the next. I'd assumed you'd kept in touch, at least for some years afterwards. It happens with plane crashes nowadays: relatives form associations, support groups, that kind of thing."

"I wasn't a relative."

156

"Of course you were! You were carrying Chuck's baby."

"I told you last night: it was a different world." Tina smiled wryly. "I was a bad girl. You're another generation, you wouldn't understand."

"I think your story is more fascinating because you weren't married. People being such hypocrites would have made it much harder for you." Kate tried to imagine how it must have been but failed. She reverted to the problem of obtaining more information and realised she wasn't enthusiastic. It was Tina's story that claimed her attention. "I suppose I'll have to go to Washington," she said. "See if I can find records of the other victims: their home towns, next of kin and so on. I've got a few names and states from the plaque that I jotted down from memory. Bill – someone was going to photograph it for me." She shook her head at the waste of his death and said tightly, "A plaque was erected at the site of the crash with all the names. Chuck was there of course: Sullivan, Montana. My friend died before he could take the picture."

"Oh, I'm sorry. A close friend?"

"Climbing partner." Kate stared at a vapour trail inching across the sky. "A lover – well, more or less; we'd got used to each other."

Tina was appalled. "This happened recently?"

"The night I left. There was a storm and he fell in the flooded burn. They thought it was me. Madeleine Bell told me when I phoned her from Bozeman. I called her to get your name actually; she was to ask Lady Lawrie, who's her aunt. Madeleine had the job of telling me about Bill. They'd buried him by then. And I knew nothing about it."

"I don't understand. How could they think it was you when they'd found his body?"

"I lent him my van and left for Glasgow without telling anyone. I thought he'd do that. They found the van abandoned at my camp site and assumed I'd had an accident on the hill. Then they found his body on the shore where it had been washed down by the river, and someone had the sense to call my publisher, so they knew I hadn't drowned trying to rescue him, or the other way round."

"Had he been drinking?"

"We'd been together earlier in the evening and he'd had one or two, not nearly enough . . . He must have had more after we parted. No way could that guy have fallen in a burn unless he was scunnered."

"Like Old Copper," Tina murmured, then, changing the subject: "Your own story would make fascinating reading." She glanced at her watch. "Why, is that the time? And Whit's due this afternoon. I wanted to make zucchini bread and sherbets and dear knows what besides."

"You've got plenty of time."

"Not to cook and go to town."

"I told you I'd do the shopping. I've got nothing else to do. I lost my watch when I was digging out the Jeep but I can go and look for it when I come back."

Some time later she came plodding up the steps to the kitchen. The Jeep had a puncture and her spare was flat. When she went to look, Tina was appalled at the state of the tyres. Kate must take her pick-up, they'd put the two wheels in the back and new tyres could be fitted while she shopped in Safeway's. And she was to take Hamish; he always went to Exito on shopping day leaving Carl, the doberman, to look after the house.

They heaved the wheels on the back of the pick-up. Kate regarded the rifle visible through the window of the cab. "You're leaving that?" she asked.

"Of course. Better safe than sorry. No one's going to bother a rancher lady packing a rifle and with a rottweiler for passenger."

At four o'clock Kate was on her way back from town with the shopping and two new tyres. Exito had turned out to be a sprawling copper-mining community with no character but a fabulous supermarket. She'd had a satisfactory afternoon and she was looking forward to the evening: delicious food, margaritas, Whit . . .

About five miles from Exito, chugging along the road towards the turn-off for the Bullion Valley, it occurred to her that the shrimps should start to thaw now in order to be ready for dinner. The ice chest was under a tarpaulin on the back where she'd thought it would be cooler than in the cab. She pulled out on the shoulder and Hamish started to fidget and whimper.

"You're not getting out," she told him, and then thought better of it; he could be in need of a leak. He leapt out when she opened the passenger door and lifted his leg on the first clump of weeds. She climbed on the back of the truck, found the bag of shrimps and considered where to put it. After driving so far it would be just her luck to have a vulture swoop down and steal it. Life out here sure was complicated, worse than the Highlands. She put the shrimps on the floor of the cab and turned to find Hamish. He was nowhere to be seen. She started to shout for him.

A mile away, in the direction of Exito, the image of a vehicle danced on the shimmering road. She shouted louder. There was no response. He'd run home? But he was thirty miles from home. A trap? Dogs barked in traps. *A rattler!* She screamed obscenities. The silence mocked her.

The vehicle approached: a white Bronco going quite fast. Hamish appeared on the far side of the road, lolloping between bushes, grinning inanely. "No," she shouted, "Stay! *Stay!*" He came on.

The Bronco loomed. Hamish reached the shoulder and picked up speed. He saw the truck, the driver saw him and braked. Dog and truck swerved. There was a screech of brakes and one anguished yelp.

Kate had covered her face, dislodging her shades. It was a reflex gesture and the Bronco had passed when she looked again. It didn't stop.

Hamish was slinking across the road, obviously cowed. She

159

swore and hugged him and made a rude gesture at the retreating truck. She picked up her shades, got in the pick-up and drove on. After a mile or so she passed a roadside halt: a grove of tamarisks and picnic tables under angled canopies. A white truck was parked in the tamarisk shade, the driver behind the wheel. She stared blankly, remembering the white Bronco on the road from Lobo. In her rear-view mirror she saw it pull out behind her.

Tina's pick-up was old and slow. The Bronco came up quickly and flashed its lights. It couldn't be the same truck, it had to be a coincidence. Of course it was! She was in a different vehicle; no way could he be the same driver who had stopped and talked to Ozzie on the road to Montezuma Springs. This was someone else: a macho tourist – but with Arizona plates – who was hassling her because her dog had been loose and she'd given him a two-finger salute. Her lips thinned; she had a rifle and a rottweiler – and then she wondered what he had.

She plugged on grimly. In the mirror she could make out the broad silhouette of the driver and the shape of a hat, Stetson or straw. She started to have qualms. There was no one else on the road, Hamish was a pussycat and the rifle wouldn't be loaded. In any case she couldn't fire one, had never handled one; this gun was for show.

The Bronco pulled out and passed. She kept her eyes on the road, ignoring the driver, sensing his stare. He pulled in sharply and slowed down. She braked, made to pass and he turned out, blocking her. She dropped back, watching to see what he would do. Suddenly he drifted to the other side of the road leaving a clear space. She stamped on the accelerator but as she drew level he was pointing right, signalling her to take to the shoulder. He was authoritative. A cop then – in plain clothes. The Bronco touched, nudging the pick-up. A rogue cop? He had the faster vehicle. She was caught – but she was on a main road, such as it was, and someone should come along. She pulled out on the shoulder, stopped and reached back for the rifle.

The Bronco came to a halt in front of her and reversed a few

A Wreath of Dead Moths

yards. There was a long pause. The rifle took up a lot of room between her and the steering wheel but she felt that she would be more vulnerable outside the truck. Beside her the stupid dog shifted restlessly, wanting to get out again. She kept the engine running.

Up ahead the driver's door opened. A boot appeared – a light desert boot, a meaty thigh. He straightened up. Yes, he was heavy. A straw hat shaded much of his face. He walked back, saw the rifle barrel, took off his dark glasses. It was Neil Grant.

"Never point a firearm at anybody, Kate, unless you're prepared to use it."

"Oh God!" The features were familiar but momentarily she couldn't place him.

He pushed the barrel aside, then took the rifle from her easily, one-handed. She was limp. "I can see the dog's all right," he said, "But how are you?"

"Jesus," she whispered. "What the hell are you doing here? Get off me, Hamish!" He was struggling to reach her window.

"Let him out," Neil said, correctly reading the eager eyes.

"Not after you nearly killed him! Why didn't you stop?"

"I was scared stiff. I'd nearly killed a rancher's dog, I'd seen the rifle. No way would I stop."

"So why'd you force me off the road?"

"Because I thought it was you when you knocked your glasses off but – the pick-up, the dog, the rifle? It couldn't be. So I had a good look when I overtook you. Then I was sure. But I didn't force you off the road, I was trying to make you stop. Why are we talking like this? Let's find some shade."

"I can't let Hamish out. Oh, shit!" The situation was beyond her. "Come on then!" He stood back, still holding the rifle, and she drove off the shoulder into the open desert. Behind her he walked back to the Bronco and followed.

She stopped a few hundred yards from the road and got down. Neil arrived, walked over and replaced the rifle on its rack. "Unloaded," he observed.

161

She felt she was being steam-rollered and took refuge in displacement activity. "First thing to do," she began bossily, "is get that ice chest down and put it in the shade. I can't stop long because the ice will melt. I'll have to take you home with me. It means one more for dinner."

"Don't sound so enthusiastic." He was suddenly contrite. "I'm sorry, I've given you a shock."

"I meant, of course you'll come back with me." She was prim. Everything she said sounded artificial.

They settled themselves gingerly on the hot sand in the shade of the truck. Hamish disappeared again. "Oh hell," she moaned, "I hope he doesn't find a rattler."

"They don't come out till dusk. Who does he belong to?"

"Why," she turned, staring in amazement, "he belongs to Tina. Sir Ian Lawrie's maid. You know her – knew her – or did you? I'm lost, Neil. What are you doing here anyway?"

"I've been following you."

"Since when? That wasn't you at Lobo? Why? How did you find me?"

"Which answer do you want first?"

Hamish returned and collapsed under the truck. "How?" Kate repeated after a moment.

He thought about it. "I must have used the same chain of communication as you: starting with Madeleine Bell and Glenn Royal's address. You might have told me you were going to do the book after all, but then I deserved it – after that last . . . encounter." He looked dejected. "I can't tell you how much I regret my behaviour, Kate."

She ignored that. "You've been to Arletta?"

"I was there not long after you left."

She looked at the Bronco. "And that was you at Lobo?"

"I came through Lobo," he said slowly. "Why do you ask?"

"A white Bronco was following me two nights ago, or I thought it was."

"It could have been me. I didn't see you. Pick-ups all look alike."

162

It hadn't been him; she'd been driving the Jeep. "So why are you here?"

They were leaning against the wheels, the ice chest between them. His legs were drawn up, his arms resting on his knees. He was looking at the mountains, his face relaxed. Her eyes softened, he was a link with home. Maybe she'd been a bit hard on him.

"You know what happened," he said. "I'm terribly sorry about your friend. But when we thought it was you, that you were missing on the hill, probably dead or badly injured, the bottom dropped out of my world. And then your publisher told us everything was all right: you were safe, you were in the States, then I knew how much you meant to me. Before, when you were there, you were a challenge, a potential conquest. It was a physical thing. Then it all changed and I had to find you, no matter what. Madeleine told me about Arletta and, well – there you are."

She frowned, uncomfortable. "I don't see how you kept track of me – or did Barbara Lomas tell you I'd gone to Arizona?"

He looked surprised. "I never asked her. But you phoned Madeleine and she told Maisie. I speak to Maisie most nights. I'd have found you anyway. You kept me going: the thought of catching up with you, how you'd look, what you'd say." He glanced at her shyly.

She could do without this, was regretting the suggestion he should come back to Tina's place. She said, trying to cool it, and only encouraging him: "And now what are you going to do?"

"Nothing." He grinned. "I'm with you. I haven't thought any further than this."

She moved impatiently. "What do you expect me to do?"

"Go on as you were. I'll tag along."

Like hell he would. Aloud she said, "No strings?"

"Why should there be? I don't want anything from you, Kate. You don't get it, do you? I'm an old man and you've bewitched me. I don't need anything, from you or anyone else. I've got it all now. Even the weather's perfect."

163

"Huh! It's obvious you've just arrived. A few hours out there" – she jerked her head at the shining desert – "and you'd die as quickly as in a blizzard."

"I know the States."

"You may know Alaska and the Rockies; you don't know the deserts."

"People live here. What was that about taking me home with you?"

She hesitated, wondering how she might get out of this. "Tina Cameron: the woman I was looking for, the maid from Armidil. Madeleine must have told you, or Maisie. It was Tina's lover who was killed in the plane crash. She was pregnant and she emigrated. She's here, this is her pick-up." She smiled sweetly. "The baby's grown up to be a cop."

His eyes hardened and it reminded her of the way he'd looked at Bill. "Neil, what happened to Bill?"

"Bill? Oh, I'm sorry. We thought it was you at first—"

"So you said, but he never walked into the burn, not Bill."

"It was a wild night. You'd left by then—"

"I left the same night. I hitched to Glasgow on a fish lorry and left the van with Bill. And he wasn't drunk when I left him."

He looked sceptical but he didn't contradict her. "It appears he went to get water and the bank gave way. There were marks . . . The burn was in spate of course."

She shook her head. "He must have had a few drinks after he left me. I wish I'd taken him to Glasgow. He wanted to come on this trip. He'd have been good company."

"You've got me now."

No strings? She tried to picture Neil at the old ferry on the Missouri; would his presence have made things better or worse? A thought struck her. "When you were in Arletta what were they saying about the guy who shot Wayne Chesler?"

"I don't know – refresh my memory. Wayne Chesler?"

"They said *nothing*? Don't you read the newspapers, watch TV?"

"Not much. I don't recall the name."

She settled herself, relishing the opportunity to tell the story to another person who would believe her. "Glenn Royal wasn't a relative, like he said, but a friend of Tina's lover. That was why she went straight to him when she reached the States. He lived with his brother in an old ferry house north of Arletta on the Missouri. I knew Glenn had died before I went down to the river but I thought his brother might give me some information on his cousin who died in the crash. But when I reached the ferry house Old Copper – that was the brother – he was in a well with the trap door closed."

Neil gaped at her. He'd removed his shades and his eyes were wide in disbelief. "What are you saying? He was dead?"

"A long time." She shuddered. "Although it needn't have been that long; there were rats. Then Wayne Chesler, another cowhand, he arrived and accused me of killing Old Copper – me! He got aggressive and I kneed him and ran. He chased me up a box canyon – cliffs all round, and those cliffs are just hard dust. Ghastly stuff. I did find a line however but when I was near the top Chesler came in sight and I thought he shot at me. But there was another guy on the rim and it seems it was him that fired, because Chesler was found shot in the bottom of the canyon. I got away and was rescued by another rancher. He said there was a stranger around, driving a Cherokee.

"The cops didn't believe me; they thought I was hallucinating because they said no one could climb those cliffs, so the rest was rubbish too. They were thick as two planks. To cap it all, when they went down to the ferry house there was no body in the well, and Old Copper's pick-up – which had been outside when I arrived – that was in the river. Now Old Copper's been washed up on a sandbar in the Missouri, Chesler's shot in the canyon, and there's a third guy on the loose. The cops say it's a gang killing. They were poaching bighorn sheep."

"This third guy . . . would you know him again?"

"No chance. And he'd know that. I was too far away. He was just a figure on top of the cliff."

165

He looked unhappy. "I don't like this. Are the police looking for him?"

"Probably not. He'll have got rid of the Cherokee and no one's had a better look at him than me. Two guys did but they're dead. What's wrong?"

He was looking past her, struggling to his feet. She heard an engine, stood up and looked through the cab. A pick-up was lurching towards them, crushing brittle weeds, loose objects in the back jumping and rattling. Hamish was barking crazily. Neil put his arm round her shoulders.

The pick-up stopped in a swirl of dust. "Hi!" Whit shouted, then quietly as he cut the engine: "Who's your friend, Kate?"

She walked to his window, Neil close behind. Hamish was leaping at his door. Whit ignored the dog and studied Neil from behind his shades.

"This is Neil Grant," she told him. "He's from Scotland." She turned to Neil. "Whit Cameron, Tina's son. We've got loads to talk about, Whit, and he's involved, to some extent. I mean, he was wanting to help with the book before I left." Which was untrue – and why was she justifying herself? She was acutely embarrassed, thinking it too ridiculous that this fat old man should follow her thousands of miles like a dog. "His father was a crofter at Cullen," she said wildly. "Right, Neil?"

"I own the hotel now," he reminded her, setting the record straight.

"So how do you come to be in the middle of the Arizona desert?" Whit asked politely, making conversation.

"I was following her."

Whit didn't turn a hair. "In that case you have to come back to our place. Providing our supper hasn't gone rotten by the time we reach home." He looked meaningly at the ice chest on the hot ground.

"We'll get back to the road right now," Kate assured him. She considered pointing out that they were off the road for Hamish's benefit, then decided that there was no call for her to explain her actions, and giggled. The hostility was palpable: poor old moonstruck Neil resenting the other man, and one who fitted his environment like a young lion. Young? Her eyes rested on Whit's shoulders where skin showed through a rent in the old blue shirt.

He was watching her intently. "I've got a good one at Mom's," he said and, in a different tone: "I'll wait till you reach the road; that truck can be a bitch to start."

He was proprietorial and intimate at the same time. Not all the hostility was on one side. She turned to the ice chest but Neil was there before her, lifting it lightly, demonstrating power. He wrapped the tarp round it and secured it with planks and the wheels, his movements watched with interest by Whit. "You had two punctures?" he asked.

"Tina insisted my tyres were clapped out."

"I see." He looked thoughtfully at the Bronco, then leaned across and opened his door for Hamish. "A lot of protection he is," he said, and she turned away, pretending not to understand.

They pulled back to the road: first Kate, then Neil, finally Whit, and when they reached the highway they stayed in the same formation. Whit was keeping a close eye on them.

Twelve

Rigoletto was ending in a welter of horror. "I adore grand opera," Tina announced, dancing into the kitchen in stone-washed denim and an apple-green blouse knotted below her breasts. Gold gleamed at her throat, there was a sheen on her hair and she reeked of Chanel. She picked up a spatula. "That guy's crazy about you," she said. "What do you propose to do about it?"

Kate spooned avocado flesh into the blender. "Use him as a guard dog? You want him? You're dressed for conquest."

"I haven't dressed!"

Kate studied her. "No more you have. You just give that impression." She peered. "You're wearing eye shadow – and blusher! Not to speak of—" She sniffed pointedly.

"You're jealous, honey."

"I don't get jealous." Kate squeezed a lime hard. "And Neil Grant? Give me a break."

"Where are our menfolk?" Tina asked brightly.

Kate grimaced, knowing she was being baited, refusing to rise. "They disappeared up the canyon."

"That poor guy will get sunstroke."

Kate looked out at the slopes where the saguaro stood tall, every spire catching the light as they did at this time of day. She was uneasy. After that ridiculous scene in his flat she'd thought she had the edge on Neil but his recent avowal of passion had unnerved her. And there was Whit, an unknown quantity. She sighed; she was an author, researching a book; everything else must be subordinated. She'd play it cool, be polite to Whit,

168

keep him at a distance, try to be nice to Neil. "How long is Whit staying?" she asked.

"I don't know. He was due some days off but if Ruthie Gilsdorf makes a fuss the sheriff may tell him to start looking just to keep Ruthie out of his hair."

"What are you talking about, Tina?"

"Didn't Whit tell you? No, he has other things on his mind, like how to cut out your fat friend. Don't look like that, he is fat. Ozzie Gilsdorf didn't come home last night and his mother's flipped. She's an alcoholic. Ask me, she never was stable. Ozzie will be with some of his pals in Exito or Montezuma doing whatever Ozzie and his pals do. Whit's not bothered about him, only about Ruthie. She's a pain."

Whit and Neil came up the steps, the dogs pushing past them. "They have grass everywhere in the Highlands," Whit said. "I can't imagine it."

"There's grass in the northern states," Tina said drily. "And heather. Go and sit yourselves down and I'll bring some beer. You can wash afterwards. You shouldn't have taken Neil in the canyon in all this heat, Whit."

"It was an education, ma'am. It's like an oasis where the water's flowing – and you've got deer! I'd like to be here for the stalking."

Tina raised an eyebrow – she hadn't called it stalking for decades. She followed them along the deck with cans of Budweiser. Neil was alight with enthusiasm and not just for the wildlife, frankly appreciative as he took in the silk blouse, the styled hair, the scent. "I should change," he said.

"Not at all." Tina dimpled. "You'll do very well as you are." Her eyes slid over Whit. "Both of you."

Subdued clicks sounded in the dim cave of the living room and, very softly, violins started to play. Neil turned wide eyes on his hostess. "*La Traviata!* You're a Verdi fan."

Whit was deadpan, Tina gave him a dreamy smile. Neil held his beer can as if he didn't know what to do with it. Tina said, "Hang on. I'll fetch a glass."

Whit sucked in his cheeks to hide a smile. It was Kate who brought the glass. "Why can't you drink like an uncivilised person?" she asked. She carried no drink for herself.

"Are you staying sober tonight?" Neil asked, as if they'd shared nights when she wasn't sober.

"You've never seen me drunk." She didn't miss the sudden set of Whit's jaw. She pulled out a chair and sat down. Whit went to the kitchen. Kate remembered she had resolved to try to be nice to Neil. "Where are you staying?" she asked politely.

"At a motel in Exito. Why d'you keep looking at your wrist?"

"I lost my watch." She glanced at the mountains. "I meant to look for it this evening. Too late now. I'll go up there tomorrow."

"What's that?" Whit asked, approaching with a tumbler containing whisky.

"I lost my watch when I got stuck coming over the Skeletons. Must have been when I was digging out the Jeep."

He placed the drink on the table in front of her. His bare arm touched hers. She looked at the glass blankly. Tina came out of the kitchen and collapsed on a chaise longue. She gestured at the mountains: "The magic hour." The shadows had climbed the slopes now and the saguaro were pale ghosts above a mysterious jungle, the last of the light flaming on the skyline. Music soared. "Just a wee bit too loud," she observed, glancing at Whit who rose and went into the living room. *La Traviata* sank to a murmur. "That's better," she said. "I can't do with being dominated at my own party." She turned to Neil. "Tell me about Cullen. Kate says Lady Lawrie is still alive."

"She lives in Edinburgh. My mother visits her occasionally. And Miss Bell – Madeleine – she still comes to Dunnas, that's the house way out on the point. And then there are the hotel guests: Alec Dunbar, Colonel Linklater – but would you remember the Lawries' friends?"

"A lot of young people came visiting," Tina said vaguely. "It was a happy place. You'll have changed a lot, put on weight maybe?"

"A little. I remember you." Neil glanced at the others. "Our local girls were very unsophisticated. Tina was different. People noticed her; still do of course."

Tina bloomed. "But you were only a boy when I was at Armidil," she pointed out, her eyes shining.

"Just a kid. You were very young too."

"You weren't a kid, Neil!" Kate exclaimed. "You went climbing with the Bells."

"That came later."

"What an adventurous life you've had." Tina was arch. "And Kate tells me you're writing a book yourself."

His glance at Kate was reproachful. "It's on the back burner."

"You're going to write a book?" Whit put in. "What's that about?"

"You've embarrassed me," Neil told Kate.

"Rubbish. He's been climbing and exploring all his life. He's *the* authority on mountain rescue. He kept journals. He's going to write his autobiography." Get out of that one, she thought viciously.

"Ah!" Tina exclaimed. "So you have a record of the Flying Fortress crash."

Kate flinched. She wouldn't have raised that subject in company, and she sensed a stiffening in the others, not to speak of Neil's reaction, which had to be embarrassment at least. How could he avoid giving pain to his hosts? She wondered how much Tina had had to drink.

"No," he said gently, "I didn't keep records until I started climbing, and even then I only wrote up incidents where I was involved."

"You weren't involved in the crash?" It was a question, not a statement.

"No, ma'am. I remember it, of course. And my dad helped – the crofters went up there – local people were used as guides." He was becoming flustered. "The rescue teams weren't all that

171

competent back in the forties; they didn't know their way around." His eyes pleaded with Kate to take over.

She guessed what was bothering him. "The Leica doesn't matter," she assured him. "I'm not going to mention it in my book. Probably the man who stole it is dead anyway. It's history."

"What's this?" Whit was fascinated. "Someone robbed the bodies?"

Kate couldn't believe it. She'd told Tina about the camera, hadn't she told her son? And one of those bodies was his own father. Had both Camerons drunk too much?

Neil broke a tense silence. He said casually, "There was gossip about a Leica disappearing. You discovered that, didn't you, love?"

She glared at him, stood up and stalked into the kitchen. Without a word Tina followed.

"Where did you buy your car?" Whit asked, blandly changing the subject.

"In Phoenix," Neil told him. "I had a Volks initially but the suspension went and I changed it for the Bronco."

"That explains the Arizona plates."

Neil smiled vaguely, lifted his glass and found it empty. "Another?" Whit asked, and went to the kitchen without waiting for a reply.

He found Kate and Tina huddled in the passage leading to the bedrooms. Kate rounded on him. "You knew about the camera! Why are you needling him?"

"Not needling. I'm a cop. I figure he knows who stole the camera."

She gasped, then nodded slowly, remembering Hector's reaction to her questions. Tina considered her son closely, the flirtatious act shed like a skin. After a moment they went back to the kitchen.

"Help yourselves," Tina ordered, lifting a lid to reveal the poached shrimps. The rice was basmati flavoured with parsley

172

and green onions, the sauce was made with cream and avocado with a touch of lime. Tina watched as Neil tasted and looked up.

"A little too rich perhaps?"

"Perfect. You can come and take over from my chef any time."

She smiled and the others murmured their appreciation. Hamish put a foot over the sill and the movement was caught by Whit. "No," he said firmly. Hamish stepped backwards and out of sight.

"Who runs the hotel when you're on holiday?" Tina asked Neil.

"I have a very good manageress. Gillean. Kate knows her."

"She's ultra-competent," Kate said. "And loyal – but then she's been with you for ever. Surely the two of you—" She broke off, raising an eyebrow. "And then there's your mother," she went on brightly. "She keeps her eye on things."

"And your father?" Tina asked.

"He died a long time ago."

"So how long have you had the hotel?"

"We took it over from Sir Ian. It was us turned the lodge into an hotel. We kept a lot of the old features – that mahogany furniture, remember it? – but we put in proper bathrooms and central heating over the years. From the outside it looks just the same. Inside it's pretty comfortable, wouldn't you say, Kate?"

"I've never stayed there."

"You've been in my flat."

"For a few minutes. Not long enough to give a verdict on it." She was furious; his tone had been suggestive.

Whit studied a shrimp as if he were considering dissecting it. "How long after Kate left Arletta did you arrive?" he asked. His flair for changing course was crude but effective.

Neil looked at her. "When were you there?"

"I don't know. It's in my diary. What makes it important?" Now she was fuming at Whit.

173

"Because," Tina reminded her, "you told me he didn't know anything about the murders. I mean, the place must have been humming!"

"I spoke to the librarian," Neil said uncertainly. "Barbara Lomas. She may have said something about poachers but I wouldn't connect them with Kate. Why should I?"

"Why?" Kate repeated, amazed. "Because you'd gone there to find Glenn Royal, and you knew I had too – and it was his brother who was one of the victims."

"But I didn't know that! I knew there was a pick-up in the river but I don't remember anything being said about bodies. Maybe people wouldn't tell me; after all, I was a stranger – you keep quiet about local scandal. Wall of silence and all that. Remember the trouble you had, Kate? Trying to get our crofters to talk?"

"That was different. Hector was covering up. Your mother as well."

He laughed. "Mother and Hector had – well, that's Mother's business. What I can say is that if Hector was a little light-fingered in his youth, Mother would shut up like an oyster once you got on the subject of missing Leicas."

Kate frowned. "I don't think I knew about the Leica when I talked to your mother."

"It was Glenn Royal who talked about the camera, wasn't it?" Tina put in. "He never said anything to me, but of course, when I was at Slaughter Creek he hadn't been to Scotland. He went afterwards."

"Why did he go?" Neil asked.

Tina said calmly: "The same reason as me: he was fond of Whit's dad."

"It could be true," Kate said absently. "No one's going to go all that way just for a camera."

Coffee was taken on the deck, the bug-light burning at the far corner: a little gold lamp eclipsed by the stars. Whit poured brandy with a steady hand. Neil looked out at the dark canyon. "Don't you feel vulnerable sitting out here?" he asked. "Exito's full of horror stories about vicious criminals coming across the border at night."

"The dogs are out," Whit said lazily.

"You mean, out as in patrolling?"

"We all do that on the border: let the dogs loose at night, although ours are loose all the time."

Kate studied her brandy, remembering Hamish fast asleep on her bed.

"Suppose the villains are armed?" Neil asked.

"We'd hear the shots. We'd be forewarned."

"You'd lose your dogs."

"We're not sentimental about animals around here. They're guards, not pets."

Kate knew Neil was being warned not to come here uninvited. Tina said nothing. From not far away, in the canyon, there came a series of banshee yelps and wails.

"The dogs don't chase coyotes?" Neil asked.

"No. Their job is to stay close to the house."

"Isn't it a strain, living like this: always having to be on your guard? Don't you worry about your mother?"

"Not at all," Tina said cheerfully. "He never worried about me in his life. Like he says, there are the dogs, and they're only the first line of defence. We have plenty of firepower – and any low life would know that. It's seldom I use a rifle."

Kate turned slowly. "You have to sometimes? Against people?"

"Not often." There was a smile in Tina's voice. "And the first time I fire low, but one can't always be accurate in the dark."

"You're having me on," Neil said.

"She hit a guy once," Whit put in. "Fortunately that time she had a shotgun and he was some distance away. Pellets don't do much damage unless you're close. Now, things being like they are, she uses a rifle."

"What was that guy doing?" Neil asked.

Tina didn't reply. Whit said carelessly, "He was probably a drugs runner, scouting for a new route. They're always doing that. Fast as one route gets plugged by law enforcement they go some place else. That one didn't come back."

Tina said, "You must stay over, Neil. It's not safe to be on these roads at night."

"Thank you, no. I'll enjoy the drive back."

"As you will."

Kate pricked up her ears at the formality. There was an expectant air about the company as if they were waiting for something to happen, or to be said. She wondered why the main lights hadn't been switched on. Tina's voice seemed to come from a distance, low and clear with the undertone of Scotland: "They were telling me that one person survived the crash, that he was still warm when the rescuers got there."

After a long pause during which he could have been waiting for someone to support or perhaps restrain his hostess, Neil said diffidently, "You're asking about the Flying Fortress?"

"What else?" Tina said in that eerie voice.

Kate distinctly heard Whit's whisper: "Humour her." Tina had to be drunk.

"Yes." Neil was at his most comfortable or comforting. "There were rumours. There always are. That at least one person survived."

"Yes," Tina repeated. "And he kept a diary."

"That too."

"And the diary was never found."

"Like the camera, yes."

"Was it true? Did someone survive?"

"No, ma'am."

"How can you be so sure?"

"I'm not," Neil said. "I'm trying to – I wasn't there."

Kate moved restlessly. "No," she said loudly. "He's right, Tina. No one survived."

"How do *you* know?" Suddenly Tina was back with them, fierce and demanding.

"There was another rumour." Kate refused to be intimidated. "About someone being on the mountain ahead of the rescuers, but that was Dr Pratt." She turned to Neil. "Alec Dunbar told you about him?"

"I know he was the chap you went to see on Skye."

She turned back to Tina. "I told you I couldn't remember when he reached the plane but I lied; he was there only two days after the crash. Everyone was dead – all of them cold. I'm sorry, Tina, Whit – but there you are. He did say someone might have survived the crash initially but he would have died soon afterwards—"

"How soon?" Tina was harsh.

"Oh, Tina! After a Flying Fortress struck? Whit?" It was a cry for help.

"She's right." He bit it off.

"Go on," Tina said. "Is there more?"

"Well, someone had survived a short time. Not Chuck," she added quickly. "Dr Pratt knew because the guy had a diary, and a pencil in his hand. He was dead when Pratt got there however. But he'd managed to write something about Chuck" – her voice dropped – "and then he died. The doctor said he could have been writing before the plane struck, of course."

"What did he write?" Tina whispered.

"There was no telling. The words were obscured – by blood." She went on quickly, "All the others were killed on impact." She didn't know but it might afford a shred of comfort.

After a while Tina asked: "What happened to the diary?"

Kate sketched a shrug. "It disappeared. Personally I think the RAF suppressed it because it could be proof that someone survived, and the thinking would be that if the team had got there sooner they might have saved him. Actually Dr Pratt said no one could have survived even if they managed to get him off the mountain alive."

Chairs creaked as people fidgeted: signs of the party starting to break up. Everyone had taken as much as they could stand of this sad old history, and yet they had subscribed to it themselves. Not Neil perhaps but even Kate had contributed to the drama, although in her case she felt she'd been driven to it. As for Tina and Whit, she viewed their interest in the plane crash as positively morbid.

They were getting to their feet now but the evening was not yet over. Neil gave events a final twist. He stopped at the head of the steps to say firmly: "See me to my car, Kate."

She was lost for words. She heard Tina's quick intake of breath. "I want a word with you," he added, and it sounded like a threat.

Whit said, as if he were included, "I appreciate that; all the same it's not a good idea. People are vulnerable at night."

"*Vulnerable?*" Neil's voice wasn't under control.

"Vulnerable to whom?" Kate asked weakly, aware that Tina had gone indoors, unable to believe that an evening, admittedly fraught, could end in disaster.

"What you have to say can be said here," Whit told him.

"It's private," Neil said thickly. "Between her and me."

"We don't have any private business," Kate said.

"Yes we have. You haven't explained our relationship to them." Tina came to stand on the door sill and he appealed to her. "We have an understanding. She can't do this to me."

"Bollocks!" Kate was livid.

Tina said brightly, "Locking-up time. I'm about to make the rounds." In the faint light Kate saw that she had what must be the rifle under her arm.

Neil turned to Kate. "Come back home with me," he urged. "It's too dangerous for you over here. You're mixed up in two murders in Montana and once the police find you the gunman will know where you are."

"You're mad," Kate said. "Or you've had too much to drink. Go back to your motel."

"Listen to me! I've only got your welfare at heart. I'm your friend, Kate; you need me more than ever. That day when we were climbing you were sweet—"

"Come on," Whit said roughly, taking the rifle from his mother. "I'll walk you to the car. No knowing what you might meet out there this time of night. You want to watch your step."

178

They went down the stairs, trailed by the dogs. The women drew together and waited in silence. When they heard an engine start Tina reached inside the living room and brought out another gun. Kate followed her down the steps and round the side of the house; at that point they heard another engine fire. There was a rush of feet as Hamish arrived.

"Where's Carl?" Kate asked.

"Seeing them off."

The doberman was on the drive, a statue planted in pale dust. Dogs and women watched the two sets of tail lights receding across the desert. "Making sure he does go back to town," Tina observed with satisfaction. "That's my boy."

"You were bowled over by Neil at the start of the evening."

"Was I, honey?" She turned and led the way back to the house.

"We have to talk," Kate said.

"In the morning. I'm exhausted. I'm going to take a pill and knock myself out so I don't have nightmares . . ." She was speaking as Kate followed her through the house. She paused on the threshold of her bedroom. "You want a pill? No? Goodnight then. Take Hamish in with you."

Take Hamish? What was she afraid of? Neil giving Whit the slip and coming back to rape her in her bed?

An hour or so later, unable to sleep, she went to her bathroom for a drink of water and became aware of a soft murmur from the master bedroom. No doors were closed in this house because of the dogs. She crept along the passage and listened. Tina was watching television. Back in bed she decided that Tina was waiting for a telephone call from Whit. Who hadn't returned.

Thirteen

The morning was warm and muggy, high cirrus veiling the sun: insect weather. Tina was preparing breakfast with the glass panels slid wide but the screens in place. "Where's Whit?" Kate asked.

"He stayed in town, honey. Did you sleep well?"

"Eventually. He followed Neil all the way to Exito?"

"Not to say followed, but he saw him to the highway and then remembered he had things to do this morning so he kept going, went to his own place." Tina wouldn't meet her eye.

"There were undercurrents last night."

"There were?"

"Oh, come on!"

Tina turned to face her, spreading her hands helplessly. "It was that camera. Neil as good as said one of the crofters stole it: 'light-fingered in his youth', remember? His mother was friendly with this Hector."

Kate was sullen. "There was more to the tension than just a camera."

"Oh yes." Tina was sure of herself now. "No doubt about that. But there, Whit's a grown man; you've got to work it out between you."

Kate's jaw dropped. "You're blaming me?"

"Blame? Of course not. It was you said there were undercurrents. How do you think Whit feels? He's unattached, so are you; you're both attracted, and along comes the fat man, making snide remarks about your relationship with him, and

180

insisting you see him to his car when you're plainly dead against being alone with him."

Kate sat down and buttered a slice of toast. "I don't want to talk about it."

Tina didn't remind her that last night it was she who'd wanted to talk. "I'm doing bacon and eggs," she said. "You'll spoil your appetite."

"Nothing spoils my appetite." Kate looked at her wrist. "Damn! I must find my watch. I'll put the wheels on the Jeep and go up there this morning. You know that pool in the little canyon east of the trail? How deep is it?"

"Who knows? The Indians say it's bottomless. Black Tinaja, it's called: 'tinaja' as in 'jar'. The water never drains out, it just evaporates some. Last year a lion fell in and drowned. The surface gets too low and the animals overbalance, trying to reach the water. God knows how many skeletons there must be at the bottom."

"Can you get to the top without walking round the pool?"

"There might be game trails. The deer feed on the mesquite in the fall so they could come down from the top, and they got more sense than try to walk round the water. What's your interest in it?"

"Only that it would be a short-cut to the top, save me plodding up the main trail in the heat."

"So long as you don't go near the tinaja."

Kate wondered why Tina didn't offer to go with her and then considered that for a woman in her sixties walking in the heat of the day could be dangerous.

It was late when she got away. She drove down the valley, passing below the Indian camp, and came to the place where the trail took off to cross the Skeletons. She was amazed to think how much had happened since she was here two days ago: Tina, Whit, and now Neil. What was she going to do about Neil?

She reached the place where people had parked below the little side canyon and halted, choking as her dust caught up

181

with her. The line of the main track was visible from here, too visible: steep and rocky and full in the glare of the sun. In contrast the side canyon was lush with little trees, at least in its lower reaches. She decided to risk the short-cut; she would go and look at it, try to find a game trail. If there was no path she'd give up, go home and come back in the evening with a torch. The stony track would be a different proposition once the sun went down.

Deer had worn a narrow way through the mesquite and in a few minutes she came out on gravel as wide and regular as a road. The layered rock on either side was in shades of brown and cream. It was very quiet, the only sound the crunch of her steps in the chippings. The air in the canyon was bright and hot; the cloud veil was thinning.

A rock step showed ahead. About a hundred feet above, on her right, was a broken crag, cliff swallows' nests plastered below an overhang.

In the wash bedrock came into view, rising gently until it was above eye level. She walked up the slab and stopped. Below her the water lay like oil, the moths motionless on the surface. Behind her, in the main canyon, she heard an engine. She listened, straining her ears.

The engine stopped. She waited for doors to bang. There was no sound. Her eyes searched the undergrowth for some sign of a trail. There it was: a broken twig and the print of a small hoof in the dust.

She moved quietly up the slope to the foot of the crag. The swallows erupted and circled like gnats, twittering in alarm. She looked down the canyon and ducked. A pick-up stood beside her Jeep, its doors wide. No one was visible.

She tried to recall the appearance of Whit's truck, of Tina's. All pick-ups looked the same. There was no reason why she should be suspicious of this one; after all, it could be the Indians. But it could be anyone.

She crouched, watching the bed of the wash through a screen of brittlebush. She could see a short section of gravel and the slabby rock below the pool. Everything else was obscured by shrubs and cacti. Above her the swallows were returning to their nests.

She heard footsteps first, no voices. Ozzie Gilsdorf came into view, treading the gravel heavily, darting nervous glances at the slopes. His hand hovered above a gun on his hip. Kate relaxed a little. On steep rocky ground she had the advantage over Ozzie.

He looked back and said something. She gasped. Neil had appeared, carrying a rifle. Where did he get *that*? And what was he carrying it for? Or for whom. She started to breathe quickly, checked, tried to return to normal, to convince herself that these two were poaching – or Neil was terrified of rattlesnakes, but – a rifle?

Ozzie stepped out of sight. He must be on the edge of the pool because Neil had stopped too, on the bedrock. He pointed, indicating that deceptive traverse round the water by way of the sloping shelf. Their voices were audible now but not the words.

She cringed as the swallows erupted again. A kestrel was perched on one of the nests, hunched against frantic onslaughts. Below her Neil was staring up at the crag. Ozzie reappeared, focused on something at his own level. He turned and spoke. Neil nodded and directed his attention to the rocky skyline, obviously scouting a route. Ozzie unholstered his pistol and moved purposefully towards the game trail that would bring him to her hiding place.

A rifle roared, the sound amplified by the canyon walls. Neil swung round wildly, losing his footing, landing on one knee in the gravel. Kate watched open-mouthed. He stood up, glaring about, glancing at Ozzie who was lurching to his feet, clutching his shoulder. They were both shouting. Neil fired in the air and they dived for the undergrowth.

The kestrel had disappeared, the swallows were going mad, the other rifle fired again – twice. Twigs shattered, gravel spattered, then there was silence except for the birds.

Kate raised her head cautiously, studying the slopes. On the other side of the canyon, above her own level, light glinted on metal. There was movement at the mouth of the canyon too, where two people were transferring stuff from the first pick-up to a second which had arrived unnoticed. The newcomers looked like Indians – and that suggested that the gunman opposite was one as well because the men at the trucks showed no concern over the firing.

Kate stayed in cover, thinking that the gunman had been watching all the time, knew she was there then, but he must be on her side; he'd fired when Ozzie was about to discover her. She wondered why she should be concerned about discovery by either Ozzie or Neil; Neil wouldn't be bothered – surely – because she'd seen them start out on a poaching expedition. And was it sinister, was it even odd, that the two of them should have joined forces? Any mystery lay with the unseen sniper, but then an explanation offered itself: the Indians could be jealously guarding their deer from incomers. But whatever the explanation Neil was trigger-happy and no way would she make a move until the canyon was clear.

She didn't have long to wait. Doors banged, an engine revved, the strange pick-up started down the track and one of its occupants yelled derisively and fired in the air.

Within a few minutes Neil and Ozzie appeared in the main canyon, Ozzie with his right shoulder swathed in his shirt. And then, to Kate's fury, as the fat boy made for his pick-up, Neil ran towards her Jeep.

They halted between the vehicles, facing each other, Neil gesturing angrily, then he moved to the driver's side of the pick-up, Ozzie climbed in the other side and they took off in a cloud of dust.

"I thought he was going to take the Jeep. I had the keys but he could have hot-wired it. What's going on, Tina? Someone was shooting at them! Ozzie's wounded."

Kate had emerged from the canyon to see dust streaming

behind the trucks, both speeding south. She had raced back to the house to pour out the story to Tina, who had listened intently but with less surprise than might have been expected. "I thought he was up to no good," she said. "Now we know."

"We don't *know*. The aggression was all on the Indians' side. Was that Lonzo and his lad stealing from Ozzie's truck? And who was it shot Ozzie? No one shot at me." Tina plucked her lip. "Well?" Kate was belligerent. "You had it in for Neil last night. Why? I can understand Whit's hostility but you said yourself: you'd leave it to us; you implied it had nothing to do with you."

"If by 'it' you mean those two guys fighting over you, it shouldn't be any of my business. What concerns me now is what happened—" She hesitated, then added lamely, "I'm expecting Whit any time. He'll tell you."

"Tell me now."

"Kate, you're a bully, d'you know that?" Tina turned to the coffee pot. "Whit called after you left," she said, pouring the coffee. "Asked where you were. When I told him you'd gone to look for your watch, he said I was to go straight to Lonzo and tell him to find you and bring you home. I guess that's how Lonzo and Tony came to be in the canyon."

"So who . . . that was Maria? Lonzo's wife was firing at Neil? No, it was Ozzie she hit. Why?"

"He could have been the easier target. She needed to hit one of them before they caught up with you."

"You're not suggesting Neil was after me! Tina, it doesn't fit. The old guy's obsessed with me. He'd—"

"He's putting on an act." They jumped. Whit opened the screen door and stepped over the sill. "You're all right?" he asked Kate, his eyes vulnerable.

She started to speak but was overborne by Tina: "Whit, Ozzie Gilsdorf's with him!"

He stared, amazed. "Ozzie? So that's where he is. But they weren't together at the motel—"

"He's wounded," Kate said coldly. "One of your Indian

friends shot him. Tina says it was Maria, she says Neil was after me! I don't believe it."

"I haven't told her, son. Anything." No 'sweetie'. Tina was serious. "What did you find out about the car?"

"It's stolen." He said it absently, staring at Kate. "Did you actually see Maria shoot Ozzie? And where's Grant now?"

"She was at Black Tinaja," Tina rushed in, and stopped. "Tell him, Kate."

They sat at the kitchen table and she repeated her story, ending with the observation she had made to Tina: "It was the Indians who were in the wrong: they were stealing from Ozzie's truck. They shot at him; there was absolutely no suggestion that Neil intended to harm me. What made you say he was putting on an act? You mean last night?"

He ignored the questions. "He saw your Jeep at the mouth of the canyon. He came after you."

"So would you have done—"

"Kate!" It was Tina, urgent and angry. "Hear what Whit's got to say."

Kate turned to him. "What have you been doing this morning?" she asked tightly.

"Telephoning. I called Barbara Lomas to find out what kind of wheels he in Montana. She didn't know; he was never in Arletta. Miz Lomas never saw him, didn't know who I was talking about." Kate was silenced. "He could have got information from the TV and newspapers," Whit went on, "but why not tell the truth; why pretend he was in Arletta when he wasn't?"

"You'd expect it to be the other way round," Tina put in, "that he'd want to distance himself from a place where there'd been two murders."

"He didn't know about the murders," Kate said. Her tone sharpened. "What was that about a stolen car?"

"The Bronco," Whit said. "I doubt that he bought it in Phoenix, even though its plates are off of a Cadillac stolen in Casa Grande last February."

"Why shouldn't he have bought it in Phoenix?"

"Casa Grande's too close. The Cadillac would have been taken across the state line, plates changed, and its original plates put on another stolen vehicle – like the Bronco. If Grant's got documents for it, they'll be forged."

"He could have bought it in good faith."

"Possibly, but not in Phoenix. Why say he did? And I need to know what he had before the Bronco."

"What are you getting at?"

"He figures it could have been a Cherokee," Tina said.

Kate's mouth opened but no sound came.

"He gave me the slip," Whit told his mother. "Must have checked out of the motel while I was telephoning. Now what's his next move? They're heading south, you said." He glanced at Kate, who could scarcely follow all this. "You have to tell her, Mom, so's she knows what we're up against. What I'd like to know is where he's hidden that Bronco. Is he making for it and a quick getaway? He knows I'll have called Arletta this morning, that I'm on to him now. There could be evidence inside that truck. I'm going after them, see what's happening. I want you both to stay here till I get back. OK?"

He left. Kate looked as if she were in shock. Tina brought her a glass of whisky with a smidgen of water, how she liked it. She called the dogs and sent them to lie on the deck. "With Lonzo and Tony on his trail he can't double back," she said cheerfully, trying to rouse Kate. "All the same, I feel more secure with the dogs out there."

"Actually it's Neil chasing the Indians."

"Ah yes." Tina smiled slyly. "So he is."

Kate drank some whisky. "'Putting on an act', Whit said. Was he implying Neil didn't mean any of it: all that stuff about me? Okay, I know it sounds like hindsight but I must admit I didn't feel comfortable out there in the desert yesterday when he was rabbiting on. It didn't ring true; he seemed theatrical, or rather, the words were, as if he'd been reading a manual on how to express passion."

187

"He could be plausible," Tina admitted. "I was side-tracked myself. I thought he was just a thief. I made a mistake; I should have told you I suspected him but, whatever he was, I did think he was in love with you, well – infatuated, and it was difficult to know how to play it. I never considered he was out to get you, although Whit didn't trust him an inch . . . Now everything starts to fall into place. Of course he was in Montana before you . . . You do realise that?"

"Whit said he was never in Arletta!"

"He would have been somewhere in the area. You said Arletta is some distance from the river. The fellow was probably camping out. Think of the man on top of the cliff, the one the police say was the third poacher. Could it have been Neil?"

Kate massaged her temples. At length she nodded. "He was heavy, like Neil. But that guy had a Cherokee and Neil's driving a Bronco—" She trailed off helplessly.

"And Whit's trying to find out what he had before the Bronco. You can change cars easily enough given you have plenty of cash and you're not bothered about documentation. Criminals do it all the time."

"A thief. You said he's a thief. You didn't mean the Bronco. What did he steal?"

Tina looked away and when she spoke it was not to answer the question, not immediately. "He killed Chesler," she said. "If it was Neil on top of the cliffs, he was the killer. He must have put Old Copper's body in the river so I guess he killed him too." Kate was shaking her head in disbelief. Tina nodded grimly. "You want to know why? I'll tell you why. He was the first man to reach the crash. The Flying Fortress."

"Oh no! Never. You're quite wrong. He was only a child—"

"He was fifteen."

There was a long pause. Kate breathed deeply, her eyes glazed. At last she said in a small flat voice: "And he used to go on the hill with his father poaching the deer, stealing sheep . . . He was a natural climber; all the Bells ever had to do was show him how to tie knots." Enlightenment dawned. "The crash! The Grants were poor as church mice before the crash. Afterwards they were rich enough to buy the lodge. Tina, *what did he steal?*"

Tina smoothed the table as if it were a cloth. "Diamonds," she said. "A diamond necklace and a brooch: diamonds and rubies. Chuck had them in a body-belt next his skin."

"No," Kate whispered. "Neil couldn't have – they were all killed on impact."

"At least one man wasn't. What did he write in his diary? 'Boy killed Chuck'?"

Kate's hand was at her throat. She was seeing new horrors. "You're saying he killed that man as well and stole the diary?"

"Took the diary, yes, and our stake in the new life we'd planned, Chuck and me. Maybe he didn't kill anyone, maybe he just walked away; he never told anyone, did he? Never alerted the rescuers to where the crash was, and one man still alive. We don't know what happened there except he took the jewels and walked away. 'Course, if he'd reported the crash the searchers might have found the guy still alive and he'd have told them a boy had been there already and robbed his mate. Either way it goes that boy was a killer."

"How can you be sure Neil stole the jewels? It could have been anyone who was at the crash."

"Because the Grants bought the lodge. And the son is in this country killing people who might tell you the truth. You know why he wormed his way in here? To find out how much we knew. Chuck might not have told me about the jewels, in which case I wasn't dangerous and there was nothing I could tell you."

"Illogical. He knew you were looking for something at the site of the crash, and you were followed by Glenn Royal. Obviously you both knew about the jewels. Last night he could have been trying to find out if you'd told me."

Tina said thoughtfully, "It was me asking the questions, not

189

him. I think we're both wrong. What he was doing last night was finding out what our security was like: dogs, firearms, who lived here, all that. Well, why not?" Seeing Kate's scepticism, she went on, "He's got ulterior motives; he followed you into that canyon. What was the rifle for? Rattlers?"

Kate held her mug in both hands as if she were cold. Neil, a killer. Tina was being melodramatic. The jewellery, the whole show was way over the top. Tina had evolved a fantasy over the years. *Diamonds and rubies?* "Where did the jewels come from in the first place?" she asked, deliberately casual.

Tina contemplated her for a moment. "What's it matter now? Whit knows, and if he can accept what we did – me and his daddy – I'm not about to be bothered by your reaction. What happened was I was working for this wealthy woman, a call-girl but very high-class. Chuck and me, we had nothing" – she shrugged – "so we stole her jewels. Not all of them, we left her some. We weren't greedy."

Kate gulped. "Redistribution of wealth? But did you really think you'd find them lying on top of a mountain? Did Glenn?"

"It was a long shot, I admit, but I thought there might be something, like thrown out by the impact? There was no word of them being found, you see, and yet the bodies were still there, more or less as they'd been sitting, so where were the stones? I realised after I'd been up there that they had to've been stolen but what could I do? We'd stolen them in the first place. After I came down from the mountain my life changed. I'd lost Chuck but the baby was on the way. I didn't make a decision, things just seemed to happen. Like I said, you can't go back, back to where I had a man I loved and we were rich and were going to live happily ever after out on the prairies. I'd lost everything except the baby and the dream of America. So I came to America."

Kate said, "You don't think Glenn—" She faltered and started again: "You didn't know he'd gone to Scotland—"

"I knew. He made the trip to see if he could find out anything from the crofters and the police. The story about the Leica was just that: a story. There never was a Leica. I kept in touch with Glenn until he died."

"You said you didn't!"

"Naturally." Tina was equable. "There was no call to tell you the truth. I might never have done so but for what's happened. I've done a hell of a lot of lying in my time. Had to protect Whit." She grinned. "What would the sheriff say if he knew his mom was a jewel thief?"

The heat built up until by the middle of the afternoon even the air seemed parched. The women and dogs sprawled on the deck, a pitcher of lemonade for the women, a bucket of water for the dogs. A rifle and a shotgun lay on the chaise longue. Suddenly Carl lifted his head and listened. Hamish gave the ghost of a growl. Tina opened her eyes and reached for the rifle. Carl stood up and trotted down the steps, followed by Hamish. "It's Whit," Tina said, replacing the rifle before either of them had heard an engine. She rose and went to the kitchen.

He was smiling as he came up the steps, the dogs falling over themselves in welcome. His eyes were on Kate and she felt her face, her whole body relax and soften, and she loved it.

"You want something stronger than lemonade?" Tina called.

"Not right now, Mom; I'm dry." He sat down. "Not half as dry as those two guys must be," he added, still smiling. Kate said nothing, absorbing the look of him.

Tina came back with a tall tumbler and ice. He filled it from the pitcher, drank and refilled it. He laughed and shook his head. "You know what Lonzo did? Drove full tilt for the salt behind that big dune there where he couldn't be seen by Grant tearing after him. Then he went round the bay and when Grant arrived there were the tracks leading straight to the salt and Lonzo on the other side so close he was almost in range. No one could fire though: one was driving and the other one couldn't use his right arm." He addressed his mother. "That was Maria, of course, winged Ozzie at the tinaja."

Tina snorted. "Grant got himself mired?"

191

"Up to his axles. They're walking now." He turned back to Kate. "There's this salt flat way down in the south of the valley: one big stretch and little bays. What Lonzo did was leave tracks to the shoreline and then drive round on pebbles that don't show tracks. If they do, Grant didn't see them and apparently Ozzie doesn't know our valley, or maybe he couldn't stop Grant. He tried to cut straight across the salt and, of course, he sank. The crust will bear a man in places, never a truck."

"What's Ozzie about, joined up with him?" Tina asked.

"They met the night I came over the mountains," Kate said. "I convinced myself then that the Bronco hadn't been following me, that I'd imagined it, but it had to be Neil driving. He saw me leaving Ozzie's house and he must have stopped and persuaded Ozzie to say where I'd gone. I wonder if Ozzie told him he'd sent me down the wrong valley. It would make a bond between them: they both had an interest in me."

"This is worse than ever," Tina protested, "the two of them together, coming after her." She appealed to Whit. "How could Ozzie leave home just like that – or did he? Was he away hunting like his mother said, and they met up again by accident?"

"More like by arrangement." Whit was grim. "For my money Ozzie'd go with anyone who promised him fun – of a certain kind, although I doubt Grant told him what he intended, maybe just that he was Kate's friend, partner, whatever. He'd say he needed a guide to follow her, someone who knew the country. Ozzie's IQ is very low; he'd be flattered, and money would make the offer one he couldn't refuse."

"What's going on in Neil's mind?" Kate mused. "He doesn't need Ozzie."

"No?" Whit's eyes were bleak. "He needs help and he needs a fall guy. You never asked what Lonzo and Tony were doing at Ozzie's truck; why they didn't come up the canyon when Mom had told them to find you and bring you back to the house. You told them to look out for Grant, Mom?"

"Yes, but I said he was driving a Bronco."

192

"That explains it. Lonzo thought Ozzie was around, not Grant. He guessed you could be in Tinaja Canyon, Kate, because there was no sign of you on the main trail. So he sent Maria after you meaning to follow himself when he'd looked to see what was attracting the flies in Ozzie's truck."

"He had been hunting then," Tina said. "He was carrying deer meat?"

"Well – meat. Two parcels of hamburger, and inside – like the beef was moulded round them – a mess of cyanide pellets."

Kate looked blank. "For coyotes?" Tina asked. "Why poison coyotes? The Gilsdorfs don't own any land."

"For these." Whit glowered at Carl and pulled Hamish's ears.

"No!" Tina cried. "Why?"

"And cans of gas on the back of the pick-up. I figure Ozzie bought that – and the pellets – in Exito. Grant would attract too much attention with his accent. Besides, they'd remember him."

"Gas?" Kate repeated. "Oh, petrol. What for?"

"We worked it out," Whit said. "Lonzo and me and Tony. The gas might be innocent but taken with the poisoned meat . . . Suppose you were planning to torch a house where there were guard dogs, how would you get past the dogs?" He looked at Tina. "Did you talk to her?"

"She knows everything, son."

He regarded Kate warily; with her now a party to the family secret he'd be wondering how she'd taken it. "The guy's crazy," he told her. "House fires aren't that uncommon in this neck of the woods – nor's arson, come to that. I don't think he'd have cared if he'd taken out two others in order to get the one he wanted."

"Of course he didn't care!" Tina exclaimed. "He needed to get you and me too. The jewellery, Whit!" She was seething with impatience. "If he would kill Kate because I'd told her that your dad was carrying a fortune on him, suppose I hadn't told

193

her? Like you said: he's crazy. He killed two men in Montana, he was prepared to kill Kate – what? What was that, Kate?"

"I said perhaps he tried."

"What's this?" Whit demanded. "He tried before this morning? When?"

She inhaled deeply. "Bill – my climbing partner back home. I left him my van. Neil said the bank collapsed and he fell in the flooded burn." She glared at Whit. "He was a climber! Fell in the burn? Never. It was a wild night, the rain lashing down; Bill would have had his hood up when he got out of the van. Neil was waiting. He thought Bill was me."

"That would make it three he killed already," Tina said. "You see, Whit, even if I hadn't told Kate yet, he would kill me because I could tell her any time. And you had to go as well, love."

"You didn't know Grant was the guy who stole the jewels; you had suspicions—"

"Guilt. He'd have a guilty conscience. He'd figure the reason we were hostile was because we *knew*. He was panicking. We had to be silenced: all three of us to die in a blazing house after they'd put the dogs out of action."

"And he'd do a runner and leave Ozzie with traces of gas and poisoned hamburger in his truck. Like I said: Ozzie was to be the fall guy. Grant's not crazy, he's bad."

"He did it to save face," Kate said unexpectedly. They stared at her. "He's a hero back home," she reminded them. "A celebrity. He couldn't live once the truth came out: that he'd robbed a body. He would have killed himself. He tried a long shot: killing the people who knew. And he's out there now." She glanced at the hot slopes. "How are you going to find him?"

"No hurry. He can't get away." Whit poured more lemonade. "Lonzo's keeping an eye on them. Even old Lucy's out on a mule. Her and Maria have binoculars – probably Grant's. They were in Ozzie's pick-up. Ozzie could have been watching this house, could have had a camp somewhere nearby. If we could find it we might find the Bronco. Could be some proof in it that he was in Arletta before you arrived: like credit slips, receipts—" He trailed off.

"Yes," Kate said, voicing his thought: "No clever killer is going to leave evidence that could incriminate him so obviously. But Grace Bierman, Chesler's employer, she said a stranger was at the ranch recently. She said he was from Texas – or Chesler said he was. But she's senile, I doubt that she'd go into court."

"You're way ahead," Tina said. "Is she on the phone?"

"No."

"Call Barbara Lomas," Whit said. "Ask her if she can persuade this lady to give us a description of the guy." He stood up. "I guess I'd better make a show of searching for them." He shrugged. "Big desert though and only one road, and they'll be afraid to use that because of the Indians. Be difficult to find them in this country, all cut up with those old washes and reefs."

When he'd gone Kate telephoned Arletta but there was no reply. Barbara would be in the library. "I'm sure it wouldn't be any good," she told Tina, "You can't believe what Grace says."

They looked at each other. "The Bronco could be quite close," Tina said meaningly. "Far enough away that the dogs wouldn't be aware of intruders, but close enough that Ozzie could watch our comings and goings, like you going out this morning."

"Neil knew. I mentioned I was going to look for my watch when he was here last night. All the same, it's something to do. Let's go and find that Bronco."

Tina took her rifle. Whit had said Neil and Ozzie were miles away in the south of the valley but it would be a long while before anyone would feel safe without a firearm.

At the bottom of the track Tina turned the pick-up north, drove for a mile and returned slowly. They were watching for the imprint of tyres leaving the road. The ground to the west, away from the mountains, was very rough: a labyrinth of dry washes and broken ridges with, here and there, a shattered reef that appeared diminutive but was probably a few hundred feet in height. Everything except the reefs and washes was covered by brush and cacti.

The tracks were obvious when they were looking for them: several sets in a wash about a mile from the house. Set back in the desert was a rock-rimmed mesa. "Ozzie could have watched from there," Tina said, and started down the wash.

The Bronco was obvious too, providing you were following its tracks. It was concealed in a grove of palo verde and all its doors were locked. Through the smoked glass they could dimly make out a blanket covering stuff in the back.

"This model has central locking," Tina said. "We'll have to force a window. Would a coat hanger work with central locking?"

"Smash the windscreen." Kate wasn't bothered with niceties.

There was a heavy wrench in the pick-up and she got to work, both of them grimly impervious to the noise and the unaccustomed vandalism. Once inside she passed out a large rucksack and a flight bag. They took the luggage to a patch of sand and started to go through the contents, looking for anything that would give them a line on Neil's movements in the States.

"He'd have his passport with him," Kate murmured after a while. "Would he risk leaving anything else important?"

Tina sat back on her heels. "He can't be thinking straight. How does he reckon to get away with this for Heaven's sake? Setting Ozzie up for a fall guy is sheer desperation – surely? He must have left a trail of clues."

"If he has, it wasn't here." Kate started on the pockets of the rucksack. After a while she said hopelessly, "There's nothing. It looks as if he destroyed all his documents."

They'd found clothing, toilet and shaving gear, sun block, sticky plasters, paperbacks. There was no airline ticket for the return to the UK and no documentation for any vehicle.

"The glove compartments?" Tina suggested.

Kate searched the interior meticulously. She found candy wrappers, an empty spectacles case, a couple of ballpoint pens, toothpicks, a corkscrew, two plastic forks and a lipstick that had melted to a mess of red grease. "Last owner," she observed. "Last legal owner."

"Try under the seats," Tina said.

Kate felt under the driver's seat and gasped. She held up a mobile phone. They stared at it and then at each other. "Lots of people have mobile phones," Kate said. "Could there be a record of its calls?"

They didn't know; they supposed there wouldn't be, otherwise why did drug dealers use mobile phones? They needed something more personal. They went back to the items strewn on the sand. Kate started on the maps, looking to see if any had been marked. Tina leafed through the paperbacks. "Here's something," she said, unfolding a yellow sheet. "It's a garage bill from some place in Great Falls, Montana – oh my!"

"Let me see." Kate crowded close, peering over her shoulder.

It was a Vehicle Purchase Order for a Jeep Cherokee priced at fourteen thousand dollars, made out to Alasdair Campbell of 1722 W. 58 St, New York, and dated 17 June.

"False name and address," Tina hazarded. "How'd he get away with not producing his driving licence? Money again, I guess."

Kate had gone pale under her tan. She said slowly, pausing between sentences: "I was still in New York on the seventeenth . . . He had a week in Montana before I got there . . . He went down to Slaughter Creek and killed Old Copper and hung around, waiting for me . . . Chesler told him when I arrived." They both looked at the mobile phone.

"Why didn't he kill you there, when you were climbing that cliff?" Tina asked.

"Because he wanted me to lead him to you? But he could have found you himself, the same way as I did."

"Then he'd leave a trail. And waiting till you reached me, he could get us both together. He planned this from way back. The guy's a serial killer. We have to find Whit, get him to call up reinforcements."

Fourteen

They found Whit fifteen miles to the south, stopped on the road and talking to Lonzo and Tony. Whit was grimly pleased at sight of the Purchase Order; if it existed at all he'd have expected it to be destroyed. "That was another mistake," he said, "like him driving into the salt. He's not that clever."

"We must have more men out here," Tina urged. "You'll never find him on your own; isn't that right, Lonzo?"

"He'll come in," Lonzo said. He glanced at the low sun. "He's thirsty now. There's no water out in the valley."

"Ozzie will be holding him back." But even as Tina spoke she knew, like the others, that Ozzie would be abandoned.

"And he's wounded," Kate said.

"Only a scratch." Whit was thoughtful. "Maria watched and saw he could move that arm. It's not broken. He lost some blood, is all." He qualified that: "Could slow him down. I guess Ozzie's a liability whichever way you look at it."

"Served his purpose." Kate was harsh. "We ought to look for him, Whit."

They knew she was right; the snag was that in searching for him they could run into Grant. "I'd like to leave it a while longer." Whit glanced at Lonzo. "Wait till Grant's a bit weaker. He could come in of his own accord, give himself up once he's dry enough."

"He might prefer to take his chance out there," Kate said. "Heat exhaustion's like hypothermia; he won't be rational after today's sun."

"So maybe we'll leave it till tomorrow." Whit wouldn't meet her eye.

199

But the women were thinking of Ozzie and they prevailed. They went back to the house and Whit called the sheriff. The others waited on the deck, listening to his side of the conversation, Tina and Kate thinking that decisions were out of their hands; someone else had the responsibility now – and knowing that this was only a cop-out.

Whit didn't ask for reinforcements; he reported developments, citing the Purchase Order for a Cherokee bought by an alleged killer wanted in Montana and now loose in the Bullion Valley with a teenager, and both of them armed. He was told Exito would get back to him.

They sat on the deck, drinking lemonade, eating sandwiches and waiting. Exito came through several times asking for additional information, and all the time the light was fading until it was gone altogether and they knew nothing would happen until tomorrow. Sure enough, the final decision was that men and vehicles would arrive at first light, with dogs, and a helicopter if one could be spared. *Spared?*

"They're treating it like two hikers lost in the desert," Whit said. "They say these guys won't hurt through the night; they can be brought in tomorrow if they don't give themselves up."

"It's hard on Ozzie," Tina said.

"He asked for it. Why did he send Kate down the wrong valley? And then he followed her. Think about it. You ask me, there was another very nasty crime there in the making." He looked meaningly at Kate.

"Neil's never going to give himself up," she said.

No reinforcements had arrived by nine o'clock next morning although the word from Exito was that they were on their way. Kate thought that the whole thing was like a badly organised rescue. Already it was another scorching day and the thought of Ozzie – slow, fat, perhaps still bleeding – outweighed the threat of Neil.

Exasperated with waiting Whit drove away to tell Lonzo to try to track the pair from the salt pan. Behind him Tina and Kate set off down the valley carrying water and a first aid box, the dogs in the back of the pick-up.

Way beyond the Indian camp Tina slowed and stopped, looking right into the valley. "Vultures," she observed. "We could be too late." She drove on, looking for a wash.

"They're soaring," Kate said. "If something was dead, wouldn't they be on the ground?"

"I guess something's alive then." Tina turned off the road onto a ribbon of sand, drove a few hundred yards and stopped. "Get the rifle out," she said calmly.

Kate twisted in her seat to take it from the rack. There was the sound of a shot. She froze.

Tina switched off the engine and they held their breath. The silence was absolute, then faintly: "Mom? Kate?" It was Whit's shout. The doberman leapt off the back, Tina switched on and sent the truck bucketing along the wash.

"I haven't got the rifle," Kate shouted, bracing herself against the dashboard. "Leave it!" Tina yelled.

Whit appeared above their level and slid down the bank of the wash, holstering his pistol. Something lay prone at the foot of the slope, the doberman a few feet away, stiff and staring. Tina stopped and they climbed down, looking from Whit to a dead coyote.

"I shot it," he told them. "But someone else had crippled it already, and recently. It was still bleeding. Lonzo and Tony are following the blood trail back. I figure Grant lost his cool and let fly. Ozzie wouldn't have been bothered by coyotes."

Not unless he was dying, Kate thought.

Tina looked up at the circling vultures. "How badly crippled was it?"

"One leg was shattered but it could have travelled a ways on three legs. Take your rig up the bank there, Mom. Ours are in the next wash. We'll stay together now. I'm waiting for a signal from Lonzo, soon as he finds something."

They sat in the shade of the trucks, the sweat trickling down their backs and chests while the sun blazed in a sky drained of

201

colour and the shadows of the vultures drifted over the sand. They didn't say much, there was no longer anything to say; they waited for the signal to move and when it came – two rifle shots – there was a feeling of relief even though they must leave the shade to brave heat like an oven, and carrying heavy weapons.

It was too rough even for four-wheel drive. They followed Whit in single file, the doberman ahead, Hamish trailing them, no longer the clown but a guard dog. Whit seemed to have taken a mental bearing on the gunshots. He moved purposefully but seldom in a straight line; they were forced to detour for craggy outcrops – unsuspected and unseen from the road – and for dense groves of thorny plants and the razor leaves of yucca. They were all wearing hats and Kate found herself wondering if Neil still had his hat, then castigating herself for being concerned. She tried changing the location, substituting the Highlands for Arizona, cold for heat. If Neil were lost on the Cairngorms in a blizzard would she be concerned? She thought of Bill falling – pushed – into the flooded burn, and knew she shouldn't be concerned. Anyway death from cold was painless, perhaps heat was the same. This bush-whacking – through thorns and prickly pear, agave, and mesquite with spines like awls – this was excruciating, and it was going on for ever. They would all die of sunstroke, didn't Whit realise? She couldn't take it, the heat was stifling. She would pretend it was cold. She reminded herself that the human system has unsuspected reserves. Or was that the mind? Both probably, they worked together. How long had they been walking? She glanced at her wrist and remembered that she'd never found her watch. Neil had cut short the search for it. Everything came back to Neil.

The world darkened. Her body seemed to hesitate and then to bloom, opening like a flower. She looked up in astonishment; they had walked into the shadow of a rock reef. She bumped into Whit who turned and put an arm round her shoulders. She smiled and took off her shades.

Ahead of them Lonzo and Tony stood close under the rock, dark faces turned to the newcomers. A hundred yards away was a large dead tree ornamented like a demonic painting with motionless vultures. Between the Indians was a body.

Which one? No one voiced it but the question was so obvious that Lonzo gave a faint shrug and looked from Whit to what the vultures had left of the head. "Stay there," Whit said, but Kate had seen climbers after they'd fallen a long way. She stepped forward.

The bony parts were as yet untouched. "Take off his watch," she told Whit.

"You should be a cop. Or an undertaker. But you make sure the labourers do the dirty work." The black humour of people accustomed to violent death. He lifted the wrist and detached the watch, wiping it on his jeans. "Grant had a Rolex. This is a Timex. I guess this is Ozzie."

Lonzo proffered a pistol. "It was under the body," he said. "Two rounds fired."

"The coyote and this guy? No way of knowing what happened till after the autopsy. Maybe not then." Whit looked around. "So where's Grant? The dogs don't think he's here." Although sitting at a distance all their attention was on the corpse.

"He's gone," Lonzo said. "Although he was here. We can track him."

Whit hesitated. "We'll wait for more firepower."

"He was fit for his age," Kate said. "He had all night to walk. He could be miles away."

The men gathered up what they could and started back with the body: poor fat Ozzie, so much lighter now. The women followed at a distance, but not too far back. Somewhere in this valley was another man, no doubt still armed, who was accustomed to stalking deer in open country. Here there was cover everywhere.

They reached the trucks without incident and put the remains on the back of Lonzo's pick-up. They remained wary as they drove out, conscious that they made prime targets, all watching for a tell-tale glint of metal in the undergrowth.

As they emerged from the brush they saw a dust cloud in the south. Their own progress must have been observed because shortly flashing lights showed against the dust. The other vehicles had turned back.

This was the sheriff's advance party: two trucks, one carrying a pair of German Shepherds and their handlers. Carl and Hamish had to be shut in Tina's cab before the police dogs could be brought out and even then discussion was impossible for the din. The Cameron animals were beside themselves at this invasion of their territory. Tina took them back to the house before they did themselves an injury.

Tony was directed to drive the body to the mortuary at Exito, despite his youth. It was either him or Kate and she flatly refused. The police left on foot: two men in mufti, two uniforms, the dogs and Lonzo leading, heading back to the rock reef, the intention being to track Neil from there.

"You're not going with them?" Kate asked Whit. She was sitting in his cab.

"I'm going north," he told her. "I figure Grant's making for the Bronco. You can show me where it is and then I'll run you home. A chopper's due any time; I'll contact the pilot and set him to fly between the Bronco and the reef."

"I'm not going home. And you're not going anywhere on your own." She was defiant, prepared for argument. "You need someone who knows how his mind works."

He didn't argue. Perhaps he thought she really did know Neil's mind. In fact she felt that he was now over the edge, and unpredictable.

"So where do you figure he is?" Whit asked, and without sarcasm. He sounded helpless. She wouldn't be surprised if he were in shock, as many rescuers are after encountering a corpse, and such a ravaged one. She felt a bit miserable herself. "Is there something to drink?" she asked, needing time to consider the question.

They drank tepid water from a gallon container. There was no shade other than in the cab so they sat there with the doors wide open to the stagnant air. "I'd love a smoke," he said.

"You wouldn't. It dulls the perceptions. And you don't smoke."

"I did."

"It makes you thirsty too." Silence. "Thirsty," she repeated. "Is there *any* water out there, like a cattle tank?"

"None in the valley, only where they mired the truck, and that's brine. There's water in the mountains; some of the canyons have springs, way back under the headwalls, but the water never reaches the valley. It evaporates or goes underground. Anyway, he wouldn't know which canyons have springs."

"Yes, he would." She turned to him in amazement. "Of course he would! They followed me into that canyon; he knows where the tinaja is."

"That's not a spring, Kate; you can't drink from it."

"He's desperate, it's the only water he knows—"

"He'd never find it—"

"He's a mountaineer, an old explorer; he's been there once, he can find it again. Let's go and look. Anyway," she went on as he turned the ignition key, "we don't have to go all the way; if there are no tracks he isn't there."

She wasn't the first person to think of the tinaja. Before they reached the turn-off to the canyon they were catching glimpses of two riders back in the brush. They were following the track and they drew aside as the pick-up approached. They were mounted on mules. One was Lonzo's mother and the other must be Maria: a pale brown woman in Levis, her black hair now in a heavy plait, her eyes large and limpid as a deer's. She regarded Kate with interest and when Whit got down, leaned towards him with a gesture like a lover. Kate frowned and saw that she was observed by old Lucy who nodded and pointed to the dust. Whit was looking too, and Kate could see from the cab: clear as a plaster cast was the imprint of a boot with a cleated sole.

Whit looked towards the canyon. "He's loco," Maria said carelessly. "Maybe with a gun."

"Irrational anyway," Whit told Kate. "He's staggering all over the place. I doubt he still has the rifle, but we have to assume he has. You follow us," he told Maria.

They drove on, stopping now and again to check the ground. Kate knew that was superfluous, Neil was heading for the water.

They left the pick-up at the mouth of Tinaja Canyon and when the mules arrived, tied them to the tailboard. In single file the four of them entered the mesquite thicket. Maria pointed to the ground. "He's here," she said. Kate could see nothing in the dust except chequered sunshine. There was a slight drop in temperature. She seemed to have got used to the heat and yet this canyon was fully exposed to the afternoon sun.

They came out of the little trees to the bed of the wash where the gravel held no tracks. They were making a lot of noise now but no one seemed worried. Did they all know something, even herself subconsciously, or did they have a collective death wish? Was he waiting for them, concealed up there, where she'd hidden herself, below the overhang and the swallows' nests?

"He's not active," she told Whit. "The swallows aren't disturbed, see?"

He nodded and squeezed her shoulder. She yawned hugely. Lucy gave her the ghost of a smile. They continued up the gravel, their eyes reverting to hunters' eyes. Kate thought Whit would have shot at anything that moved. She had Tina's shotgun; he had given her a quick lesson in how to aim and fire but not to reload. Perhaps he thought she wouldn't need more than two rounds.

The bedrock appeared ahead. They stopped and clustered, staring up the empty wash, looking over the slopes, then they advanced again, scrunching through the chippings, stepping up the rock like cats, fanning out as if to confront the tinaja united.

At the last moment Kate was thinking that there were no vultures so there was no body, but the body was there, splayed out, seeming to fill the circular frame of rock: a still life floating in a wreath of dead moths.

Fifteen

The autopsies revealed that Neil had drowned and that Ozzie had been shot in the head with the pistol that was found under his body. Death by accident, and suicide were the verdicts. The Camerons and Kate were inclined to agree, thinking Neil would not have been bothered to shoot Ozzie, more likely the boy would have been abandoned to die of thirst.

Kate returned to Scotland. She had to see Maisie. Whit was against it; Tina was vehemently opposed. "She's his mother! How can you tell her he killed two guys here, apart from Ozzie, *and* your friend, if he did push him in that creek? She could be dangerous, Kate."

"It could kill her," Whit amended – more reasonably in view of Maisie's age.

"I liked her," Kate said. "Besides I owe it to her. She'll know the basic facts by now but she has a right to – well, some kind of explanation."

"But why is it you have to provide it?" Tina protested. "You don't owe her anything. It's the other way round."

"I'm involved. It seems like a duty."

"Rubbish—" Tina snapped, and stopped short.

"Suppose Whit was a killer," Kate said earnestly. "Suppose he was hunted through a strange country and died thousands of miles from home, wouldn't you want to know the details, to have the gaps filled? Be told what happened?"

"You'd tell her all of it?"

"Of course not; I'm used to editing reports of accidents –

208

and I'll take someone with me, someone she knows: Madeleine Bell. There, I'll have support and a witness. Does that satisfy you?"

"I'll come with you," Whit said.

"I'm sorry." Kate wasn't surprised. "This is between me and his mother." She regarded him fondly. "I'll be back."

It was still August but there was an autumnal nip in the air the morning she came down the glen to Cullen, driving her old van. She'd picked it up in Strathmor. She'd left Bill's motorbike at the police station but she had his rucksack in the back of the van. Its presence was familiar, hardening her heart, putting her on the same level as Maisie. She had lost her son but the bond between climbing partners is closer than that between lovers.

The meeting had been arranged by telephone with Madeleine. "But she wants to see you," Madeleine had protested when Kate tried to explain her motives for the visit. "It's ages now since she heard and all she knows is that he drowned in a canyon after getting lost. Which everyone knows is ridiculous. He could swim like a seal and Neil was never lost in his life. No one can make head nor tail – you want me to come with you? I assure you she doesn't need anyone to support her . . . Yes, of course I'll come; to tell you the truth I'm all agog myself. I mean, to drown in a canyon in Arizona!"

"If you hadn't come I would have come to you." Maisie set down a tray and poured coffee with a firm hand. She was composed, too composed in the circumstances, and she had lost weight, her eyes sunken under the hooded lids. She didn't smile, and she hadn't smiled when Kate and Madeleine arrived at her door, but her courtesy was so impeccable as to be suspect.

It wasn't until they were settled in the gloomy dining room that the purpose of the visit was broached. There was no finesse. "I don't believe a word of it," Maisie said flatly. "He couldn't be lost and he couldn't drown. It must have been a stroke or a heart attack. Was it a warm day?"

209

"It was a hundred and twenty in the shade," Kate said.

"That's very hot, Maisie," Madeleine put in.

"Drowned," Maisie intoned. Kate's guts contracted. The eyes pinned her like a moth to a board. "You were there—"

"No, he was alone."

"So he could have been pushed."

"Like Bill." It slipped out: thought made audible. Kate stared at Maisie, detecting a flicker in those fathomless eyes.

"What was it?" Madeleine tried to ease the tension. "Quicksand? It couldn't have been a deep river surely, not in Arizona."

"It was a pool," Kate said. "Like a limestone pot: very deep, completely enclosed by rock. Some water had evaporated, making it more like a well."

"If he wasn't pushed," Maisie said heavily, "how did he come to be in it?"

"I wasn't there. He must have tried to reach the water to drink and fallen in, or perhaps he went in deliberately – to get cool, and didn't realise he couldn't get out again. He wasn't rational at that point."

"How do you know if you weren't there?"

"Because we followed his tracks and he was staggering."

Maisie winced. "What was he doing on foot? He had a car, a big one like his Range Rover. A Cherokee, he called it."

Kate licked her lips. She found herself staring at a photograph of Neil – a younger, slim Neil – cutting his way up an ice wall on the north face of the Matterhorn.

"When did you separate, Kate?" Madeleine asked. "You *were* together?" But Kate looked blank.

"He was following you," Maisie said, regarding her intently. "Where did he catch up? Because he did. He telephoned me from Arizona. He phoned every few days."

"Did he?" Kate's tone was hollow. "In that case you know he was staying in a town called Exito. That was where we met – that is, all of us: Tina Cameron, Neil, me. You remember Tina Cameron." She was gentle. Of course Maisie remembered;

210

she'd been a link in the chain that kept Neil informed on Kate's progress across the States.

"She was one of the maids at the lodge," Maisie said. "She had nothing to do with Neil. He was a child at the time."

Kate's mind supplied the missing part: the time of the plane crash. But Neil wasn't a child then, he was fifteen. No one made the correction and Kate reflected that this was going to be something other than an edited account. She could, she would, suppress his crimes. There need be no mention of Old Copper and Wayne Chesler.

Maisie was watching her like a cat. She knows I'm keeping things back, Kate thought, and she's considering whether to ask what they are. "Neil came to dinner at Tina's," she said evenly. "He didn't stay at the house. At the end of the evening he went back to his motel. I didn't see him again." A gross lie; she'd seen him twice again, the first time he was stalking her, the second he was dead.

"What happened between then and when you *did* see him again?" Maisie asked, the emphasis indicating her contempt for evasion.

Kate said, "Tina's son is a policeman. He was looking for a local lad, Ozzie Gilsdorf, who was missing. Actually he'd joined Neil as a guide. To do a spot of hunting." Eyes sharpened. Hunting in July? "The morning after Neil came to Tina's, he checked out of his motel and met Ozzie again." She paused. This was another tricky part. "Apparently they were out in the desert and they got their truck bogged down in a salt pan. After that they were on foot. That's how they came to be lost, trying to walk back to their camp."

"Where were you when this was happening?"

"I was staying with Tina. No one knew what had happened until someone saw the stranded truck. Then Whit – that's Tina's son – he got a party together and we started looking for them. We found Ozzie first. He'd shot himself." She was amazed at the ease with which that slid out.

Maisie didn't query it, and that was significant. "Go on,"

211

she ordered. "So then you looked for my son?" It was said delicately, almost pleasantly.

"He had found the canyon with the water in it."

"You followed him there."

"We followed his tracks."

"You were alone."

"No, there were four of us." Kate was edgy but she tried to make allowances for a bereaved mother. She glanced at Madeleine, wondering how soon it would be over, relieved that the confrontation had gone off comparatively peacefully. She wasn't worried that Maisie should voice suspicion of her own part in Neil's death, that was natural in the circumstances. She thought of Bill and her eyes narrowed. It was time to go, before she said something she'd be sorry for later.

"How much did he tell you?" Maisie asked.

"Who – Neil?" She was startled, disorientated. "He didn't tell me anything."

"What was the name of Tina's friend who was killed in the crash?"

"Chuck Sullivan."

"Neil did tell you."

"No, Tina told me—" Kate looked from Maisie to Madeleine who was plainly bewildered. She said slowly, "Yes, he did tell me. What happened to the diary?"

"I burned it."

Kate fixed her eyes on the table, her mind racing. "You read it first. You washed off the blood. It was a propelling pencil so there would be indentations. What did it say: 'Chuck' – did what?"

Maisie's face was desolate. "The blood was at the start of the words. It was 'Kid robbed Chuck'."

"This was in the *wreck*?" Madeleine grasped the seat of her chair. "It was one of the rescuers? A kid? Not—" She glanced guiltily at Maisie then away.

"He panicked," Maisie said drearily. "When he found the wreck he had no thought of . . . none at all . . . he didn't dream

212

. . . He was a good lad . . . a *good* lad," she repeated fiercely. "He did it for me. He loved me, he did it out of love. You've no idea how poor we were in those days: no electric, carrying all our water, beds always damp . . . He did it for me, to give me a better life."

Kate couldn't stand such a spectacle of guilt. She said dismissively, "Chuck was dead; he had no use for the diamonds." Tina had, but she suppressed the thought.

Madeleine's lips moved but she didn't speak.

"He thought they were all dead," Maisie went on. "And he put the jewels in his pockets and looked around and there was that one: alive and smiling at him. And then he spoke. Neil was terrified out of his wits. He scrambled out of that plane and he ran all the way down the mountain."

Kate frowned. "So who took the diary? And the pencil?"

"Neil went back. He thought about it and he reckoned he could have been mistaken, that he only imagined someone was still alive. There was a strange light inside the plane, and there was all the snow, and the wind howling. He was surrounded by dead men. Some trick of sound could have made it seem a corpse spoke. So he went back to make sure. Didn't tell us till afterwards. When he got up there early the next day the man was dead but he'd written in the diary, so Neil brought it away with him. He missed the pencil. It was Hector Stewart who took that – and threw it away when the rumours started. Hector told me a long time after."

"Why did Neil give you the diary?"

"I made him. He told us everything; forced to, wasn't he? How could a lad of fifteen turn jewels into cash? His father had to do that; he was the one went to Glasgow." She looked away. She wasn't going to tell them how Rory Grant came to know where to find a fence. "So Neil told me about the diary, and gave it me to burn."

"And you cleaned the page and read it," Kate murmured, and stopped there because it occurred to her why Maisie was compelled to clean it; she had to find out if the missing verb was 'killed': 'Kid killed Chuck'. Perhaps that was what it *had* read. She remembered Tina suggesting that he might have started killing then. How many men had he killed?

"Your friend's death was an accident," Maisie said, as if she were telepathic.

Kate's lips parted and she waited for the next blow.

"He thought it was you," Maisie explained. "He didn't say so, but I knew."

"Neil thought Bill was me?"

"You wouldn't have anything to do with him. You were no better than you should be – he thought – and you turned him down. He was devastated."

"You're saying I was responsible for Bill's death?"

"Of course she's not." Madeleine fought for order. "Maisie doesn't know what she's saying. She's still shocked. It's only a few weeks since Neil – since Neil. Your friend fell in the burn, Kate. He'd been drinking. I told you."

Kate studied Maisie: gaunt, bereft – mad? She thought of Old Copper and Wayne Chesler, of Neil vowing his life wasn't worth living without her, and following her into Tinaja Canyon with a loaded rifle. She thought of the crumpled wreckage on Am Bodach.

"You must give me Tina Cameron's address," Maisie said.

"Do you mind telling me why?"

"I have to send her money. Armidil will be sold and then I can repay her. We bought it with her money; it goes back to her."

"Suppose Chuck hadn't come by the diamonds legally?"

"That has nothing to do with me. It's Tina's problem."

No, Kate said, she wouldn't go back to Dunnas with Madeleine; she must return to Glasgow, she had a flight booked through to Tucson. They sat on a bank above the shore and looked across the loch to the mountains basking like fat grey cats in the sunshine.

Madeleine broke the silence. "Neil didn't kill Bill Hoggart. Maisie's unbalanced, shocked."

"Unbalanced yes, but she's not in shock." The pent-up tension broke. "She knows how Bill died, and why: it was in mistake for me—"

"Kate! Neil was mad about you—"

"Neil was mad, full stop. You don't know half the story." Sitting there, in the bitter-sweet atmosphere that marked the end of summer, she told the rest: the murders below the White Cliffs of the Missouri, Neil stalking her through the West and coming after her at Black Tinaja. She told it all: his fervid protestations of love, the cans of petrol and the meat laced with cyanide, the intention unmistakable. "All that puzzles me," she concluded, "is why he didn't try to kill me sooner. Surely I was more of a threat than anyone else?"

"He had a terrible secret." Madeleine ignored the question; she had listened to the story in disbelief that deepened to a kind of appalled resignation. "He'd clawed his way out of poverty, become a celebrity, a hero, and it was all built on one shameful action: he'd robbed a body. I don't think he was mad, I think he went mad; that's the only way I can account for his behaviour in America."

"It started here. With Bill. If he loved me why kill—"

"Impulse. And you were starting to sniff around that aircraft crash. You could expose him."

"Then why didn't he shoot me when I was on that cliff above the Missouri? He had the opportunity – but he killed Chesler."

"The way you tell it Chesler could have been about to shoot you. Neil stopped him."

"Why? Neil wanted me dead. He'd killed Old Copper because he could have told me that his brother came over here to try to trace some diamonds that had been on the plane. He killed Chesler because the fellow knew he'd killed Old Copper. But after shooting Chesler why didn't he shoot me? He didn't even try, there was no second shot."

"He loved you."

Kate gave an angry laugh. "It was an act."

"No." Madeleine was firm. "I think this is the cause of all

215

the trouble. The man was in love with you and at the same time terrified that you could ruin him. This on top of the shame of what he'd done, never mind that it was nearly half a century ago, the horror of it stayed with him, could well have got worse the more celebrated he became. He'd not only robbed a body, he'd left a man to die – and this is the chap who went on to perform outstanding acts of courage . . . trying to compensate? You could expose him but he adored you; why else should he follow you to Arizona and never attempt to harm you?"

Kate gaped at her. "What about Bill? What about the petrol and the poisoned meat? I'll tell you why he didn't kill me on the way to Arizona: because once I'd phoned you from Bozeman – or shortly afterwards – once you'd told Maisie, he knew I was on Tina's trail but he didn't know her address. He let me live because I could lead him to Tina."

"And you reckon he was out to kill you when he followed you into that canyon. Perhaps you're right." Madeleine shook her head in despair. "The man didn't know where he was; he was doomed from the start." Her gaze wandered. "From that night," she amended. "D'you remember my telling you someone broke into our cottage and stole food one winter?"

Kate was bewildered. "You said something about tins of sausages."

"That could have been the night the plane crashed. It was how Neil knew: he was out on the point, stealing food, and he saw the plane go into the mountain – saw a flash in the clouds."

They were silent. A heron stepped along the weed, head down, intent.

"What are you going to do now?" Madeleine asked. "What's there, in Arizona?"

"Unfinished business."

"Your book? But you can't turn Tina and Chuck into a story."

"Of course not – although perhaps one day, in fiction . . ."

"That's the unfinished business?"

"No, I wasn't thinking of writing. I want to explore the

deserts. Funny thing, I've been monopolised by mountains all my adult life but there's another whole new world: canyons, deserts, particularly the deserts. And the sunsets, Madeleine, the sky flames" – her eyes were bright – "and the cicadas, and the coyotes singing—"

"I've been to America too," Madeleine reminded her, wondering why she was stroking the face of her watch.

"I lost it," Kate said, seeing her interest. "It must have fallen off in the sand when my Jeep got stuck. Whit went up there with me, to where I'd slept on the mountain. He found it." She smiled. "That's why I'm going back."

Madeleine understood. She had been there too. The flaming sunset, the coyotes' song, the softness of deep sand, the smoothness of a watch face and a lover's skin. On Am Bodach the broken wing was just discernible through the haze. Something good had come out of that old tragedy after all.